Blades of the Empire

Matt Penrose

Contents

CHAPTER 1

"You must stop with this childish antic of pretending to be ninja warrior just to join violent brawl. It is unladylike and look at what it has done to your pretty face," Princess Li Lei Shuang admonished her younger friend while rubbing a balm gently on the latter's bruised cheeks.

"Ouch, Lei Shuang!" Yan Mei Ling exclaimed. Just what did Li Lei Shuang put on her face - a chunk of burning coal? "Go easy on whatever you are putting on my face; it's supposed to make me feel better not terrible!"

Li Lei Shuang let out a gentle laugh as she continued putting the balm on Yan Mei Ling's cheeks. The latter, however, never stopped complaining about its stinging effect on her cheeks.

Despite the obvious differences between the girls, the two had become remarkably close friends.

Li Lei Shuang was a gentle and thoughtful soft-spoken girl with impeccable manners that she attributed from being the Emperor's daughter.

Yan Mei Ling, on the other hand, was her royal cousin's opposite. She had the tendency to do outrageous things and she was utterly stubborn. If you forbid her from doing something, the more that she would be tempted to do it no matter the consequences. She detested people who underestimated her and, she would do everything and anything to disprove those who doubted her abilities. With her daredevil attitude, it was not surprising that she had put herself in harm's clutches several times but despite it she was innately kind-hearted and well loved by those who were close to her.

While Mei Ling continued with her rants, an old maidservant came in with the tea set. She curtsied to the two girls before laying down the porcelain pitcher and cups on the low table. She discreetly gave the younger girl a look of distaste. Once done, she bid her farewell and exited the princess' receiving room.

Yan Mei Ling did not pass on the opportunity to make a silly face at the back of the retreating old maidservant to whom she considered her nemesis in the palace. Disappointed at the former's actions, Li Lei Shuang gave her a frown of disapproval.

"Please stop getting yourself in trouble, Yan Mei Ling. I am worried that something worse might happen than what has happened to your cheeks right now."

Yan Mei Ling snorted childishly to express her displeasure at what Li Lei Shuang said. Did she not repeatedly tell her best friend that it was her greatest goal to be the best warrior Chixian Shenzhou ever had? Besides, she loved and found joy in what she was doing. As her best friend, she should be the most supportive person in her every endeavor.

"You know what - you sound like a teacher! How many times have I told you that nothing worse than a bruise will ever happen to me? Well, many times! You need to remember that this is the worst thing that ever happens to me since joining the tournaments!" She pointed to the biggest and most painful bruise on her cheeks.

"Yes, but I can never forget that one time when you came to me with a dislocated arm," Li Lei Shuang reminded gently as she placed the ointment on the table. She took the pitcher and poured some hot tea into the porcelain cup. When the cup was full, she carefully served it to Yan Mei Ling.

"You don't have to make me remember that! It happened when I was still an inexperienced warrior," she said while receiving the tea offered by Li Lei Shuang. "You should have seen me fight- look how I put down the big, fat man on his back with my adept and stealth skills."

Yan Mei Ling mindlessly drank the tea and, suddenly, spit the contents from her mouth. What the heck?

"Oh, I'm sorry I have forgotten to remind you that the tea is still hot." Lei Shuang said. Her cheeks reddened deeply, feeling extremely guilty for her failure to warn her best friend about the tea's temperature.

Yan Mei Ling gritted her teeth, not because she was angry, but to suppress the surge of blood from invading her cheeks. How embarrassing - no wonder her best friends fretted over her joining tournaments because she could not even take the heat.

"It is my fault! I know that I should not have put my guard down whenever that old witch serves us tea!" She said with irritation referring to Li Lei Shuang's former wet nurse, now one of the latter's maidservants.

The old crone never really warmed up to her because she always thought that she was a bad influence on Li Lei Shuang. In retribution, Yan Mei Ling devised several ways to pull mischievous pranks on the witch. Well, the old hen had had her time today but then victory was her twin, and the old woman would someday have her day of reckoning.

"I'm really sorry about everything but you should not say such things against Chunhua, Yan Mei Ling," Lei Shuang told the younger girl as she stood to retrieve a cloth from her cabinet. She knelt in front of Yan Mei Ling and started to wipe her best friend's mouth, but the latter hurriedly moved away and angrily wiped herself with the end of her silk sleeves instead.

Lei Shuang gently shook her head in disappointment at Yan Mei Ling's unladylike manner. "You must stop acting as if you're still a child but be a noble lady that you are, Yan Mei Ling."

Yan Mei Ling rolled her eyes in disgust. "Act like a noble lady that I am? And how does a noble lady act like-do those gentle, tedious and extremely ladylike manners a princess like you is trained to do and have always done? Cut that silly talk, Li Lei Shuang; while those things may have suited a princess like you but stop thinking of the day that I will ever emulate you. We are different and I will become the greatest warrior in Chixian Shenzhou!"

Yan Mei Ling's caustic and unfeeling remarks about Li Lei Shuang's ladylike manners deeply smeared the latter's heart but she decided to keep what she felt to herself.

Yan Mei Ling ascended to go to the balcony of Li Shuang's room, woefully ignorant of her best friend's hurt feelings, to stare and revel on the different trees and plants of the Imperial palace that could be seen outside.

"Li Lei Shuang!" she enthusiastically called her best friend from the balcony. "The flowers are in bloom today - quickly, come, look!"

Li Lei Shuang immediately stood at Yan Mei Ling's excited voice and smiled upon seeing the magnificent landscape. Their eyes feasted on the beautiful and colorful hues of the flowers, and then followed the shape of the upward sweeping arches of the grand pavilion as if those arches would lead them to the heaven.

A moment later, their stares descended to the silver glimmer of the huge pond's greenish grey water where the lotuses twirled like tiny parasols.

As if indulging their eyes even more, the praying bamboos and humble willows swayed rendering the big garden an enchanted air. Thoroughly mesmerized, the birds began to sing harmoniously as if to serenade them.

"The nature's deities bestowed greatness in today's spring season, Yan Mei Ling."

"Yes, even the plants in our garden and the village are in bloom."

Li Lei Shuang smiled with affection at Yan Mei Ling and started to gently caress the latter's soft cheeks with her fingers.

Something came to Yan Mei Ling that she stood petrified at what might have been considered her best friend's normal action. In panic, she warily put some distance between them. What was happening to her? What was this strange thing that was budding in her heart's core?

"Did my touch hurt you, Mei Ling?"

This was sublime folly.

Yan Mei Ling remained motionless and silent because she was still trying to discern what exactly Li Lei Shuang's touch had provoked within her.

This was insanity.

She slowly stared into Li Lei Shuang's face and, for the first time in her fifteen years of being a silly child, she was in awe of her best friend's beauty. She had always thought that Lei Shuang was beautiful but to look at her now in an entirely different light was something surprising to her.

It was such a jolting experience for her to notice that the simple mint green silk robe gown with floral patterns Li Lei Shuang wore elevated her best friend's beauty to that of incomparable; it seemed hysterical for her to notice that the morning light made Li Lei Shuang's dark liquid eyes shone like the precious gems from the other oriental countries brought by the Empire's trading junks; and it was an abject horror for her to feel the need to touch Li Lei Shuang's braided long black hair with her fingers, freeing it from its bondage like a shimmering black waterfall.

Li Lei Shuang seemed unreal, ethereal - utterly captivating. No flowery words could be remotely adequate to describe the realness of her beauty - she was amazingly awe-inspiring. But all that she was feeling right now did not sit well within her.

This can't be!

"Did I hurt you, Mei Ling?" Li Lei Shuang asked again, her voice laced with worry. She was alarmed because her best friend had stayed silent for so long. It seemed unusual.

"No, you did not," Yan Mei Ling stammered - her eyes confused, her expression uncertain. "Nothing hurts, Li Lei Shuang," she managed to emphasize her last phrase despite the havoc within her heart. She wanted to get away from here; she wanted to get as far as possible from Li Lei Shuang.

What sickness had came into her?

What kind of lunacy had addled her mind?

Li Lei Shuang smiled in relief and hugged Mei Ling. "For a moment, I was under the impression that your silence meant that you were angry because I'd done something to hurt you."

Mei Ling trembled nervously and cautiously removed herself from Li Lei Shuang's embrace. "No, you did not, and I could never be angry with you, Li Lei Shuang - you are my best friend!" She took a deep breath to pacify the clamorous beat of her heart. "I become silent because I just remember that I have to go to the mountain today. Master Tang Jiao Quon will teach me a new skill. Yes! He will teach me a new skill!"

Li Lei Shuang simply nodded her head. She disapproved of Yan Mei Ling learning violent skills, but she did not voice what was inside her mind because her best friend would never listen to her.

For many years, she had tried talked her best friend out of training martial arts, but all her words had simply fallen into deaf ears. Yan Mei Ling was person with unbreakable conviction; once she made up her mind, there was nothing that one could do to change it.

"Be careful and stay safe, Yan Mei Ling," Those were the words that she could only say.

CHAPTER 2

The sun's harsh noon rays struggled to overwhelm the thick, shrouding leaves of the tall trees. Fortunately, the sun light that penetrated through the trees softened as it landed the forest ground; giving the entire lair a misty vibe which reminded one of the weather during the spring season.

Everything felt solemn, untarnished by unwanted human noise as compared to that of the town's clamor. One could hear the orchestral sounds from the birds and animals; soft whispers of the swaying grasses and plants that carpeted the ground; and of course, the everlasting flow of the stream rushing against the bed rocks.

At the heart of the deep forest, a humble hut stood unperturbed. Not far from it was a spartan training ground filled with these amenities: a bamboo beam buried in the ground held by medium-sized rocks where one could practice the improvement of balance; myriads of fat cotton sacks filled with decaying leaves and earth were hanging on the branches of the tall trees used for strengthening one's fists and feet; a few wooden squares were erected to serve as targets when practicing one's skills in archery, and there were also several obstacle courses to improve one's speed and agility.

At the training ground, an old master stood tall and dignified in front of his student despite the limp in his other leg. He wore a simple black cotton training robe with a white sash tied around his thin waist, it cascaded down his dull white trousers which was weathered by time. His student wore the same except for the color- the robe and trousers were dull white while the sash was pristine white - this was to give a distinction between their status.

"You may think that your body is fragile and weak but don't be disappointed for it is only a shell. If you work hard towards the goal in uniting the elements of the nature and the forces around you, then you can utilize a power that has always been within you. Although it may have been latent but with practice and determination, you can harness the energy and use it to subdue opponents who are bigger and stronger than you." Master Tang Jiao Quon, an ancient man with intelligent small eyes and stern features said with certainty.

"Do you hear me, young lady?" He asked when he sensed that Yan Mei Ling's thoughts seemed to waver out of nowhere.

Yan Mei Ling shook her head from the peculiar thoughts that had continuously bothered her and gave her attention back to her master. "Yes, I hear you, Master."

Master Tang Jiao Quon stared intently at his only student as if trying to see through her thoughts. "It is a good thing that I am not holding my stick or else I am going to beat you back to your senses."

Yan Mei Ling bowed her head in contrition. "I am very sorry, Master."

Master Tang Jiao Quon walked around the grassy ground of his lair which was conveniently shaded by bamboos, beech, Ailanthus Altissima and many different varieties of trees.

His thoughts went back to the past when he used to have a training ground situated within the Imperial palace grounds.

He was once a highly regarded master of combat techniques and trained the best warriors of the empire, including the Emperor and his officers in the past. His training ground in the Central Capital used to be filled with strong and eager young man. However, after the cold and brutal war against the barbarians of the North; he, unfortunately, incurred great wounds and injuries that permanently paralyzed his other leg. With one working leg left, he saw himself unfit to teach martial arts.

His perspective had dimmed and since he could not set himself as a perfect example to his students, he decided to leave the Central Capital without informing anyone. He led a hermit life in the mountains, channeling whatever strength left in him through meditation and understanding how the nature works with one's body.

With the passage of time, the great name Grand Master Tang Jiao Quon had been erased from the minds of the people. While his courageous deeds might have been immortalized in the scrolls of the empire but just like the most famous myths, they all seemed like a fictitious tale now.

His forty years of silent solitude and meditation had been disrupted when a young child had managed to climb the perilous mountain of Dark Skull. It surprised him how someone found him but what had not prepared him was when the child begged him to be her master.

He had initially declined because he did not have any interest to each anyone and, not just that, the child was a girl. How could a delicate-looking little girl possibly learn combat skills? But the girl was persistent. Not only that, when he stared into her eyes, he could undoubtedly sense the warrior within her with an unfathomable power waiting to be harnessed. It had shocked him for he had never came across anyone with such latent power and it would be a shame to not cultivate her skills. Since she was full of determination, he agreed to teach her.

For the past five years, the little girl, named Yan Mei Ling, had proven her eagerness to learn even the most difficult ones. She was different from her former male students. Despite the physical limitations of her body and her vexed soul, she became true to her word to follow his words and teachings without any complaint.

He greatly admired Yan Mei Ling's extreme fortitude and willful desire to learn despite her age and sex. Thus, her seemingly distracted mind was a surprise to Master Tang Jiao Quon.

"I know that something is bothering you, young lady. I may be your teacher, but I can also be your confidant - you can tell me all the things that are bothering you. As I have always reminded you, bottling up intrusive thoughts can impede your focus in learning."

Yan Mei Ling stared at her old master's firm countenance and quickly bowed her head to hide the flushing of her cheeks. She certainly did not want to tell him what was bothering her - what would he think of her?

"Ah - I am truly in a state where my thoughts are in a muddle, but I think I can perfectly handle myself. My eagerness to learn has overshadowed those thoughts. Please teach me now, Master Tang Jiao Quon."

Master Tang Jiao Quon stared at Mei Ling and slowly nodded his head. "Do you see those huge stones on the stream, young lady?"

Yan Mei Ling followed the direction of where her master's gaze. It was at the stream where the trees bowed in reverence, creating a shade on the clear water. "Yes, Master."

"I want you to meditate on the smallest of the huge stones for three hours using one foot."

Yan Mei Ling's mouth went agape in shock. It was impossible! She could not even imagine herself standing for an hour on one foot - how much more three hours? What was her master thinking? This was not the kind of training that she had in mind.

"To be able to achieve balance, you must relieve yourself from all of the intrusive thoughts in your head. Can you do it, young lady?" Master Tang Jiao Quon challenged.

Yan Mei Ling stared at the huge stones at the stream and the strong determination to succeed overwhelmed her apprehension.

"I can do it, Master."

The wind descended softly from the Eastern morning sky tracing gentle steps on the long, dull brown brick path leading to the big Imperial Garden's heart.

Feeling utterly amorous, the wind continued its path sending side wise kisses to the parading flowers - chrysanthemums, forsythia, peonies and others - until it reached the drawbridge connecting the other side of the garden to the arched pavilion shrouded with wisteria, hibiscus, and plum trees.

The thin bamboo trees and cascading willows swayed causing the lotuses on the wide lake-like pond to stir and create miniature whirlpools on its greenish grey water. As if enticed by the playfulness of nature, the gold fishes and carps danced beneath their liquid domain, gliding gracefully under the shadows rendered by the lotuses.

At the far-right side of the arched pavilion, a wonderfully crafted low bench shied away from the subtle morning light. An ancient big tree with mottled silvery trunk and pine tree obliged it by basking shade on the bench. Just a few steps away, a tree with contorted stem and twisted roots leaned almost against the imperial garden's smaller pavilion.

Li Lei Shuang stood from her room's balcony while staring silently at the scene nature created in the imperial garden; her elbows propped against the balustrade while her left hand rested on the right.

She could hear the soft swinging sounds of the circular white lanterns hanging on the ceiling. The wooden lattice doors were pushed at both sides of the paneled entrance baring her bedroom to the gentle morning light and breeze.

When the gentle zephyr sweetly caressed her soft cheeks, the door beyond the paneled entrance of her room earned an instinctive glance. But she decided not to heed the impulse though the prospect of sauntering at the imperial garden proved to be tempting. She merely contented herself with watching the magnificent bloom of the different garden plants from her balcony while drowning herself in the thoughts inside her head.

She and Yan Mei Ling had always loved colorful flowers and the fresh breeze brought by the spring wind. However, she could not stop thinking about Yan Mei Ling. Being older than her best friend, she felt a sense of responsibility towards the latter.

Li Lei Shuang never approved of Yan Mei Ling going up the dangerous mountains to train and dreaded the thought of the latter being hurt during the competitions. Unfortunately, she knew that her voice of disapproval would appear mute to her best friend's ears. The only thing that she could do was to pray for her best friend's safety and change of heart in the future.

She should be very understanding and patient to Yan Mei Ling. She knew why her cousin had this intense desperation to become a warrior.

It rooted from the fact that Yan Mei Ling's lineage descended from the Empire's greatest warriors. And, more importantly, her desperation to prove to her father, Unit Commander Yan Bao Rong that she was capable of being a great warrior as their ancestors had been. Yan Mei Ling had believed that her father did not want a daughter but a son because he thought that women were not capable of bringing glory to the family.

Yan Mei Ling's father was widowed after her mother died giving birth to her. Although he could have married again, he never considered it because of the dedication that he had to his deceased wife. He poured all his attention to his duties to the Emperor and the Imperial Palace, leaving Yan Mei Ling feeling neglected and in dire need of parental affection.

'My father has never loved me because I know that he always wanted a son. He may not say the words, but I can sense it every time I express to him my desire to be part of the Imperial army.

He tells me that women are weak and will never have the chance to become great warriors but should tend to household duties instead. But I will never give up; I am going to disprove his stance about women because being a woman does not only mean getting married, raising a family and then attaching oneself to a lifetime of domesticity.' Yan Mei Ling had said with gumption and intelligence uncommon in her age.

'I was able to climb the mountain of Dark Skull that my maid-servant's grandfather told me where the greatest warrior of the Empire had stayed. I saw him and his lair. I knew that he was the only one who could help me to become a great warrior, so I beg him to teach me. He refused at first because I am a female. Can you just imagine the kind of condescending perception all the males have towards the females? But in the end, I successfully persuaded him to teach me. If you could only feel the happiness that I felt when he agreed to teach me, it was just so surreal. I will finally be a warrior, Li Lei Shuang!'

'You don't have to put yourself in grave danger just to make your father recognize your worth, Yan Mei Ling! You could prove yourself in other means than being a warrior; you do not have to be one. It is too dangerous for you and it's not even worth it.'

'My father will never recognize my worth if I'll just engross myself in all feminine and domestic duties, besides, what happiness will it bring me? You know that I have always wanted to become a warrior - it is in my blood!' There was a different flare in Yan Mei Ling's hard eyes - a conviction that could never be dissuaded. 'Li Lei Shuang, you should support me because it will make me happy. Are you not my best friend?'

Li Lei Shuang silently sobbed in disappointment. She could not bring it in her heart to oppose Yan Mei Ling.

'Sometimes one does not always have to support everything that her best friend wants to do. However, if that will make you happy, then I will not object. But please keep this in mind, I will always pray for your safety, Yan Mei Ling'

Yan Mei Ling happily hugged Li Lei Shuang. 'I know you will understand, Li Lei Shuang. However, I beg you please do not tell anyone especially my father about my plan. As of now, only you and Yeng know about this.'

'I won't. I promise you.'

Li Lei Shuang wept silently in her heart every time she remembered Yan Mei Ling's decision to become a warrior. She tended her attention back to the beautiful plants and flowers dancing gracefully against the zephyr from her balcony, but their beauty failed to lighten her up - she was too worried for Yan Mei Ling.

A knock from her door took Li Lei Shuang's attention. She saw a group of female attendants came and bowed to her; one of them came forward and bowed again. "Good day, Princess, the Son of Heaven calls for your presence at the family room."

Li Lei Shuang nodded gently and then the group of attendants came near her to escort her to the family chambers.

CHAPTER 3

Li Lei Shuang walked regally along the long and wide red-tiled hall; it was outlined by several columns supporting the high ceiling with entablatures sculpted with gilded dragon's head to emphasize the dynastic symbol - the golden serpent dragon.

The end of her magnificent flowing royal pink silk robe was held by two royal attendants. The princess' majestic pink robe had yellow borders on the sleeves; its hems were designed with miniature circular geometric patterns that depicted their culture. A sash with a darker shade of yellow was tied around her slim waist. It was so soft that it felt like the river's cool water.

Two royal attendants walked behind her, left and right, to watch for any disfigurement on her royal headdress. The headdress was designed with dangling pearls and silver; it added to its majestic flair. Her plaited long black hair which was obscured by the headdress was tied in a chignon with small jade pins, but a considerable amount of hair was allowed to fall gracefully at her back.

The rest of the attendants walked behind her back lining like dutiful imperial army soldiers on a royal march. All of them were dressed in identical dark orange robes designed with minimal circular patterns on the flowing sleeves and hems; bright orange sashes were tied around their waists. The head attendant, distinguishable by her different hair style, led them to the royal family chamber. The elegantly dressed Imperial Eunuch walked in front of them.

When Li Lei Shuang walked inside the family chamber, she and the attendants bowed in unison the Emperor and the Empress. She had also noticed that the Emperor was having a serious discussion with her mother at the tea table as marked by the soberness of his face. As she came near her parents, she felt that something was not right - both of them seemed to be mourning over a terrible fate.

All of them dutifully kowtowed to the Emperor as a sign of respect. "Greetings, Son of Heaven, Lord of Ten Thousand Years! I present to you, the Imperial Princess, Princess Li Lei Shuang."

"Good day, Son of Heaven; good day, Imperial Empress " Li Lei Shuang greeted and bowed respectfully to both of her parents again.

The Emperor anxiously stared at his only child, Princess Li Lei Shuang. After a moment, he turned his gaze to the Imperial Enunuch and attendants, and commanded them to leave. Everyone left hastily at the Emperor's orders.

When everyone left, the Emperor stood from where he was kneeling and hugged his daughter as if he was shielding her from all dangers. At the other side, the Empress was weeping with great remorse.

Li Lei Shuang was utterly confused with her parents' unusual behavior but she did not voice her thoughts.

"My daughter, you are my one and only beloved treasure. All I have in my Empire will never amount to you. I will never allow anyone to hurt you - they should have to face me first." The emperor said.

"Is there something wrong, bà ba?" Li Lei Shuang asked in confusion. She was unable to understand what was amiss - everything felt lugubrious.

The Emperor led his daughter near the tea table and directed her to sit.

Li Lei Shuang's parents' looked morosely dejected as tense silence filled the room. Suddenly, she could not bear the situation and curiosity won the better out of her as she asked her father to break the uneasy silence, "Please tell me what is wrong, bà ba."

At her question, her mother broke into another wave of whimper and the Emperor's eyes glistened with tears. It was as if he was bracing himself over something dreadful yet unavoidable.

"Lord Hsien Mao Dong of the Hsien Clan," the Emperor finally started. "is planning to wage war against our Empire."

"Did he not visit the Imperial Palace to forge an alliance with us, bà ba? I don't understand why he plans to wage war against us." Li Lei Shuang asked utterly confused by her father's statement.

The Emperor paused for a while; the tension never left his face. "Yes. But two weeks after his visit, he sent a letter demanding someone precious to seal the alliance."

Li Lei Shuang became more perplexed by her father's words; her mother never ceased crying. She came beside her mother to comfort her.

"The Hsien clan became the strongest of all the feudal lords of the Empire - they have incorporated several feudal states to theirs through their own brutal means. The feudal states they have accumulated held several people in authority that will possibly crush our Empire if a war will ever take place." The Emperor narrated helplessly. His eyes mirrored intense fear of what could possibly be a future outcome.

"What is there demand, bà ba?" Li Lei Shuang's voice trembled when she asked.

The Emperor lovingly stared at his only daughter. Suddenly, tears began to trickle down from his eyes. It was the first time that Li Lei Shuang had seen her strong father cry. "They demand someone that I can never give them."

The Emperor tried to hold on to what feeble strength of control that despair tried to take away from him. "Lord Hsien Mao Dong wants to you to be a part of his harem. He wants you, my beloved daughter, as his wife."

Li Lei Shuang shuddered as terror razed her body; her father's words thoroughly shocked her. She could not utter any word as if her tongue lost its sense. She could not believe it.

The thought of being married to a man such as Lord Hsien Mao Dong made every living fiber of her body jolt with so much revulsion. There was not much to do after a long moment of silence but to break down and cry. Her mother embraced her and wept along with her.

"Not my daughter!" The Empress sobbed.

The Emperor thought after a moment of tears - a lot had been lost to crying. Suddenly, the Emperor's façade became implacable as if a new strength dawned in him. "I will never allow my daughter to be married to a selfish traitor. If the Hsien clan wanted a war, then I have no choice but to give it to him."

The sun took its descent and the sky looked like a white canvas splashed with a flurry of the lightest shade of blue-grey, silver and orange. It precipitated down the dense moutain, giving it an enchanted aura.

Yan Mei Ling was delighted to go down from the mountain after a very long and grueling meditation. Despite its tedium, it was the certainly the most painful of all her training since she repeatedly lost her balance and fell hard on the stones of the stream.

Yan Mei Ling arrived home feeling drowned with fatigue, her meditation had finally taken its toil on her. She bathed to wash herself out of grime and perspiration.

Yeng, her loyal maidservant, came after she washed herself and put salve on all of the bruises in her body. Unlike the balm that Li Lei Shuang used on the bruise of her face, the salve was soothing creating a cool sensation wherever it was applied.

When the maidservant was done with her task, she left leaving Yan Mei Ling entirely alone in her room with nothing but her own vexing thoughts for company.

'Your bothered thoughts have impeded your concentration. If you are unable to control the chaos within your mind, then you will never find serenity in order to achieve balance.' Yan Mei Ling remembered what Master Tang Jiao Quon told her.

'A great warrior is not only skilled in the arts of physical combat; she knows how to control one's feelings and minds in such a way that she can achieve unity with herself.' Master Tang Jiao Quon explained when Yan Mei Ling took her third fall on the stream.

'Meditation is the highest form combat skill because when you are under its trance, you are not fighting someone else but rather the most difficult enemy one can find who is yourself. You must know that, young woman.'

Yan Mei Ling sighed despondently - she did not learn a real combat skill today because of her Master's insistence on meditation. Well, life was certainly damned with that boring meditation; she might as well swept and scrub the palace floor clean.

'Myself? My own enemy? That is certainly absurd.' Yan Mei Ling berated in her mind. She was disappointed because she did not achieve the balance that she had strived hard for. She was absolutely furious with herself because of her inability to get over the terrifying emotion that struck her at Li Lei Shuang's house. It was absolutely unnatural and she would never welcome such emotion - it was immoral!

Yan Mei Ling walked back and forth her room utterly disturbed. She remembered the feeling of her best friend's touch which was something akin to being struck by a thunder only it was gentle, heart-sweeping similar to the caress using a peacock's feathers.

No - she should not feel that way! It could not be. It was unimaginable and utterly insane! She shook her head in denial. How many times should she shake her head to completely purge herself of the lunacy that was trying to control her mind? The lump in her throat was suddenly becoming heavy as if she swallowed the biggest stone in the stream where she had meditated.

She anxiously walked back and forth again, this time thumping heavily on the floor like a warhorse's furious stomp. Her thoughts sank deeper still drowning her mind, making her want to take her heart off her chest to finally put an end to her misery. 'Why do I have to feel this way?' Yan Mei Ling wailed to herself pathetically. 'I can't feel this way to Li Lei Shuang. She is my friend and a friend she shall always remain.'

Yan Mei Ling's distressing thoughts was put momentarily sidetracked when Yeng called in a low voice, warning her, "My lady, your father has arrived. He called you for dinner."

"Oh, no!" Yan Mei Ling cried in panic. "Yeng, you have to help me.. I need to hide the bruises on my face - there should be nothing visible! Quick, we need to put rouge on my face."

Moonlight was spilled generously on the terrain. It even eclipsed the light emitted by the lanterns hanging on the ceiling outside the huge open windows of the Yan's dining hall. Its sweet glare made the burning oil lamp in the dinner table seemed superfluous.

Yan Mei Ling had done essential preparations before dinner. She made certain that her make-up was thick enough so that her father, Unit Commander Yan Bao Rong , would not notice the bruises on her face. She did not like to be bombarded with sermons if he did.

Dinner between Yan Mei Ling and her father had always been silent and stiff - even uncomfortable at most times. If not for the discreet sound of the chopsticks against porcelain, everything would have been eerily silent.

At every stretch of silence, Yan Mei Ling longed to break it and share the things she'd been doing to her father but every time she glanced at his cold and inscrutable face, she knew she'd regret after. Idle talks were not tolerated in the dining hall except perhaps if it was about imperial or household duties. However, all the talks were mostly her father's, all she had to do was to nod like a brainless and obedient daughter.

With a flat voice and impassive face, Unit Commander Yan Bao Rong started a conversation which surprisingly made Yan Mei Ling silently sighed in relief. "I heard of a boy who dressed himself like a ninja. He always won the town brawls. It would have been an honor in the imperial army to have someone as good as him."

At her father's words, Yan Mei Ling stared onto her father's face. She could not believe that the news about the ninja boy would reach her father. It was quite a shock but it seemed that his stare was rebuking her, as if he knew of her secret. Because of that, she felt guilt razed through her that she choked on her food and hastily drank her tea from her cup.

Unit Commander Yan Bao Rong eyed her daughter with extreme disappointment and firmly admonished her, "You are almost a lady but you have not polished your childish manners yet. You never do anything good but to disappoint me."

Yan Mei Ling was hurt by her father's words and tears started to form from her eyes, "I don't want to be the lady that you want me to be, bà. Why won't you just allow me to join the imperial army?"

Nettled by his daughter's plea, he slammed his fists at the table and stared scathingly at her. "You must know that women will never have any purpose in the military. What kind of foolish thought has come into your mind to tell me of that absurd wish of yours?"

Yan Mei Ling's tears longed to fall from her eyes but she dared not to for that would only prove her weak in her father's eyes. "I am going to prove myself, bà, if you will just give me a chance."

"Stop talking of foolishness and try to put some sense into your head. When will you understand? I do not raise you to become a part of the military. I want you to become the lady that you ought to be."

"But.."

"No buts," Unit Commander Yan Bao Rong sternly cut his daughter's words. "Be as I wanted." He left the dinner table without finishing his food.

Yan Mei Ling was left alone with a heart full of anguish and frustration. The wall that she painstakingly built finally collapsed leaving her defense open. She was left with no other refuge but to succumb to the tears that she had been holding back.

CHAPTER 4

Li Lei Shuang felt utterly hopeless despite the beautiful song of the spring wind in her garden; she felt as if that fate had been extremely unfair. Adding to her despair was her solitude for Yan Mei Ling had forgotten to visit her today.

Li Lei Shuang had inquired several times to her maidservants if Yan Mei Ling had come to visit but to her utter dismay, her best friend hadn't. It was simply unusual of Yan Mei Ling to forget visiting her every day because it was what her best friend had been doing for many years - Yan Mei Ling did not even bother sending her a letter to explain her absence.

A stray flower darted on Li Lei Shuang's face as she wiped the tears forming from eyes. She felt extremely lonely ever since her father had told her of Lord Hsien Mao Dong's demand so that a war would not break.

A heartbroken sob formed deep from her heart, the thought of war along with its ruthless violence and its tremendous bloodshed terrified her so much - she loved the empire and its people.

Her father would never succumb to Lord Hsien Mao Dong's demand but then she was prepared to sacrifice everything for the Empire. She would do anything even if it means compelling her life to a loathsome and loveless marriage to an old and ugly barbarian.

'All of the males o the Hsien clan are nasty perverts - they had plundered several states and raped all of the woman they could see be they toothless or not. There are actually a widespread suicide of women who survived after being raped by the Hsien clan probably because no woman could live up to the shame brought by those filthy and ugly pigs. He had several wives and mistresses, and he made each of his woman's life a living hell!' Li Lei Shuang remembered Yan Mei Ling's hideous description of the Hsein clan.

If Yan Mei Ling's description about the Hsien clan was true, then Lord Hsien Mao Dong would certainly be a terrible husband.

Ghastly hopelessness pervaded Li Lei Shuang which left her no hope to cling upon. As tears dulled her eyes, a vision of fallen empire, lying corpses of the innocents and crying people came to her.

She cried harder feeling terribly defeated by the demons of her mind and for knowing that she was trapped. She had no right to put herself first because it only meant the death of more people. She even doubted if her father's army had a chance against the Hsein clan.

'They have gone stronger after incorporating a lot of feudal states.' The hopeless words of father came to taunt her.

"Oh, no," she sobbed harder - everything seemed hopeless no matter where she looked at. She had to tell her father that she already made her decision. But before incarcerating herself to an extremely bitter fate, she had to see Mei Ling, for all days before her dreaded day would finally come. "Oh, Yan Mei Ling, where are you? I need you."

Yan Mei Ling along with her maidservant, Yeng, passed outside the enormous gates of the Imperial palace but she deliberately walked past it.

"Are we not going inside the Imperial Palace, my lady?" Yeng asked, there was wonder in her voice.

Yan Mei Ling wearily shook her head though from the look in her eyes, going inside the imperial palace was what she really wanted to do. "No, let's go straight to the town, Yeng. We will find out when is going to be the next fight of the Ninja boy."

"As you wish, my lady"

As they walked away from the gates of the Imperial Palace, Yan Mei Ling felt extremely lonely; she also felt guilty - guilty over the things she felt for her best friend and guilty for taking the coward's way of not showing up without any explanation. But she had no choice; staying away was the only known sensible solution to avoid falling deeply in love with her best friend.

The realization that she loved her best friend had certainly knocked her away despite the fact that she didn't want it to happen. She could not - would not - relinquish herself to such. She didn't want to feel that way, and if only she could extricate herself from such emotion, she would gladly do.

"The young and valiant Jinzhou Lu Wang Wei of the Imperial Palace Military has enlisted himself for the town's upcoming brawl." Mei Ling heard an old vendor shared to one of his customers as Mei Ling and Yeng walked past his store in the bustling and lively cobbled street market.

"Who could be the probable opponent?" His customer asked as he waited for the vendor to finish computing the amount of the goods he brought on the abacus.

"I don't know - ah, that costs you 3 pieces of copper" The vendor said to his customer. "Oh, but I have seen the list and all of the names there are nothing but weaklings."

"Jinzhou Lu Wang Wei is certainly a strong man. I have heard that his unmatched strength helped greatly in pacifying the invading pirates of the south." Another customer joined in.

The old vendor scratched his chin as if in deep thoughts before nodding his head slowly. "True," he affirmed to the other customer. "but if the ninja boy will enlist himself in the town's next brawl, then, I think, Jinzhou Lu Wang Wei will have a formidable opponent."

"The ninja boy has great skills but I think that he will have no match against the battle-trained Jinzhou Lu Wang Wei. I think I will put my bet on Jinzhou Lu Wang Wei."

"Me too," another agreed.

Yan Mei Ling's ears hang to the every word that the vendor and his customers said. Jinzhou Lu Wang Wei - she heard of his numerous glorious feats and even though she had not seen him yet, her father had talked about him as if he was someone of great worth.

'Jinzhou Lu Wang Wei had brought immense glory to the empire even at a young age. I wish I have a son like him - it would have been a great honor.'

Yan Mei Ling had remembered the pride in his father's voice whenever he mentioned the name Jinzhou Lu Wang Wei. She never heard her father talk about her with such great pride that she felt extremely jealous and full of spite to the faceless man.

'I am going to fight you Jinzhou Lu Wang Wei, and I'll mark the first taint in your seemingly immaculate honor,' she said to herself with intense determination.

"Yeng," she quickly called the attention of her maidservant who was busy hovering over the goods put on sale by different vendors.

Yeng immediately went to her. "Yes, my lady?"

"I want you to find someone who will enlist the ninja boy for the upcoming town brawl." Mei Ling instructed her maid-servant, and gave her a few copper coins for the registration and payment to the man who would enlist ninja boy on the list. She did it this way to avoid being discovered and maintain the anonymity of the Ninja Boy.

Yan Mei Ling continued walking around the town. She would like to stroll before going to Master Tang Jiao Quon's lair up the mountains. She sauntered above the cobbled street and saw several vendors in their lively and colorful stands; at the other side, she saw someone plucking his ruan hoping that the music emanated from the stringed instrument would lure customers into buying vases from him; and on a farther side, she heard a squealing pig desperately struggling against the cursing burly man who attempted to drag it into the caravan.

Despite the simplicity of everything she saw, she felt that each activity all added up to form the word: Life. Beyond the walls of her house, everything seemed so free and lively, and in wonderful symphony - this was life should be. Amidst the townspeople, she never realized that she would feel the pulse of life.

So very unlike her home...

She doubted that her house should have the honor of being called a home. A home should be a place filled with the music of happiness, love and laughter not the not the eerie song of tension, insecurity and coldness. She even regarded the Imperial Palace more of her home because there, she felt loved especially in the arms of her best friend, Li Lei Shuang.

Yan Mei Ling's heart clenched despairingly at her thoughts. She would never experience how it felt to have a home anymore; she had finally decided to confine herself to the cold prison of misery now that she would avoid Li Lei Shuang forever. Maybe it was for the best. She should not cry even though that was exactly what she wanted to do - wasn't it her decision? She would rather take it as the most selfless act in her entire life.

Yan Mei Ling was so absorbed in her thoughts that she didn't notice a horse speeding to her direction.

Fortunately, the rider of the horse was keen on his senses and was quick to stop the animal before it ran over her. Terror momentarily seized Mei Ling's senses - what happened was certainly a near-death experience.

'Even if you are in the midst of self-absorption, you must still be perceptive and conscious of what is happening around you. Heedlessness can be your possible downfall,' Master Tang Jiao Quon words came to taunt her panic-alarmed state.

The rider came down from his mount and hurriedly checked on the girl that he almost ran over. "My apologies - are you fine, my lady?"

Yan Mei Ling remained stunned for a few moments but was pulled back to reality when she realized that someone held her shoulders. She flared up immediately when she recognized that the one who held her was the rider of the horse that would have permanently stamped her life away. "Take your hands off me! You have no right to touch me!"

The man was surprised by Yan Mei Ling's reaction but then he also smiled because he was in awe of her beauty. "I hope you will accept my apology, my lady. I never intend for my horse to nearly hit you."

The gall to deflect his misdeed to an animal - the gall indeed! She furiously looked at the smiling man with dagger eyes hoping that simply staring at a person could kill. But, unwillingly, she also noticed how tall and handsome he was - nape-length straight black hair, darker than the moonless night sky, tied neatly in a pony tail fashion, beautiful and sparkling almond eyes regarding her both with admiration and concern. Oh, she never thought that a nose would seem to be a work of art but his was; never had she seen such wonderfully sculpted aquiline nose.

To make thing's worse, the wide breadth of his shoulders filled his imposing armor which was worn above his finely tailored silk brocade. She would have swoon over his overwhelming male beauty if not for her anger at almost being killed due to his recklessness. "Do not blame your horse if it happens to hit me because it's just a loyal animal that goes wherever and whenever his master wants it to, and picks up the speed whatever its master pushes it to!"

"I am truly sorry, my lady; both for blaming my horse over my inability to control its speed and for almost hitting you with it. I swear I have no intention of harming you. Now, I would like to make sure of one thing - are you fine?" The handsome man humbly asked looking genuinely contrite though his admiration over her beauty was still in his eyes.

Yan Mei Ling felt absurdly shy but then she displaced it by snorting at the handsome man petulantly and left him without bothering to answer his question.

"Can I bring you to the place where you are heading, my lady? I have a horse" The man called the beautiful girl who furiously turned her back at him.

"I am fully aware that you have a horse, you have almost killed me with it!" She sarcastically answered not bothering to look at the man. "And, you only have one horse which means that only one person should mount it. Besides, I am capable and old enough to go to any places where I want to go!"

"Well, mind if I could ask for your name then, my lady?" He desperately tried to catch her attention. He had followed her leaving his horse in the middle of the street unbridled.

"I do not give my name to a clumsy stranger!" Yan Mei Ling angrily burst out, stopping in her tracks to face the man who followed her. "And, please, do not follow me!"

The man did as he was told and remained standing in his place for a moment watching the girl who hurriedly walked away from him as if his nearness offended her.

"Keep safe, my lady" he said to the wind hoping it would convey the message to the girl who had earned his admiration with both her overwhelming beauty and sharp mouth.

The noisy warble of the townspeople and the massive stone walls of the town suddenly became a very picturesque scene as the girl walked farther and farther until she was finally nowhere in sight. The man smiled once again, as if in trance, before returning to his horse and drove toward the Imperial Palace gates.

CHAPTER 5

As the man walked swiftly on top of the long and wide red-tiled hall, the ferocious-looking dragon's head entablatures seemed to smile at him. Even the ornamental javelins, displayed on the walls at both far sides of the tall columns and punctuated by huge open windows, twinkled like stars known only during the cloudless night sky.

Truly, the place might had been enchanted... or was it he who was still under some kind of enchantment?

He couldn't forget about her - she was very beautiful like the wildflowers gracing the high mountains.

Her beautiful face unmarred even by an angry scowl. Her cheeks rosy probably from the eager kisses of the sunlight; her eyebrows were like trimmed feathers though he suspected them to be uncut; her pretty little nose which complimented her face perfectly; her expressive beautiful almond-shaped eyes shone like black diamonds. Unfortunately, during the time that they had met, they were shining only because of anger.

If only he had seen her eyes shone not only in anger, he could have believed that his ancestors had been extremely indulgent on him; and her lips - he believed that he was not under some exaggerated imagination but he thought it had the color of the prettiest hue of pink.

Truly, the beautiful virago taught him to have a mind of a poet. Never had he been this attracted to a female though he had seen several beautiful faces such as that of the Imperial princess. But where the princess looked divinely ethereal and pale, the girl he met at the market was nature's gift and basking with life which made him thoroughly captivated.

She was indeed beautiful.

He wondered fervently when fate would cross their paths again as he took a right turn and headed to the imposing massive doors of the Imperial palace meeting chamber.

Two hall guards wore their lamellar armors with pride over their black cotton sleeves barely covering their dull brown cotton trousers; the armor had a circular plate on the front designed with two serpent dragons spiraled against each other, their heads facing apart. Both of the guards greeted him with respect due to a superior ranked official despite the swords held in their hands.

The massive doors were opened and he saw the emperor and his trusted officials as well as alliances gathered.

He kowtowed respectfully to the Emperor and said, "Son of Heaven, Lord of Ten Thousand Years, please forgive my error in the judgment of time, an unexpected circumstance has come along my way. I shall promise to be more heedful of the time in whatever circumstance that may come my way so as not to commit the same mistake again."

"Take your rise and take your place among the seats, Jinzhou Lu Wan Wei; you are forgiven." The Emperor said.

Still saddled with the irritation she felt for the man she had encountered at the town a while ago, Yan Mei Ling furiously removed her travelling silk robe and donned into her combat attire when she arrived at Master Tang Jiao Quon's domicile.

She knew that she should have eradicated negative emotions before coming here, as what her Master sternly advised so that she wouldn't get distracted but, at this moment, it was almost impossible.

She almost got hit by the horse and the fear she felt from the near-death experience had turned into a festering ire. She understood that he might be in a hurry but he should at least be considerate that the street leading to the Imperial Palace wasn't paved as it was crowded by people. Oh, she remembered his armor - judging from the way it was crafted, he might probably a palace official but she was skeptical for she hadn't seen him before.

Well, she hadn't really known everyone in the Palace except for a few. And, if he was indeed an imperial palace official, he should still not let his horse run so fast on a crowded street for he might hit someone. He was such an arrogant and unthinking man.

She took a deep breath to calm herself, and went outside of the hut. She saw her master meditating with his eyes closed and balancing on one foot. She was amazed - that was exactly the spot where she did her unsuccessful meditating stance. How did he do it? He seemed in perfect balance despite being crippled in his other leg. Ah, no wonder he insisted in using one foot.

Sensing the arrival of another person, Master Tang Jiao Quon opened his eyes and saw Yan Mei Ling. "Can you finally be in harmony with your body?" He asked her.

"I don't know, Master, I did try the last time but it seemed so difficult in the current state that I am now." Mei Ling answered ruefully.

Master Tang Jiao Quon stepped out of the stone where he held his meditating stance and, with the ease of the wind, he stood in front of Yan Mei Ling. "Do your thoughts still distract you, young lady?"

Yan Mei Ling remained silent unable to answer her master - her face looked dismal. She was in the trance of inner battle with herself - to tell or not to tell?

Master Tang Jiao Quon silently but keenly observed his young student and sensed her inner struggle. "I am your teacher, and as your teacher, I am concern about the things that will hinder your focus in learning such as what is currently inside you mind right now."

Yan Mei Ling swallowed audibly - a pandemonium of different opposing thoughts came to her but she was at lost the moment that she spoke. "I think I am in love, Master. The emotion is so new to me that my mind can't seem to imbibe it yet."

"Every living creature on Earth is susceptible to different emotions - one of which is love. You must know that loving is the most natural phenomenon on earth. Take courage to understand that emotion, young lady."

"But not in my case, master," Yan Mei Ling objected.

Master Tang Jiao Quon stared silently at his student and, then, a frown further creased his wrinkled forehead. "What is your case then, young lady?"

The question pushed Yan Mei Ling into the brink of hysteria making her heart shudder guiltily. How could she tell her Master about her predicament? She couldn't possibly tell him that she was in love with her best friend - he would certainly condemn her.

"I just find being romantically in love unnatural in my case because I'm still too young to feel such. I mean. . ." She stammered over her words trying to think of an idea that wouldn't invite more censorious questions. "I found such emotion as great impedance to my goal and focus as a warrior, Master."

Master Tang Jiao Quon momentarily reflected on what his student said then he stared at her. "I must explain an important thing that you must know, young woman; emotions, depending on how you perceive or handle them, can either be a catalyst or impedance in reaching your goals. The same thought applies to love."

"But I am not ready to experience such an emotion"

"It is not about you being ready or not; all unexpected things can happen such as being or falling in love. You need to understand that our emotions," he pointed to his chest, " although unseen are something that we can never compromise."

The whimsical music sang by the birds and the different colors of the spring flowers and plants in the Imperial garden reunited in the hopes of easing a quelling heart - Li Lei Shuang's heart.

She stayed the whole day at the Imperial Palace Garden in the hopes of relieving herself of the emptiness that she felt. She missed her best friend who hadn't visited since the past two days, and she was depressed with so much worry - what if Yan Mei Ling was fatally ill? Her best friend never forgot to visit her despite the onset of a bad weather or even during an unexpected illness. The thought already prompted her a while ago to go to Yan Mei Ling's house but her parents forbid her in fear that the Hsien clan might happen to attack the Empire in surprise and take her captive. But, what if the Hsien clan had attacked Yan Mei Ling's village first - what would happen to her best friend? Suddenly, dread had attacked Li Lei Shuang's entire senses so instantaneously that tears fell down from her eyes even before she knew it would came.

She walked to the garden's pond and was surprised to see its tranquil water disturbed by the relentless out-pour from her eyes. She felt utterly morose and full of fear despite the gayness of the scene in the garden brought by the spring season.

She couldn't help it. Visions of the enemies' monstrous siege and terrible waste of her people's lives came to taunt her even more.

'Li Lei Shuang, help me!' She could hear the frightened shout of Yan Mei Ling's voice in her head.

"Oh, Yan Mei Ling," she wept with a shattered heart. "There is nothing I could do - everything seems hopeless.. Oh, no."

All was lost indeed for the only panacea to avoid the terrible war from happening was to sacrifice her own happiness and tie her life eternally to the lecherous old warlord Hsien Mao Dong.

'If you feel sad during spring, just call me and we will watch the newly budding flowers caressed by the gentle wind while hoping for a glimpse of a butterfly that only comes during summer.' Yan Mei Ling had said gaily. 'But if winter comes and you also feel sad, just call me again, and together, we will reminisce the wonderful memories that happened during the last spring season.'

The memory of Yan Mei Ling's assuring words came back like a balm to a lonely heart but where was she?

"Where have you been?" Unit Commander Yan Bao Rong Di frigidly asked his daughter who had just arrived.

Yan Mei Ling silently swallowed the nervous lump in her throat and awkwardly looked at her father's hard and inscrutable features. "I strolled around the town with Yeng. We are looking for some things that we would like to buy, Bà."

Unit Commander Yan Bao Rong coldly looked at his daughter and told her, "I forbid you to leave the house ever again." He abruptly turned his back to go to his study chamber.

"Bà, you can't forbid me to go outside; I detest being incarcerated here!" Yan Mei Ling desperately cried after her father.

Unit Commander Yan Bao Rong stared back at her. "You have to follow my order because it is for the good of your own sake."

Bitter tears escaped from Yan Mei Ling's eyes and she felt a deep angst over her unfeeling father. "You never know what is good for me. How would you? You barely do your duty as a father to me."

Unit Commander Yan Bao Rong 's impenetrable eyes became bleak but before his daughter could see that her words had affected him so much, he turned his back. "You have no choice because you are just my daughter; you will follow whatever I say. No more arguments."

"I hate you, Bà!" Yan Mei Ling retorted in desperate anger and hastily ran to her room.

The Unit Commander went to his study chamber fully aware that the sorrowful sound he heard was his daughter's cry. His heart wrenched in great sadness and regret over his inability to fulfill his duties as a father to his only child.

The gauzy silk curtains embroidered with auspicious patterns were draping lazily around the wooden awning of Yan Mei Ling's four-postered bed. Though the shelter provided by the drapes seemed to provide comfort to the throb within her heart, it was only temporary because with every passing moment, the pain just kept on escalating.

The wind passing freely from her lattice window might have been comforting but it reminded her that she wasn't as free as it, and the thought only made her feel suffocated with too much envy. She had nothing else to do but to rage the contents of her heart to the pillows.

Every thing in her house, even her room, seemed to intensify the sadness she was feeling-from the wide yellow fan painted with exotic mountain flowers hanging on the wall above her canopied bed to the gilded red coromandel screens lacquered with golden geometric patterns.

'If you feel as if your heart is troubled, don't hesitate to come to me; I shall embrace you and all your troubles will be suppressed, Mei Ling'

She remembered Li Lei Shuang's words which made her cry even louder. She would never go back to her best friend's loving arms unless the insanity that was boiling within her heart would ebb.

Amidst the storm of her heart, the night was not entirely oblivious to it. The nightingale began to sing - the melody heartwarming and soothing. She took her face away from the pillow as if hypnotized by the bird's song but the moment she did so, the moonlight struck her straight in the eyes making her flinch away from it. As she swiveled her head to the other side, her eyes were drawn to the unfamiliar scroll on top of her wooden drawers.

Driven by curiosity, she went out of her bed and immediately took the scroll. She slowly unrolled it while walking around her room. When the scroll was completely opened, her legs seemed to lose its strength and, just in time, she sank down to the corner leg stool beside her tea table.

My dearest Yan Mei Ling,

How are you?

I have written this letter to express my concern about your absence in the imperial palace during the last few days. I terribly miss your jovial presence which never fails to lighten up my day.

As much as I would have loved to visit you, I was not given the luxury to do so. Actually, a lot of ghastly thoughts have troubled my mind such as the thought of you being ill. Oh, I hope you are not! I would never be there to take care of you. But it is not only that, since the past few days, my mind has been on constant wondering. I feel utterly sad that I think my eyes would never be dry again. My spirit is hopelessly despondent that I want someone to confide my troubles to. Though the Imperial palace might have been filled with wonderful people but I prefer no one to confide my troubles to but you.

Oh, my beloved best friend, I really miss you. If you are indeed afflicted with an illness, please write to me so that I may have a very good reason to tell my parents of the need to get out of the Imperial Palace.

Please be well and always be safe. I love you so much.

Li Lei Shuang

After reading her best friend's letter, Yan Mei Ling's heart swelled with so much emotion that she found herself drowning in her tears again. She had resolved to shut Lei Shuang from her life but it seemed so hard. She would always feel guilty especially when she had no logical reason to tell her best friend why she did so.

'All unexpected things can happen - that is something that we could never compromise.' Master Tang Jiao Quon's words echoed in her ears like a bell's clear shrill sound.

Li Lei Shuang might have been in deep anguish as what the letter seemed to imply. As her best friend, Mei Ling didn't have the heart to deny her the comfort that she deserved.

Remembering her Master's last words to the heart, she felt like braving the worst of all storms.

'Love is not only for two lovers in a romantic bliss - there are other kinds of love; some are unimaginable but uncontrollable.'

Chapter 6

The bird's melodious voices on a beautiful spring morning never failed to hit the perfect note. To complement the enchantment brought by the avian song, the breeze felt tranquil, pleasant and invigorating. But then no matter how beautiful the nature's deity tried to paint today's spring morning, in the Yan's dining table, it had only been deemed an abominable irony.

The only audible sound, aside that of the birds', where the hiss brought by the dancing lanterns on the ceiling outside the windows. As what had always been, just like in a stringent military formation, Unit Commander Yan Bao Rong and his daughter ate their breakfast in rigid silence.

During the entire duration of the meal, Yan Mei Ling had eaten with her head slightly bowed down, like she was avoiding looking straight to her father. Her thoughts, at that moment, were occupied; her dilemma was difficult but then she had her resolution - and the latter weighed more than the former.

She slowly lifted her head to finally stare at her father but the moment she did, she only felt dwarfed by the sheer authority she sensed in him as the imposing ornately-decorated heavy armor he wore above his long-sleeved black silk robe. The empire's dragon dynastic emblem carved on the armor looked as powerful as he was. Yan Mei Ling started to feel her resolution waning faster than she thought deeply about it yesterday - doubts and fears had loosened her resolve.

The Unit Commander stiffly excused him self from the table and stood.

"Bà," she softly called him before he turned his back.

The Unit Commander remained standing in his place to look at his daughter. He merely regarded her with an impassive stare.

"Uhm," Yan Mei Ling awkwardly faltered but then she must say what she wanted to say. "May I come along with you on your way to the Imperial Palace? I need to visit Li Lei Shuang."

The Unit Commander remained silent as he continued staring at his daughter stolidly. "I will not come back home tonight. I will not be able to accompany you back here."

"Yeng can go with us," Yan Mei Ling suggested - desperation was evident in her voice.

The Unit Commander remained unmoved and started to turn his back.

"Bà, please," she called again. "If you won't come back tonight, then please allow me to stay at the Imperial palace. Surely, I will be safe there."

At Yan Mei Ling's last words, her father faced her again and said, "Yes, you can go with me."

Yan Mei Ling felt extremely ecstatic with her father's consent that it took a lot of her strong will to control the urge to hug her father but then she managed to say, "Thank you, bà."

"Oh, Yan Mei Ling, I am so happy to see you!" Li Lei Shuang exclaimed delightedly the moment Yan Mei Ling entered her room. She rushed to embrace her best friend. "I was so worried about you. How the thought of you being ill had distressed me so much, and it pained me that I was not there to take care of you. But I am so happy that you are here - I miss you so much, Yan Mei Ling."

Yan Mei Ling went rigid with what her best friend said to her. She felt guilty for ignoring Lei Shuang. The truth was she did not want to stay away from her best friend but then her feelings had plagued her so much. She was in denial from the time that she realized the extent of her feelings, and thought at first that staying away would purge whatever she felt but, unfortunately, it did not. In the same way that her feelings intensified, her guilt had escalated.

After a moment of rigidity, Yan Mei Ling returned Li Lei Shuang's embrace - trying to fight the awkwardness that threatened to swallow her being. Surely, this cannot be wrong when being in her arms feels so right?

"I am very sorry, Li Lei Shuang," Yan Mei Ling said remorsefully when she tore herself from her best friend's embrace. "I was ill and I don't want you to be afflicted with it." She lied and even pinched her nose for added emphasis. "But now, I feel perfectly fine. I.. I miss you too."

"I'm happy to hear that," Li Lei Shuang beamed.

Yan Mei Ling smiled back and could not help but notice how utterly beautiful Li Lei Shuang was. Her best friend was majestic and beautiful beyond any words. Her best friend was also good and kind. But no matter how great the extent of her feelings for

Lei Shuang was, she knew only too well that the love she felt could be reciprocated in a way that a friend would to her friend.

She could love her best friend but only in silence for she would never have the guts to tell Li Lei Shuang the depth of her feelings - such feelings were unheard of. She was afraid that her best friend might alienate herself from her. It would certainly kill her if Li Lei Shuang would spurn their friendship.

Yes, that was it. Love Li Lei Shuang in silence would be the most sensible thing to do. At least, despite the unrequited love, she still had a consolation - Li Lei Shuang's friendly affection.

"Oh, I truly miss you, Yan Mei Ling." Li Lei Shuang said and embraced her best friend again as if she was afraid of letting her go.

Yan Mei Ling's heart fluctuated nervously that she was afraid that Li Lei Shuang might hear the thumping inside her chest. She almost tore herself from her best friend's embrace again but when she felt something hot and wet soaked through the silk on her shoulder, she she tightened her arms around Li Lei Shuang.

"Please remain in my arms, Yan Mei Ling. I am very lonely."

"Is there something wrong, Li Lei Shuang?" Yan Mei Ling asked in wonderment.

Li Lei Shuang remained silent but the tears from her eyes never ceased from falling.

Yan Mei Ling reluctantly removed herself from her best friend's embrace after a moment. She stared at her best friend and saw the great sadness that was lingering in them - a sadness that she could not decipher the cause of; a sadness that curiously made her feel guilty.

"Was my absence for a few days the reason why you are crying, Li Lei Shuang? If so, I am really sorry. I will never leave you even if I am ill."

"No, it is not the reason, Yan Mei Ling."

Yan Mei Ling stared at her best friend trying to figure out the reason behind her best friend's sadness. Her heart clenched painfully when, apparently, she did not know at all. She felt utterly helpless to comfort her best friend.

For years, Li Lei Shuang had been the one who always guided and lectured her. Her beloved best friend was always the one who was there whenever she felt sad, and even consented to her childish follies despite the fact that her best friend did not always agree with all of them.

Li Lei Shuang was her happiness. But now that the tears in her best friend's eyes were dimming the happiness she had always seen in them, it was her turn to make Li Lei Shuang happy.

"Please stop crying, Li Lei Shuang. I will never leave you even if all of the black strands from my hair would turn snowy white." Yan Mei Ling said lightheartedly.

"I love you so much, Yan Mei Ling, but you must know that not at all times that we are going to be together. But if I will be granted with just one wish, I want to be with you forever."

Yan Mei Ling was confused with Li Lei Shuang's words. Suddenly, she felt a sense of foreboding - as if those words were another way of telling her farewell.

"Of course, I love you, Li Lei Shuang!" Yan Mei Ling blurted out. When she realized what she had just said, her heart shuddered guiltily that she looked at her best friend, expecting for a look of condemnation. When she saw none, she continued,

"I mean, yes, I truly love you, Lei Shuang - you are my dearest friend. If you are happy, I am happy. If you are sad, I will also feel sad. So, tell me the reason why you are crying, we will try to sort that out together so that you won't cry anymore."

Li Lei Shuang was touched by what Mei Ling said that she took her best friend's face between her palms and tenderly kissed her best friend on the forehead.

Yan Mei Ling almost leapt at Lei Shuang's gesture but then she knew that it would only be foolish. Li Lei Shuang kissing her on the forehead had never been unusual for that was her best friend's gesture of affection for her. Reacting differently would only give birth to suspicions. But everything is different now.

"The Hsien clan plans to attack my father's empire." Lei Shuang finally said - her voice was full of agony and fear. Her eyes were greatly swollen from the tears that were destined to perpetually flow.

"Didn't the Hsien clan come to the Imperial palace banquet several weeks ago to discuss about a peaceful alliance between your father's empire and theirs?" Yan Mei Ling asked; she was enraged by what she heard. "Now, my instinct about those ugly pigs was right - they could never be trusted."

"It is not the only reason, Yan Mei Ling." Li Lei Shuang sobbed brokenly. "Oh, I never felt so strangled and helpless in my entire life."

"What is the other reason?"

"Lord Hsein Mao Dong, the head of the Hsein clan, won't push through with the war if I consent to be his wife."

Yan Mei Ling entire body froze. If Lei Shuang would marry the old pig, then he could be next to the Emperor or, worst, become the next emperor. And what had become of the places that he ruled? Chaos and fear ruled! No, it could not be! Something came to Yan Mei Ling that made her want to kill Lord Hsein Mao Dong - was this what they call blood lust? She would never let that ugly pig have her best friend. She would rather have a war to take place.

A memory of the Hsien clan's visit came to Yan Mei Ling:

'His most radiant Son of Heaven has such a splendid empire,' Lord Hsein Mao Dong said meaningfully to the emperor then he turned his avid gaze to Lei Shuang. His eyes were looking at her with longing. 'And an equally exquisite daughter'

Now, everything was clear to Yan Mei Ling. The way Lord Hsien Mao Dong looked at Lei Shuang only mirrored his avarice to possess the empire. The thought was unthinkable and obscene - he was an extremely lecherous pig!

"What did Son of Heaven say about Lord Hsein Mao Dong's demand, Li Lei Shuang?"

"My father said that he would rather have a war to take place than give me to Lord Hsien Mao Dong." Lei Shuang sobbed brokenly. "Oh, Yan Mei Ling, I am so afraid. You know that I hate war, the violence it brings, and the lost of innocent lives as a result of it." The tears from her eyes never waned. It was as if that all hopes had been pointed out and ended up as nothing. "I don't want the war to happen especially if there is a way to prevent it. If I have to marry Lord Hsien Mao Dong for the peace of the empire, then I will even if it means compelling myself to a lifetime of misery."

Upon hearing Li Lei Shuang's decision, Yan Mei Ling's stomach reeled that she felt sputtering with disgust. This was too much. No, this was utter insanity. Seeing her best friend being married to the devil himself was disgusting beyond any words.

"Peace?" Yan Mei Ling asked in furious incredulity because she could not help it. "Do you want me to enlighten you once again as what happen to the places that the Hsien clan ruled? There is no peace there - only fear and cruelty! Do you want it to happen to your father's empire; to your people?"

"Yan Mei Ling it was the -"

"No, I will not allow you!" Yan Mei Ling shouted angrily interrupting whatever Lei Shuang was about to say. "Do not do it, Li Lei Shuang," she whimpered softly as if she was exhausted from extreme desolation. "Do not do it. I beg you, Li Lei Shuang. If a war will take place, then so be it. You are far too precious to wed that morbid swine. Oh, you are so special to me. Please do not."

Li Lei Shuang embraced her crying best friend, comforting her. "I love you so much, my dearest friend, but I could not always think of my own welfare - that would be selfishness on my part. I have a duty, and my duty is to protect the empire and its people."

"You are not being selfish by not consenting to marry that vile swine." Yan Mei Ling cried in explanation. Her heart was breaking, breaking into fine pieces. "I told you: if you marry that pig, fear and cruelty will surely reign. Listen and try to understand what I am telling you; marrying him will only hasten up the degradation of the empire! Please trust in Son of Heaven's army, they will win. Fear not of violence, for being married to Lord Hsien Mao Dong is worst than the most lurid violence.

Fear no more, I will never leave you; I will protect you. You can always count on me."

Chapter 7

Sneering and laughing masculine sounds mingled with the opium haze assailing through the gambling den. Not to be outdone, clicking wooden chips, soft paper whispers and clinking coins added to the noise.

At the right of the tavern, near the wonderfully-crafted paper calligraphy art, a pot-bellied man named Liang Zhu stood frowning disappointedly to the poker-faced gamblers playing Ma Diao Pai. Much to his utter dismay, everybody seemed to do his best to ignore Liang Zhu's existence.

Well, the reason wasn't that hard to figure out: Liang Zhu was considered a tavern fool for seeking too much attention from the people in the gambling den. If his ugly smirking face was not the reason, then it was most certainly his irritating mouth which did not seem to have the ability to stay close even for a short period of time. His overbearing narration of his latest venture or whatever menial deed he had done for the day had already grated to the people's nerves.

"My bet on Jinzhou Lu Wang Wei had been extremely profitable. I know that he will make it to the championship unscathed. And, let me predict, the championship fight will be between him and the Ninja boy." Liang Zhu announced hoping to get some attention from the disinterested gamblers.

"It is expected," one of the gamblers sneered distastefully but not directed to the news but rather to Liang Zhu whom he deemed a plaguing nuisance.

Sensing that he could not get an ounce of the attention he sought than what he had just received, Liang Zhu added slyly, "Oh, I forget to mention that I placed equal bets between Jinzhou Lu Wang Wei and the Ninja boy. Isn't it extremely fortuitous of me?"

The statement caught the attention of another gambler who disgustedly remarked, "Only a coward without honor will bet on two opponents - that is pure stupidity."

The gambler's companions agreed and diverted their attentions back to their game leaving Liang Zhu in sneering silence.

Feeling even more neglected and sneered upon in addition to being irritated as one of the gamblers purposely released the opium smoke in his direction earning a sputtering cough from him and humorous laughs among the gamblers, Liang Zhu persisted in talking, "In gambling, you need to be wise and practical even if it means being a coward. And besides, there is no honor in gambling - only gains and losses."

"Are you implying that placing equal bets on two matching opponents as wise?" One of the gamblers sarcastically questioned him.

Feeling belittled but still determined, he answered, "Partly"

"Partly? Bah! Half wise and half foolish would never be wise - that would be the most stupid thing I have ever heard." Another gambler jeered loudly that the gamblers from the other tables heard and guffawed at Liang Zhu.

Liang Zhu merely smiled in an indignant way ignoring the jeering laughter aimed at him. "It doesn't really matter what you think of me now. I know each of you bet on either Jinzhou Lu Wang Wei or the Ninja boy but I tell you loyalty to one fighter won't make you gain more money. Now, I may have placed equal bets on both of them which technically mean that I will not earn a copper this time. Who cares if I might not earn this time, I already won betting on the two fighters during their previous fights anyway. At least, in the end, no matter the outcome of the fight, I will always be a winner."

"That is if you call a half loser a winner!" One of the gamblers said which intensified the laughter inside the gambling den.

Liang Zhu realized that he would never get the kind of attention he sought from the gamblers but only more insults so he left the gambling den in haste.

When he was gone, the place became eerily silent as if gamblers are suddenly locked in their own reflective thinking. At first, they were disgusted with what Liang Zhu said to them considering how twisted his logic of being wise and practical seemed to be. In the end, they all agreed albeit silently, to avoid being dubbed as stupid, that Liang Zhu despite being foolish was being practical and somehow wise - that was if partly wise could be accepted.

The wind was gentle as it kissed the balcony like a mother cradling her baby. Over the horizon, a shooting star passed by the jeweled cloudless sky. In another time or in a different circumstance, such a sight would have been wonderful but still not enough to hamper the tears streaming from Yan Mei Ling's eyes.

She was supposed to clear her mind from all murky thoughts for the championship tomorrow but she was buried in the pit of despair. She couldn't help but think of what would happen should the Hsein clan attack the empire. And, what bothered her most was Li Lei Shuang's absurd though unselfish sacrifice of her self.

Sacrifice - such a terrifying thing! If only things would not be as complicated as they truly are; if only war had not only existed, then she would not be sitting outside her room in the balcony crying against the night; continuously pondering on a future that represented danger.

Had she been given a chance to change even a thing in the past, then she would see to it that the evil tyrant, Lord Hsien Mao Dong, would never be born. He was the root of all evil and, simply thinking of him made her want to do things that could only be deemed as evil. He was the reason why she could never paint beautiful colors in her life; he was the reason why she'd never have peace in her mind.

As she continually thought about things, her reflection brought her back to a beautiful memory - something that she would never forget:

The street on the market was congested during that time. Wonderful wares and mouthwatering meals were on display.

The sun didn't feel harsh, just perfect for a stroll. Yan Mei Ling and Li Lei Shuang were walking as if they were part of the common folks wearing simple identical white gowns they borrowed from the maidservants - Yan Mei Ling took the pains of convincing and bribing them.

'Look, Li Lei Shuang, a wonderful sword! I have never seen such a beauty!' Yan Mei Ling said exuberantly pointing to the direction of the merchant who sold several weapons. Her eyes glued avidly to the biggest sword with intricate dragon design on the grip.

'Your father will not be pleased if you buy that,' Li Lei Shuang reminded her gently.

Yan Mei Ling snorted childishly and began sulking.

Li Lei Shuang looked at her friend seriously for a moment before walking to the merchant who sold arm-wares. She took her time examining the different weapons put on display while Yan Mei Ling continued sulking, oblivious to everything.

She smiled when she saw a small knife. Its hilt was made of black lacquered hard wood, encrusted with pearls and jade. It also had miniature dragon paintings done in lustrous gold. It was perfect. She politely asked the merchant to wrap the thing.

The merchant's eyebrows rose skeptically obviously doubting her ability to pay for the knife considering the type of clothes she was wearing. He purposely told her the price even though she did not ask for it. When the penniless-looking beautiful girl remained undaunted, he became amused. She nodded respectfully, took her purse and gave it to him. He disinterestingly opened the purse and his small eyes dilated with shock when he realized the amount of its content.

Li Lei Shuang smiled at the merchant and told him that he could have everything in the purse if he would wrap the knife nicely. He immediately complied, took his best silk and wrapped it. Extremely grateful, she thanked him as she took the knife and went back to the sulking Yan Mei Ling.

Li Lei Shuang gently tap her grumpy friend's back.

'What?' Yan Mei Ling asked in irritation.

'I have something for you,' Li Lei Shuang gently answered.

Yan Mei Ling looked at Li Lei Shuang's hand where she saw something wrapped wonderfully in a red silk.

'If that's a mirror or a comb or even a sweatmeat, then I am not accepting it,' Yan Mei Ling exclaimed childishly, crossing her arms in her chest.

Li Lei Shuang smiled patiently and said, 'Why won't you take and open this so you will know what I am giving you?'

Yan Mei Ling's curiosity was piqued but remained skeptical. 'What is that? I know I'll be sorely disappointed.'

'I have this specifically wrapped to surprise you. Won't you take and open this?'

After a moment's hesitation, Yan Mei Ling relented and accepted Lei Shuang's gift.

'Open it,' Li Lei Shuang gently urged her.

Yan Mei Ling immediately opened the parcel and looked surprised upon realizing what it was. She marveled at the knife's exquisitely painted containment and unsheathed it. Though small, it looked formidable. Its steel shone when the sun's ray kissed it. Her palm could snuggly hold its majestically-designed hilt, extravagantly encrusted with jade stones and pearls.

'This looked even more wonderful than the sword that first caught my fancy!' Yan Mei Ling exclaimed happily as she sheathed the knife back.

'I know you would like it - it reminds me of you. At least, it will be easy for you to hide it from your father.' Li Lei Shuang explained. Her heart bursting with joy upon seeing Yan Mei Ling's ecstatic reaction of having the knife.

'Oh, Li Lei Shuang, you really are my best friend!' Yan Mei Ling hugged Li Lei Shuang in supreme gratitude.

Li Lei Shuang smiled and gently kissed Yan Mei Ling's forehead. Then she paused when she remembered something. 'It is almost time for tea, Yan Mei Ling, and we have not brought any sweetmeats yet.'

Yan Mei Ling broke from their embrace and said, 'Oh! Let's buy now and be quick.'

'I have no money left,' Li Lei Shuang told her.

'Oh,' Yan Mei Ling blushed guiltily upon realizing the reason why her friend had no money anymore. 'Ah. . I have a few coins. I will pay for the sweetmeats'

Li Lei Shuang smiled and they went to the store that sold sweetmeats. They brought everything that looked and taste delightful and happily went out of the store.

Yan Mei Ling was happily testing each sweetmeat when Li Lei Shuang ran and went to an old beggar. Her mouth went agape when she saw her friend took the little silver combs from her own hair and gave them to the old beggar who in turn smiled gratefully.

Li Lei Shuang smiled when she went back to Yan Mei Ling, her lovely long hair unsecured and was swept by the wind.

'Why did you give your combs to the beggar? Look at you,' Yan Mei Ling asked.

'She needs the combs better than I do.' Li Lei Shuang simply explained.

'Huh?' Yan Mei Ling exclaimed - confused by her friend's answer. 'Whatever would she need the comb for? The beggar wore her hair down and probably never comb it. You should have given her a sweetmeat.'

'Oh, I also gave her a sweetmeat.'

'Then, what is the purpose of you giving her the combs when you already gave her a sweetmeat? She obviously doesn't comb or tie her hair.'

Li Lei Shuang remained silent for a while then look at Mei Ling. "You are right, Yan Mei Ling. She doesn't need the combs to make her hair looks nice but those are made of silver. The sweetmeat would only feed her for a day but she can sell the combs and make her fare better."

Yan Mei Ling was dumbfounded with what Li Lei Shuang said. A blush guiltily crept her cheeks and she felt ashamed. 'You could have asked me some coins to give her.'

'It's fine, Yan Mei Ling. You've purchased the sweetmeats and somehow you've helped her. Isn't it nice to help someone?'

Yan Mei Ling smiled happily at what Li Lei Shuang said - her heart was overwhelmed with too much emotion.

Yan Mei Ling smiled at the recollection. She would never forget the way Li Lei Shuang humbly bared her kindness to her people. She was the kind of person that do good deeds without telling others who she really was. There was even a time when she gave her jade bracelet to a poor family while they were visiting the town square.

Li Lei Shuang was the most generous and loving person Yan Mei Ling had ever known. She would definitely make a wonderful Empress. At this time, the thought might be a bit shaky but Yan Mei Ling was bound to make it a reality. Not only was Li Lei Shuang the Son of Heaven's daughter thus made her the heir to the throne but she truly deserved the throne. Her kindness and generosity were the things that the people needed. And if Lord Hsien Mao Dong would marry her, then the Empire's peace would be forever thrown among the winds of peril.

Yan Mei Ling would never want that to happen. She must protect her best friend at all cost. She would be willing to lay her life for Li Lei Shuang.

The moon's light momentarily took her attention. The sheer beauty and clarity it presented were overwhelming. She noticed how it illuminated the darkness behind it; she marveled at how its light never dim even at night. A ghost of cloud threatened to cast upon it but the gentle zephyr blew the latter and its light continued to reign.

A thought came to her upon realizing the meaning of what the moon seemed to represent. If she wanted to protect Li Lei Shuang, then she should be like the moon. Someone that could never be defeated by the darkness.

Happy New Year 2014! Vote and comment! Thanks

'I am not perfect but so are you.'

Chapter 8

The tournament was filled with a kaleidoscope of emotions but two certain ones dominated the crowd's hearts - tension and excitement.

They were tensed because they were afraid of going home empty-handed should their favored warrior lose; and they were excited because a new champion was about to emerge.

"Jinzhou Lu Wang Wei is such a great warrior and I have been earning more betting for him than I do when working as a butcher for a month." A man shared to his companion.

"Hmm," the other exclaimed. "My small bet, for the ninja boy though, gained fairly well enough for me a sample of a taste of life's luxury."

"Luxurious living, eh?" someone remarked disgustedly. "You could do better with what you had won. But, then who cares about betting? I am just here to watch the fight and find out who will win. I didn't even bother risking a coin on nonsense things such as gambling."

"Bah, we did not ask for your opinion, and what you are doing is a waste of time. You might as well didn't pay to watch the fight if you are not gambling. You could have waited tomorrow and ask who wins."

"I want to witness firsthand who will win. This is an event that one should not miss. Besides, gambling would be a waste of my time if I am only here to enjoy the fight." The antagonistic man countered indignantly.

The trade outside the arena flourished. A lot of merchants were crowding outside the thick red walls of the arena. Tents were set-up, vases of different designs and varying colors were displayed; accessories made of precious and semi-precious stones were flaunted, even fake duplicates were displayed together with the real ones; and the food stalls were swarmed by the crowd who were about to enter the arena.

"The thieves really know when to start their nasty business," a fat merchant said to his only customer who wore bright red silk brocade of obvious great quality, colorful intricate patterns were printed on his dress.

"You are right," the customer agreed as he slowly examined the pearl necklace; and when found no fault on it, he smiled. "I'll take this necklace. How much?"

"It is of perfect quality, we got it from the oriental continent of the south. You can have it for 3 pieces of gold." The fat merchant said excitedly to the customer.

"3 pieces of gold for this pearl necklace? Obviously, this is not first grade. That is too much!" The customer sneered in disbelief.

The merchant's brows rose indignantly and said, "You are wrong! It is of unmatched quality and you will never find it in the sea of Chixian Shenzhou. We even traveled the oriental seas to obtain it. I say, if you can't pay the price, then please place it back to where it is displayed."

"Fine," the customer relented as he reached for his purse. "I will take it." He handed three gold coins to the merchant and immediately took his leave.

The merchant smiled contentedly as he held the gold coins in his hand. He enjoyed his private amusement of having outwitted his customer. The pearl necklace was actually not of first grade quality as what he claimed, and it was originally valued at 10 copper coins when it reached the shores of Chixian Shenzhou. But his ingenuity had convinced the foolish customer into buying it at a price too extravagant for its value.

He flipped one coin, and the sun's ray reflected over its shine. He leisurely examined it and then, rubbed it but was flabbergasted when its golden color faded revealing a dull copper coin beneath. He furiously rubbed the other coins and saw the same thing. Cold sweat started to form on his forehead and tears fell from his eyes as he cried hysterically, "I have been duped!"

A few minutes before the championship began, more and more people were putting their bets on their favored warrior. The betting area was so congested that it was as if you could not throw a needle in between the people due to lack of space. People of different stations - rich or poor - did their best to advance in the line just to get their names and bets registered. Different human smell permeated through the air that one old man fainted due to suffocation, various curses were also heard as arms hit each other and feet stamped upon another.

It was busy indeed.

Chou, the one who was in-charge of listing the names and accepting bets, was almost on the verge of losing his patience as one man shouted at him arrogantly.

True, he loved the privileges of being in-charge of the betting list but encountering different attitudes of varying insolence sometimes made him want to quit his job. If the pay wasn't just so big, he would never take this job - it was most stressful. Life, in all its essence, was flawed.

By the time the betting registration was officially closed, much to Chou's relief, a lot of people were protesting angrily, demanding that the registration time should be extended. But that couldn't be simply done so Chou just bore their curses with a wry smile as he closed the list triumphantly, and went to the room where the monies and list were kept.

The mob angrily shouted at Chou and attempted to go after him but the big guards immediately pacified them by threatening them with their swords. Some people weren't as violent as the others even though they were just as unfortunate of not making it to the registration. They simply formed a group and made bets against each other.

The gong was finally hit thrice heralding the start of the championship. Pandemonium momentarily came to a halt as tension came to the crowd but then the excitement that they previously felt came back so the noise filled the arena once again.

The announcer, dressed in blue dragon-embroidered silk brocade, climbed the stairs of the 3-foot long circular arena made of red marble tiles. Despite the heavy plain black head dress that he was wearing, he was able to efficiently climbed onto the arena and began shouting, "Good day, people of Chixian Shenzhou. We are gathered here today to witness the rise of the new champion of the biggest fight the empire ever has."

The crowd paused and listened attentively.

"This fight that we are about to witness will be between two of the strongest warrior across the empire. You all have witnessed their unmatched strengths as they defeated one strong warrior after another." The announcer proclaimed, then he added light-heartedly, "Well, not all are strong though. Some are just pathetic delusional warriors who merely wanted their asses whip."

The crowd laughed at his humorous statement. The announcer raised both his hands as if to silenced the crowd. When silence reigned, he continues, "Without a doubt, people of Chixian Shenzhou, these two warriors whose fight you are about to witness are formidable and of great skills. But then, there could only be one champion and you will witness him today. So people of Chixian Shenzhou, hold your breath as I will introduce the warriors of this year's most anticipated fight!"

The crowd went wild with excitement and began cheering loudly.

In the midst of the vexated crowd, at a secluded and silent corner of the east wing of the arena, Yan Mei Ling, who was already dressed in her plain black ninja costume, talked to Yeng. Her maid was also dressed in a simple male cotton strolling robe; her hair tied in ponytail fashion so that no one would recognize them.

"Have you seen the way Jinzhou Lu Wang Wei fights, Yeng? What are his fighting techniques?" Mei Ling whispered to Yeng.

Her eyes cautiously drifted to the different parts of the corner to make sure than no one would overhear them.

With dreamy eyes, Yeng replied, "Oh, yes, he is handsome and charming, my lady."

Yan Mei Ling's brows rose in surprise at Yeng's far-fetched answer. "Do you hear my question well? I did not ask if he is handsome or charming; I asked you: what are his fighting techniques."

Yeng remained stuck in her fantasy that Yan Mei Ling shook her maid and impatiently said, "Won't you come back to your wits and stop behaving like a fool so that you can answer my question?"

"I am not behaving like a fool, my lady," Yeng explained, still caught under the spell of Jinzhou Lu Wang Wei. "You might be surprised to find yourself drooling over him when you meet him in the arena."

Yan Mei Ling rolled her eyes in disgust and irritation but she wasn't angry with Yeng though. She considered Yeng as a friend and confidant aside from Lei Shuang. "Who is Jinzhou Lu Wang Wei and what did he feed you to make you act in a bizarre way?"

"He fed me nothing," Yeng answered dreamily, clasping her hands to her heart. "He lured me with his unbelievable charm, undaunting strength, and exceptional fighting skills. Why, he could even match the legendary dragon warrior when it comes to fighting techniques."

Yan Mei Ling paused upon hearing Yeng's description of Jinzhou Lu Wang Wei. The legendary dragon warrior, according to her Master Tang Jiao Quon, was sent by the gods to protect Chixian Shenzhou against its enemies, many centuries ago. It was said that he single-handedly defeated more than a hundred enemy soldiers using his dragon technique. How other people learned the dragon technique was still a mystery but it was fabled that the legendary dragon warrior taught a peasant boy before he went back to Heaven as his mission was fulfilled. The peasant boy after learning the dragon technique became a great teacher of martial arts though his name was never known.

The dragon technique was one of the several techniques that Yan Mei Ling's master taught her, and it was the only technique that she had not fully mastered yet. One of the components of this technique was the ability to meditate on one foot and attacking enemies at a lightning speed without opening one's eyes - relying only on hearing the sound of the motions executed by the opponent.

If indeed Jinzhou Lu Wang Wei had matched the legendary dragon warrior's skills, then she shouldn't take him lightly. She suspected that this fight would be the most challenging one that she'd have but she was determined to win.

CHAPTER 9

The arena was situated at the right side of the market, it was about a few kilometers away from the imperial palace.

High rectangular-shaped stone walls, painted in ivory, surrounded the arena. The massive entrance was made of heavy wood sculpted with the big imperial dragon emblem, and was painted in orange except for the emblem which was done in gold. The big knobs were dragon's head made of brass. A multi-inclined gabled roof, made of blue ceramic tiles, covered just the width of the huge entrance doors.

The arena was very huge with several bleachers that could accommodate more than a thousand people. It was divided into four wings: North, South, East and West. Each wing had a tower where a guard was assigned to look for any discord except the East wing tower. If any disturbance was observed, the guard assigned in the tower would hit the big gong to warn the other guards. There were several rooms in the arena namely: book-keeping room where the monies and lists were kept, two arsenals, warriors' lair and the guards' chamber.

The East wing tower, the biggest, was made for the exclusive use of the Emperor and his officials. It was the only tower that had a roof which was done in pagoda-style though each layer had carvings that looked like dragon's claws at the tips. The walls were painted bright red and the entablatures were gilded dragon's head.

The main attraction of the arena was the area where the warriors fought - the battle stage. It was a big circular stage made of stone bricks with red marble tiles on top. The size was about 3 feet long with a radius of 1 kilometer.

As opposition to its main use, the arena connoted a wide sense of architectural grandeur primarily to please the Emperor. If not for the battle stage, you couldn't feel any suggestion of violence. In fact, the way the sun's ray kissed the ground almost made it a picturesque scene - a paradoxical implication.

The excited people stood from their bleachers ignoring the heat that was furiously licking their skin. As the gong was hit again followed by the sounds of the firecrackers, screams of anticipation grew three pitches high.

The people who did not make it to the registration hastened in finalizing their illegal bets. Others were more of spectators probably due to lack of funds or distaste for gambling or, maybe, for mere curiosity of knowing who would become the next champion; but some watched primarily to divert themselves from their patterned drudgery. And, let us not forget, some people came to take advantage of the event to thrive in their dirty and nasty businesses.

By the time that the sound of the firecrackers stopped, Jinzhou Lu Wang Wei climbed on the battle stage after his name was called. The first thing he did was to bow respectfully to the Emperor and his officials at the direction of the magnificent East wing tower; the Emperor, in turn, raised his hand to acknowledge Jinzhou Lu Wang Wei. After the Emperor's acknowledgement, he did the customary warrior's bow to the cheering people.

Yan Mei Ling was extremely shocked to find out who Jinzhou Lu Wang Wei was. She could never forget that face. How could she, when he was the arrogant and reckless man who almost killed her with his horse at the town market. The anger she felt for him during that almost tragic day came back, making her feel desperate to bring him down to his knees.

'I'm going to taint your seemingly immaculately honor', she remembered the promise she made to herself. But she needed to control the anger that had gripped her heart or else it would blind her and, eventually, distract her focus.

Yan Mei Ling was so absorbed in her thoughts that she did not hear the announcer calling for her name.

"Where is the ninja boy? What took him so long?" someone from the crowd fulminated impatiently. The other people become frustrated and started shouting for the Ninja Boy to come out.

The announcer stammered as he tried to pacify the crowd or else the Emperor might deem him and the people who were in-charge of the arena as incompetent. While the announcer was trying to soothe the impatient crowd, the ninja boy jumped onto the arena as if he magically appeared from a place of nowhere.

The unbelievable display of his entrance thoroughly amazed the crowd that they did a standing ovation. The ninja boy, amidst the noise, bowed to the Emperor who also acknowledged him before he did the customary warrior's bow.

After the Ninja boy was done with the customary warrior's bow, he faced Jinzhou Lu Wang Wei who seemed fascinated at him due to his almost magical entrance.

Jinzhou Lu Wang Wei bowed respectfully to the Ninja boy and said, "I am extremely grateful to be given the opportunity to fight one of Chixian Shenzhou's greatest warriors."

Despite the genuine light in the Jinzhou's eyes and the sincerity of his voice, Yan Mei Ling, deep in her heart, felt suspicious. 'What a deceptive man - you could not bait me with your pleasant smile and flowery words.'

She remembered Lord Hsien Mao Dong in Jinzhou Lu Wang Wei - of the time of the evil tyrant's visit to the imperial palace.

Lord Hsien Mao had greatly praised the empire's outstanding beauty and the wonderful hospitality shown by the imperial family. He even promised a peaceful alliance but everything he said was a lie. He was merely making a good impression to the imperial family by baiting them with flowery words and false promises when in fact, he was seeking for the most vulnerable part of the Empire that he could use for his advantage. Now, he had finally discovered it, he used it by threatening to attack the empire if the Emperor would not succumb to his demands.

Yan Mei Ling curbed her fists angrily at the recollection and controlled herself from crying in front of the crowd.

Jinzhou Lu Wang Wei studied the masked ninja boy who was dressed in black outfit. His attire was not common among the warriors of the empire but rather with the spies of the other countries located at the Northeastern part of Chixian Shenzhou.

Could the ninja boy possibly be a spy from another country or possibly sent by Lord Hsien Mao Dong? But the latter seemed vague for Lord Hsien Mao Dong's army or spies did not wear the same thing.

'Maybe the ninja boy is a foreign warrior who merely wants to prove his fighting skills,' he concluded to himself.

He heard of some warriors who traveled from one place to another to fight with the renowned warriors in the area merely for the joy of proving themselves the world's greatest warrior. But no matter the identity of the ninja boy, he would use this opportunity to study his fighting techniques and enrich his knowledge in martial arts.

He continued looking at the Ninja boy until he felt the latter stiffened. A sudden awareness came to him when he found himself staring into the boy's eyes - the only feature that was not covered. Those eyes, he thought for a moment, seemed familiar but he couldn't exactly remember where and when he had came across with someone who had those eyes. He frowned when he remembered someone. . Of the girl he'd almost hit in the town market. But he dismissed the thought as it seemed impossible.

Although the girl he had met at the market seemed a bit fiery as compared to the other women he knew, she was too beautiful and fragile to mask herself as a warrior so that she could fight with the big and strong men.

'But the ninja boy was slender and fragile too just like the girl you'd met in the market,' an unbidden thought came to him. He mentally shook his thought aside. It was ridiculous and impossible.

He frowned at his thoughts. Maybe, it was his obsessive desire to find the girl once again that had played illusions on his mind. Heaven knew how he had yearned for her, and the time he'd spent searching for her. But then, how the fiery girl captivated him, despite the fact that she had momentarily made him feel like an ass when she scolded him in a public place, was still a mystery to him.

Shaking the thoughts that had momentarily distract him, he studied the ninja boy again and concluded; despite his small and fragile frame, his appearance was just a facade hiding an incredible and stealth warrior. He'd watched the boy's previous fights and knew well that the latter relied on his intelligence and speed so he should outwit the ninja boy.

Yan Mei Ling was curious why Jinzhou Lu Wang Wei remained standing while frowning at her as if trying to figure out who she really was. She stiffened when she realized that he might have recognized her.

She felt distraught thinking even of that possibility. What if he would know her identity and tell her father? Her father would definitely not allow her to go out of the house even to visit Li Lei Shuang - that thought deeply saddened her and made her want to leave the arena right now.

The crowd was silent, thinking that the two warriors were scaling each other. But they became bored when the warriors merely stood while staring at each other for too long - no one even made a move to start the fight.

"Hey, you both start the fight!" A man shouted impatiently. "We did not pay to come here and watch you as you stare at each other on the arena!"

The other crowd shouted the same thing.

"Yes, start the fight!"

"What do you think of us? Paying you to entertain us with your staring contest?"

Jinzhou Lu Wang Wei became irritated with the crowd and looked at them with deadly calm eyes. As if the crowd were admonished by his arctic glare, they became silent.

Yan Mei Ling was surprised at how Jinzhou Lu Wang Wei effortlessly pacified the crowd by simply staring at them. It was as if that he had celestial powers in him.

When Jinzhou Lu Wang Wei sensed that the ninja boy was in deep thoughts, he seized the moment and started to attack the ninja boy with multiple fast kicks but the latter had quick reflexes, as what he expected, and managed to avoid his attacks. He was impressed at the stealthiness of the ninja boy that he threw another series of swift attacks which, again, the latter successfully avoided.

"You are a great warrior indeed," Jinzhou Lu Wang Wei exclaimed before he aimed another series of flying kicks to the ninja boy.

Of the numerous kicks that Jinzhou Lu Wang Wei released, three had finally landed on Yan Mei Ling. She winced at the unbearable pain she felt but she tried her best to ignore. Obviously, he was using the Wind Horse technique: it was a technique that combined both speed and strength to release numerous number of kicks with the same fatal intensity as that of a speeding horse.

But she would not allow him to intimidate her without even showing what she was capable of. She jumped mid-air until she landed at his back. She did a lightning fast turn and kicked the jinzhou.

Jinzhou Lu Wang Wei was thrown on his knees at the intensity of the ninja boy's attack. He gnored the pain by swiftly standing on his feet. The boy despite his size had unbelievable strength but he could manage it.

Meanwhile, Yan Mei Ling was disappointed at how fast the Jinzhou was able to stand when, in fact, the kick that she had just released was The Mountain kick technique. It was a kick that was so fatal that it would be impossible for the opponent to stand directly after receiving the attack. How the Jinzhou ignored it as if her kick was a mere feather landing on his back greatly frustrated her. A fast transition of words came to taunt her:

'Jinzhou Lu Wang Wei had brought glory to his clan - I wish I have a son like him.'

'Jinzhou Lu Wang Wei will defeat the ninja boy'

'He is the greatest warrior the empire ever has.'

The words echoed and hammered through her brain painfully making her extremely angry. Her anger was driving her mad that it blinded her sensibilities. Adrenaline rush pumped into her vein that enabled her to release a series of attack to Jinzhou Lu Wang Wei.

She could not seem to stop. She would not seem to stop. She was panting for breath but it was as if that she would die if she stopped raging attacks on Jinzhou Lu Wang Wei. She had to hit him; she had to hurt him and made him go down on his knees in a gesture of defeat.

'Get him down!' Her mind cried.

Yan Mei Ling made a cartwheel to Jinzhou Lu Wang Wei's side and kicked him at his side ribs. He retaliated by propelling his knee to her but she dodged him.

'Be calm, Mei Ling,' she could hear her master telling her. 'Have full of control of your emotion. Be its master; don't let it dominate you.'

Kick, punch, dodge!

Kick, punch, dodge!

Kick, punch, dodge!

Kick, punch, dodge!

'When anger arises, think of the consequences.' She oddly remembered the Confucian thought.

Yan Mei Ling continued her mindless assaults until she felt a fatal blow landed between her chest and stomach. It felt excruciatingly painful that the air she breathed seemed to desert her.

She saw a nebulous sky slowly blinding her vision until her knees melted like water, and she felt her back hitting the ground. She was evaporating, it was sucking the life out of her.

Something warm and liquid was on her mouth but she was wearing a mask trapping it within. She would drown then asphyxiate - pathetically killed by her own blood.

'I want to be with you forever, Yan Mei Ling,' a voice told her.

That voice.

She recognized it; it belonged to Li Lei Shuang. Oh, she wanted to see her best friend now but she would die on the arena.

She would die when the sun looked so beautiful and the bamboos outside proudly danced with the wind.

She would die without even saying goodbye to the people she loved.

She would die when she felt that she was not ready to die.

I need to protect, Li Lei Shuang! I cannot die. Her mind screamed but her voice appeared silent as darkness ultimately enveloped her entire senses.

Jinzhou Lu Wang Wei watched the ninja boy sprawled on his back for so long and, then, something gripped his heart - compassion.

It was odd to feel such emotion when you were fighting against your opponent but undeniably, he felt it. The ninja boy looked vulnerable and innocent despite the fact that he was a warrior. He was possibly a mere child trying to prove himself that he could be the greatest warrior. And, he felt genuinely sorry for the boy for this fight would possibly shatter the young warrior.

Jinzhou Lu Wang Wei was about to leave the battle stage after the announcer declared him the champion when someone from the crowd shouted, "Unmask the ninja boy!"

He would have ignored it but soon the other crowd joined in convincing him to unmask the ninja boy. He stared at the fallen young warrior and felt curious. Aside from his curiosity, he feared that the kick he threw on the boy might possibly be too much than he could handle. He immediately walked to the boy to check if the latter was still breathing. But when he was about to remove the mask to allow the boy to breathe properly, another ninja, an adult, kicked him hard enough to throw him off the arena.

Jinzhou Lu Wang Wei's went agape with shock when the adult ninja quickly carried the unconscious ninja boy in his arms. He jumped out of the battle stage and they both disappeared from the arena as if by a gasp of magic.

CHAPTER 10

The wind was soft as it descended on Yan Mei Ling's face. There was no glaring heat but rather a misted air. She longed to open her eyes but her body seemed opposed to it.

She could feel someone was cradling her lovingly while its unfamiliar yet soothing voice sang to her.

She tried opening her eyes to look at the face of the person who was singing to her but the moment that she opened her eyes, there was no one. All that she could see was the bamboo beams on the ceiling and the trees outside the window of her master's hut. Surprisingly, the only voice that sang to her was nothing but the birds' endless chirping.

Yan Mei Ling began to feel that an unfathomable emptiness was swallowing her being. She sighed wearily and tried to get way from the bed when Yeng came and rushed to her.

"Oh, my lady, please do not move yet!" Yeng, her faithful maidservant said. Her voice was laced with concern.

Yan Mei Ling was confused as to why Yeng seemed overly concern when in fact, she felt wonderful. She looked at her body and gasped when she found several needles on the different parts of her body. What greatly astonished her was the absence of pain in the punctured parts of her skin.

"What are these, Yeng? What are we doing in my master's hut when we are supposed to be in the arena?" Yan Mei Ling asked in confusion. She frowned as if trying to understand her situation. "Has the fight been nothing but a dream?"

"No, my lady," Yeng answered; she went near Yan Mei Ling to serve her with a cup of tea. "The fight is real and you are injured. Here, drink this tea; it will make you feel better."

"No," Yan Mei Ling refused. "You have not answered some of my questions. What are these needles on my body for and what are we doing in my master's hut?"

"Uhm, but, my lady," Yeng tried to protest but when she looked at Yan Mei Ling's determined eyes, she surrendered. "You were unconscious when Jinzhou Lu Wang Wei defeated you at the arena. He was about to unmask you when Master Tang Jiao Quon kicked him, carried you away from the arena and brought you here in the mountain. He also brought me here and taught me about acupuncture - it was a way of piercing specific points in the body to stimulate healing process. I was the one who pierced the needles on your skin."

Yan Mei Ling blankly stared at Yeng for a moment. She released a jaded sigh and asked, "Where is Master Tang Jiao Quon?"

"He is outside, meditating, my lady," Yeng answered while holding the tea for Yan Mei Ling.

"Take these needles off my flesh, Yeng; I already feel better." Yan Mei Ling told Yeng. "I need to talk to Master."

"But, my lady, you need to let the needles seat for a few hours more so that you won't feel sore. Why won't you rest first and drink this tea? I will get the needles after and we can talk to Master Tang Jiao Quon before we go home."

"No, Yeng," Yan Mei Ling sternly shook her head, determined to have her way. "I can't wait for a few more hours. If you won't get these needles off my body, I will."

Yeng looked dejected with worry as she set the tea at the simple low wooden table beside the unadorned bed. "I will take the needles off your body, my lady, but please drink the tea after I'm done."

"Fine, I will drink the tea so hurry and take these needles off my body now."

The afternoon light seemed filtered as it passed through the thick forest trees. The ground was covered in soft grass with several bald patches of forest ground and, the stream looked as serene and eternal as the clear water passing through it.

Amidst, the otherworldly feel of the forest, Yan Mei Ling anxiously approached her Master who was silently meditating on one of the stones in the middle of the stream.

As always had been, his stance was the same: eyes closed, arms in gesture of selfless surrender as if offering oneself to the celestial gods in heaven, the thumb and forefinger touching each other while the remaining fingers in stiff horizontal position. And, just like that of the holy Buddha, he was using his right foot to carry all of his weight while the heel of his left foot was placed upon his front right thigh.

Even until this moment, Yan Mei Ling, still found it hard to imagine how her Master was able to maintain a good level of balance incorporated in such a difficult stance. The strength he had achieved in order to maintain this difficult level of balance was the very thing she had aspired and worked hard for. Indeed, the body was a mysterious shell with unknown great power - a power one would fully yield once the external and internal forces of the body were in harmony.

"Master," Yan Mei Ling called in a soft voice.

Master Tang Jiao Quon opened his eyes and turned his unreadable gaze to Yan Mei Ling. "Yes, young lady?"

"I have failed you," Yan Mei Ling said in a voice filled with remorse as she bowed her head in shame, not willing for her Master to see the very evidence of her shame - her tears; the manifestation of her weakness.

Master Tang Jiao Quon leapt from his stance and landed softly in front of Yan Mei Ling which had amazed her inspite of her tears.

"You did not fail me, young lady," Master Tang Jiao Quon said quietly. "You failed yourself. You have allowed your emotion and your mindless desire to defeat your enemy to obscure your mind."

Yan Mei Ling stared in confusion at her Master with teary eyes. "I thought that I will die in the arena."

"No, you will not," Master Tang Jiao Quon simply said as he slowly walked around the forest ground. "The attack made by your opponent is strong, true enough, but it is not meant to kill you; it is meant to keep you unconscious for a few minutes. He has no intention to kill you; he meant to win without giving fatal injury on your person. His techniques and self-control are truly remarkable: the marks of a skilled warrior."

Yan Mei Ling's heart sank at her Master's words. True, she had failed herself - she had failed the promise she made to herself. And, true, the Jinzhou's skills were indeed legendary just like the dragon warrior. How utterly foolish was it of her to even think that she could defeat him! She had been so foolish that she allowed her emotions to be the cause of her defeat.

"I can sense your frustration but you should not let it overrule you. You must take what happens in the arena as a lesson so that you will not commit the same mistake, young lady."

"But it is not just that, Master," Yan Mei Ling explained. When she realized that her voice was too loud, she humbly whispered, "I'm sorry, I forget to control my emotions once again, Master."

Her master looked at her for a moment. "Is it the same problem that you have before the fight started, young lady?"

"No, master, it is different."

"What is bothering you, young lady?"

Upon hearing her master's question, all the emotions she'd been holding had finally came out through a torrent of tears. She weakly stumbled to the ground as she covered her face with her hands in anguish.

Master Tang Jiao Quon knelt beside his student and asked, "What is bothering you?"

"The war, master; oh, it is threatening to destroy everything I hold dear - everything. And, I don't know what to do."

"A war?" Master Tang Jiao Quon's brow rose in puzzlement. "Why is there a war?"

"The evil tyrant, Lord Hsein Mao Dong, threatens to attack the Empire if the Emperor won't yield his daughter, Princess Li

Lei Shuang, my best friend, to him so that she will be his wife. Oh, I love my best friend and, I don't want her to go to someone as cruel and evil as Lord Hsien Mao Dong. What should I do?"

"Lord Hsien Mao Dong," Master Tang Jiao Quon uttered the name as he recalled a memory during his youth.

'Stop it, Hsien Mao Dong! You had hurt Hong Lee-Hwa terribly enough.' Tang Jiao Quon beseeched Lord Hsein Mao Dong, son of a nobleman, as he rushed to Hong Lee-Hwa's unconscious body.

'Hmmp,' snorted indignantly. 'Get away from that weakling, Tang Jiao Quon; I will finish him off.'

'What do you mean finish him off?' Tang Jiao Quon's eyes widened upon realizing what Baron Hsien Mao Dong intended to do. 'Are you mad? This is just a practice duel, Hsien Mao Dong. Can't you see that you already win? There is no sense in killing Hong Lee-Hwa; our master don't tolerate cold-blooded murder and I won't allow you!'

'Oh, really? How heroic of you,' Baron Hsein Mao Dong sarcastically sneered. 'I am tired of following our old master's foolish rules! The world has no place for weak people; all of them should die. And, if you won't get away from Hong Lee-Hwa, I will kill you too, Tang Jiao Quon.'

Baron Hsien Mao Dong unsheathed the sword from his waist and threatened Tang Jiao Quon with its evil gleam.

Sensing that no words would enlighten the dark mind of Baron Hsien Mao Dong, Tang Jiao Quon stood and unsheathed his sword, matching the murderous gleam of Lord Hsien Mao Dong's sword. 'I will not allow you. You have to defeat me first, Hsien Mao Dong.'

A look of contempt filled Baron Hsien Mao Dong making his face looked like an evil demon. 'You are giving me no choice, bastard!'

Tang Jiao Quon closed his eyes tightly at the tragic recollection. He remembered the hatred and frustration he'd seen in Lord Hsien Mao Dong when the latter was defeated.

'I will kill you for this, Tang Jiao Quon! And, I will kill everyone you hold dear and you will come, crawling to me like the pathetic worm you are; begging me to spare your life and, then, I will slice your foolish head off.'

Tang Jiao Quon had ignored everything that the injured and incensed Baron Hsien Mao Dong said, thinking that the latter was merely nursing his injured ego by making threats but he was wrong. The next day, the whole training class were shocked to learn that their Master Ming Liao was poisoned, and he was also called by one of his neighbors to return to his village because his entire family was ruthlessly murdered.

Tang Jiao Quon remembered the inexplicable anguish that he felt - the agony of living each day blaming yourself for the tragedy that had happened to the ones you loved.

He would have took the path of vengeance but unfortunately, Baron Hsien Mao Dong disappeared from his stately house. It would have been fitting to kill all of Hsien Mao Dong's family members as what he did to his family but it wasn't right to kill innocent people just because he'd like to appease his thirst for vengeance. Instead, he joined the Imperial Army when he learned that Baron Hsien Mao Dong had gathered a considerable number of bandits who plundered the unconquered places on the Northern part of Chixian Shenzhou and ultimately established himself as a war overlord.

"I think we should do something to stop whatever Lord Hsien Mao Dong is planning, young lady," Master Tang Jiao Quon seriously said to Yan Mei Ling when the fog of memory disappeared from his thoughts. "He is the kind of man who won't stop unless he gets what he wants. He is evil and, if the Emperor changes his mind and allow Lord Hsien Mao Dong to marry his daughter, the empire will be thrown into chaos."

Yan Mei Ling stopped crying upon hearing his Master's solemn statement. She looked at her Master and, for the first time, she was able to witness the emotional side of her usually aloof master.

"Do you know him, Master?" She asked softly.

Master Tang Jiao Quon stood then looked at the sky as he quietly answered, "More than what you have heard of him."

Jinzhou Lu wang Wei was sitting on the low bamboo bench of the inner courtyard of his house. He had been in deep thoughts ever since his fight with the Ninja boy a few weeks ago.

Who was he? Who was his adult companion?

He stood from bench and, walked back and forth in front of the huge stone altar dedicated to his ancestors. He could smell the sweet scent emanating from the burning incense.

Could there possibly be more ninjas hiding within the Empire? Or were they spies from another country gathering information about the Empire? Were they possible threats to the security of the Empire?

Questions. A lot of questions. But, unfortunately, there were no answers.

Jinzhou Lu Wang Wei frowned more as he raked his hands to his untied long hair, flowing freely down his shoulders. He could hear the soft rumple of the end of his informal orange silk brocade long robe as he walked in frustration.

Whatever degree of curiosity he'd felt about the ninja boy's real identity was compounded when another took him away. The way they disappeared as if they were nothing but a wisp of smoke still astounded him. No normal human being could possibly be as fast as them or disappear just like that.

Jinzhou Lu Wang Wei breathed deeply when he realized what his thought seemed to conclude:

Could they possibly be celestial beings sent by the gods to protect Chang'An from its enemies? Just like the legendary Dragon Warrior?

The thought might sound a bit superstitious if not impossible but who could possibly be those two ninjas were? They were obviously superhumans.

Jinzhou Lu Wang Wei stopped walking when he remembered the ninja boys eyes. Those eyes. . Those curiously familiar eyes. Those eyes - oddly similar to that of the beautiful girl who had captivated his heart.

'What is happening to me? I am becoming a lunatic,' Jinzhou Lu Wang Wei said to himself while he kneaded the side of his temples to ease the headache that he'd experienced due to overthinking.

A moment later, a servant came to Jinzhou Lu Wang Wei and said, "My apologies for disturbing you, my lord, but the Emperor's herald is at the West corridor waiting for you. He has an important message from the Emperor."

Jinzhou Lu Wang Wei seemed to stareat his servant for a moment, disoriented by his thoughts, then he said, "Show him in to the west corridor study; I'll be there shortly."

The servant bowed to Jinzhou Lu Wang Wei. "Yes, my lord."

Yan Mei Ling was practicing calligraphy at her house inner garden pavillion when she noticed her father and one of the Emperor's herald in serious discussion at the northern corridor's veranda.

"The Son Heaven has requested for your immediate presence along with empire's high officials at the Imperial palace, Unit Commander Yan Bao Rong." The herald said and handed Unit Commander Yan Huang Di a scroll containing a message with the Imperial dragon seal.

"Thank you. I'll be there in haste." The Unit Commander answered.

The herald bowed respectfully before a servant led him to the house's exit.

When the messenger was out of sight, Yan Mei Ling ran to her father and asked, "Father, where are you going?"

The Unit Commander stared at her daughter for a moment before he enveloped her in an affectionate embrace.

Yan Mei Ling was curious as to why her indifferent father seemed acting in an odd way. "What is happening, father?"

The Unit Commander released his daughter from his embrace and tenderly rumpled her hair. "I will go to the palace, daughter."

"Please let me go with you, ba."

The Unit Commander gently shook his head and, in a soft yet firm way, he said, "No, my daughter, you can't go with me this time. Please stay here where it is safe."

"But I need to know if Li Lei Shuang is safe too, baba, please," Mei Ling beseeched her father.

"We will make sure that the princess is safe. There is no need for you to worry. Just stay here and trust me, my daughter."

Yan Mei Ling looked at her father, a bit disappointed at his refusal of her request, but then she understood so she hugged him instead and said, "I will be safe but be safe too, baba."

CHAPTER 11

The start of the war.

Yan Mei Ling watched as the clear white sky had turned dark from her room's balcony. How everything in her house seemed at peace, considering that a terrible war was brewing outside the empire, was still a wonder to her.

Among the infinite glowing gems scattered across the dusky sky, one shone brightly. Thinking it was a sign from heaven, Yan Mei Ling hurriedly knelt down and clasped her hands together. She prayed hard to her ancestors and to the gods that they would always keep her and the people she loved safe from the evil tyrant, Lord Hsien Mao Dong.

While she was pouring her heart to her prayer, a tear slowly found its way out of her eye. She immediately wiped it away but it became incessant. Tears came down her eyes like the rain brought by a violent storm.

The war was immensely stressing her that she did not know if she could handle it. Deep inside, her mind was troubled and her poor heart was restless. Peace, at the moment, seemed unattainable.

When she was done, she stood and went inside her room to the study table. As she was about to review the letter that she wrote for Li Lei Shuang, she heard a soft knock from her door.

"It is open. Come inside," She said.

Yeng timidly came inside, her eyes full of worry. "My lady"

"What is the problem, Yeng?" Yan Mei Ling asked with concern and gestured Yeng to go near her.

"I have heard that the Hsein clan had started attacking the Empire. They had razed several villages at the Eastern border." Yeng started with a broken sob.

Yeng's grim news had terribly distraught Yan Mei Ling's already fractured heart. "My father? Has he arrived?"

"Not yet, my lady"

Yan Mei Ling swallowed the lump on her throat, and bit her jaws together so that Yeng would not notice how the news had thoroughly shattered her.

A lot of murky thoughts formed her head. She could feel the enemies marching to the village - attacking and killing everyone. In her mind, she could hear the desperate cries of the villagers, the burning houses and maniacal laughter of the enemies.

Yan Mei Ling curbed her fists in fierce determination. She would not let that happen, not when she could do something about it.

A sudden thought came to her and, in a desperate voice, she said, "I need to go to the palace tonight, Yeng. Please stay here in my room, sleep in my bed. I need you to cover for me so that when baba arrives and decides to check on me, he will not notice my absence."

"What if your father open the curtains to look at you? He will find me instead of you!" Yeng said in panic.

Yan Mei Ling smiled in affection and gently held her maidservant's hands. "My father does not open the curtains. He just goes inside the room and watch me sleeping from afar. Please, Yeng, I need your help."

"What you are planning is extremely dangerous! What if your father will not arrive tonight, my lady?" Yeng asked worriedly. "Please - it is not safe to go out at this time."

"You have always been more than a maidservant to me; you are my best friend. You have helped more than anyone else. In this very moment, I beseech you to help me again as you always did." Yan Mei Ling appealed to Yeng. "I need to send a letter to Li Lei Shuang. It is very important."

Yeng sobbed. Her fear for her lady's safety and their friendship had played upon her heart like a tug-o-war. "If you want to send a letter to the princess, then let me do it instead, my lady."

"I know that you are concern about me, and I am grateful, Yeng." Yan Mei Ling said softly. "But I want to see Li Lei Shuang. I desperately want to see her."

"Can't you do it tomorrow when the sun sets high up in the sky, my lady?" Yeng's voice was full of anxiety.

Yan Mei Ling sadly shook her head. "No, Yeng, there is no other better time than now. Tomorrow may be too late."

The Hsien army advanced to the next village at the Eastern border after burning the previous one to the ground.

Under the blistering heat of the sun, all of the houses were consumed by the fiery monsters of inferno. Men were killed like dumb animals; women were utterly ravaged and violated beneath the glaring heat of the sun to abate the monstrous lust of the Hsien soldiers; and children were brutalized in all devious forms imaginable or some were hurled thoughtlessly like mere logs to feed flaming houses.

Some villagers, especially the males who fought back, were flogged until their back were bloody and raw. Their skins were flayed like cattles when their flesh became tender - this made the pain more agonizing, utterly unbearable. The method was so inhumane and brutal as the victim died from the shock of losing too much blood.

The others were subjected to another severe type of torture by having the nails removed and then pricking the fingers with sharp needles. The victims were then thrown to fire when the amusement of the sadistic Hsien torturers began to dissipate.

Thick black smoke rose above, overwhelming the pureness of the white sky with the devil's breath. The clear running water of river was soon tainted with red and black soot. The air smelled strongly of roasted human bodies and burning establishments. Cries and shouts for help filled the entire place but were hastily subdued after the silence, caused only by death, engulfed them.

The imperial army sent by the Emperor had soon arrived but the Hsien army outnumbered and crushed them like a pathetic worm beneath a man's boot.

The Hsien soldiers had already expected their arrival and had prepared a trap to defeat them. All Imperial soldiers were rained upon with arrows and cannons. Those who survived were immediately seized and beheaded.

It was an unfortunate day. Tragically unfortunate. . No words could describe the wickedness that had pervaded the entire village. It seemed that the Hsien army was the manifestation of the devil himself who only brought terror and death.

While the soldiers of the Hsien army destroyed what remained standing in the village, TongJun Linghua, one of the generals of the Hsien army, emerged from a small hut that wasn't burned yet. He licked his lips wickedly and adjusted his trousers; he felt carnally satisfied after raping the mother and daughter who lived in the hut. He flicked his finger to one of his soldiers who was holding a burning log. Throwing a meaningful look at direction of the hut, the soldier immediately complied to his silent command and set it on fire.

"Emperor Li Huang Di, you are a fool for refusing Lord Hsein Mao Dong's simple demand; now, you are next," TongJun Linghua muttered devilishly as he watched the bestial fire consumed the hut.

With the knowledge that her father had not came back yet, Yan Mei Ling sneaked stealthily into her room, like a thief in the night. She expected Yeng to be awake, waiting for her return, but then she found her maidservant sleeping soundly on her bed covered with several embroidered silk bedsheets.

The first thing that came to her mind was to shake Yeng until she woke up but she did not do it because of guilt. She felt that Yeng needed an uninterrupted rest after all the stress she put her poor maidservant into.

She sighed restlessly in her room and sat on the wooden chair near her study table with a rolled paper in hand. She thought about how she got the letter and its contents.

Yan Mei Ling had disguised herself as the Ninja boy again when she was walking along the cobbled street of the empire. She noticed several papers posted on the walls. Out of curiosity, she read it and was surprised that it was an announcement to call on men, experienced warriors or not, to join the Imperial army in haste.

She knew that it wasn't easy to join the army as one needed to pass the Imperial examination and, then the rigid military training before being admitted to the imperial army. But now qualifications were not important anymore as long as you were an able-bodied man.

She mentally scoffed at the discriminating qualification but she knew why more soldiers were needed. The Imperial army needed reinforcements to ease the dwindling number of imperial army soldiers due to the ongoing war.

After reading the entire announcement, a thought came to her but then she quickly dismissed it. Instead of going to the mountain, as she previously planned, she headed to the Imperial Palace after tearing one poster from the wall.

Still disguised in her ninja garb, she finally arrived at the Imperial Palace. With her extensive knowlege about its architecture and stealthy skills, she was able to elude the multitude of Palace guards.

She reached the Royal Princess' wing, she frowned when she saw the door of Li Lei Shuang's chamber slightly ajar. She tiptoed to make sure that no one would hear her. She saw a maidservant finally closing the door and eliminated the light inside.

Yan Mei Ling pressed her ears upon the wall and when total silence finally engulfed the chamber, she silently opened the door of the chamber and went inside. She carefully put her letter on Li Lei Shuang's desk. She was about to leave when a certain part of her beckoned her to take a look at her beloved best friend. She followed her heart for somewhere, deep inside, she felt that this would be the last time she would see the person that she loved. It maybe a sad thought but it was not far from impossible.

She slightly opened the silk curtains that covered Li Lei Shuang's bed.

Yan Mei Ling's breathing was arrested the moment that she laid eyes upon her best friend. Despite the shrouding darkness, Li Lei Shuang's beauty stood out like the vivid full moon against the expansive canvas of sable sky. Her straight long hair was like a jet-black ocean, glimmering wonderfully like a black onyx. Her melodic murmurs were like a divine song sang by the sweetest nightingale - it felt like a balm to her wounded heart.

Li Lei Shuang ethereal face shone with an incomparable radiance - she was, in every essence, like a goddess. She was so sweet, pure and delicate like an exquisite flower. No one should despoil her pristine sweetness. A sweetness that was inherently her.

Yan Mei Ling smiled through the darkness as she continued to watch her sleeping best friend.

Li Lei Shuang looked so peaceful and beautiful while sleeping. But, at the same time, she looked so fragile and vulnerable.

Her endearing qualities always sparked out a deep sense of protectiveness within Yan Mei Ling.

The need to protect Li Lei Shuang was so strong that she was willing to lay down her life for her best friend. She was even willing to walk into the gates of hell if that would secure her best friend's happiness in heaven. Yan Mei Ling would do anything for her - anything and everything.

'I swear that I will protect you with all my life, Li Lei Shuang,' Yan Mei Ling whispered before planting a soft kiss on Li Lei Shuang's milky cheek.

Yan Mei Ling looked blankly into the wall of her dim room. She was thinking - thinking utterly hard. Her hands were unconsciously rolling and unrolling the poster that had been reading. If she was going to take the plunge into the ocean of danger, there would be no turning back. This thing she had been ruminating over was not something a child would play and easily get away with. If she would do this, she would be force to be an adult. She breathed in deeply hoping to calm the irrational beating of heart.

She stood from her stool, anxiously pacing back and forth. However, her steps were as light as a feather so as not to disrupt her slumbering maidservant, Yeng. She sat back to the chair after a moment, contemplating deeply. She sighed again and again.

'Think. Think hard. It's not going to be easy so think!'

A few more moments passed by and, finally, a decision had came to her mind. But she already fell asleep on the chair with her head resting on the table.

CHAPTER 12

Jinzhou Lu Wang Wei wasted no time in summoning the soldiers under his command to find and gather the men on the conscription. Most of the men in the list up to this critical time, did not show up yet. Aside from tracking the names in the conscription, he campaigned in every village of Chixian Shenzhou - near and far. He called upon all men, noblemen or peasants, to join the Imperial Army.

After a tough and tiring campaign around the Empire, Jinzhou Lu Wang Wei returned to the Imperial Army training ground. He saw only a few men lining up to have their names registered. He felt disheartened with what he saw for he expected a great number of men willing to offer their lives for the safety of the Empire. He quickly came down his horse, and handed the bridle to a servant boy who rushed to assist him.

He sighed deeply as he watched the boy put his horse to the cavalry stables. He riveted his eyes to the afternoon sky and, hopelessly, contemplated on its pink and orange hues.

Time was dwindling.

"Jinzhou Lu Wang Wei."

He heard a soft and low voice calling his name, extricating him from his thoughts. He quickly turned to the direction of the voice, and was stunned with whom he saw.

"Ninja boy," he exclaimed in awe. The boy's presence in the imperial army training ground was indeed unexpected.

"I came here to offer my help to the Imperial army in fighting against the Hsein Army," the ninja boy declared as he raised a poster for Jinzhou Lu Wang Wei to look at. It was the poster that was posted in all walls of the Chixian Shenzhou calling for men to join the Imperial army.

Jinzhou Lu Wang Wei was momentarily silenced by ninja boy's statement but he also felt curious. Why did his voice sound odd? It was as if that the boy was controlling the timber of his voice. Was he an ally or an ememy?

"Shall I fall in line and write my name on the list?" The ninja boy gestured his hand to the direction of the registration table.

Jinzhou Lu Wang Wei frowned absentmindedly. He was still skeptical as to the real intentions of the Ninja Boy. Could he be trusted?

"Do you still need to drape yourself in your ninja costume? The imperial army can provide you with better armors and weapons."

Yan Mei Ling was not surprised with Jinzhou Lu Wang Wei's question for she had anticipated that and thus came prepared.

"I will remove my mask," Yan Mei Ling offered without any trace of hesitation.

Jinzhou Lu Wang Wei's body became taut with anticipation. He could hear the strong and furious beat of his heart like a hammer upon a metal.

When the ninja boy finally removed his mask, Jinzhou Lu Wang Wei's eyes widened in shock. It was unbelievable. Truly, unbelievable.. He could not believe that the warrior he had fought on the arena was still a child - possibly a boy of 12.

Jinzhou Lu Wang Wei's gaze narrowed with disbelief as he stared intently at the ninja boy. Judging from the boy's thin and slender body, he almost looked like a female.

If not for the boy's short hair and flat chest, Jinzhou Lu Wang Wei would have swore that he was staring at a girl. Of course, the boy's slender appearance looked deceiving; for in reality, his strength was unbelievably great.

"How old are you?" Jinzhou Lu Wang Wei asked. He thought that his curiosity about the Ninja boy's identity would be alleviated after seeing the boy's face but then he was wrong; in fact, it was intensified.

"I'm 15 years old, Jinzhou," the ninja boy answered in his oddly low voice.

"15?" Jinzhou Lu Wang Wei skeptically asked then he looked at the boy's face to check if he was lying.

A sudden jolt of familiarity came to him - those beautiful eyes, the small wonderfully-shaped nose, and the lips, why were they so temptingly pink?

He felt like running to the Yangtze river and drown himself to death there when he realized that he had been staring at the ninja boy's cheeks for too long. The boy's face flushed deep with embarrassment.

'What could he be possibly thinking? This is absurd! What is happening to me, am I becoming a lunatic like Lord Hsein Mao Dong?'

Jinzhou Lu Wang Wei turned his back at the ninja boy to calm himself. He softly inhaled and exhaled several times before continuing his queries. "What is your real name? Who is your family? Where are you from?"

"I'm Tang Lao Fang. My family - I. . I have no family anymore. They all died after the Hsien clan attacked our village. I lived at the Eastern border of Chixian Shenzhou" Mei Ling answered, trying so hard to hide the nervous quiver in her voice. What if he recognized her? What if he realized that she was lying? Heaven forbids!

Jinzhou Lu Wang Wei could hear the lonely inflection in the boy's voice and, felt sorry for what had happened to the boy's family. He was too young to experience such pain; such loss.

"How about the other ninja, where is he?"

Yan Mei Ling heart almost leapt from her chest due to nervousness but she persisted in appearing and sounding brave. "He is my father. I lose my family - all of them. I am the sole survivor."

"I am sorry, Lao Fang," Jinzhou Wang Wei said sadly when he faced the ninja boy. Genuine remorse was etched on his handsome face.

Yan Mei Ling was momentarily tongue-tied when she looked at the Jinzhou.

Why did he have to be so kind?

Why did it have to be him who would head the campaign where she planned to enlist herself to?

Was this how fate planned to mock her?

"There is no need to apologize for tragedies that can never be undone, Jinzhou. Please allow me into the army so that I can seek revenge and bring back honor to my murdered family."

Jinzhou Lu Wang Wei curiously frowned at the boy's words. "Did you only want to join the army just to seek revenge? For someone as young as you, that is not a good reason. By law, we admit only men who are at least 17 years old and above to the army. I am sorry but I can't allow you to join the army, Lao Fang."

Yan Mei Ling was flustered upon hearing the Jinzhou's refusal to admit her into the army. "Really? I thought you are looking for able-bodied men who are willing to lay their lives for the safety of the Empire. I am a man, and I am able-bodied. Have I not proven myself enough in the arena?"

"Of course, you are a wonderful warrior but you're not a man," Jinzhou Lu Wang Wei said firmly - his eyes doubtful.

Yan Mei Ling stiffened in fear at the Jinzhou's vague statement. Had he discovered her real identity? "What do you mean that I am not a man?"

The Jinzhou critically looked at her for a moment before saying, "You are a still a young boy, a child, and I know you are not 15 years old as what you claimed to be. Judging from the way you look, you could be 12 or possibly younger. Don't concern yourself with the war; enjoy your childhood and let the adults take care of this serious matter. I promise you, Lao Fang, the revenge you seek for your family will be realized."

"Enjoy my childhood?" Yan Mei Ling echoed with incredulity. She opened her mouth as if she was about to blurt a caustic missive. Eventually, she decided to settle for a different approach. "The war does not choose what to destroy or kill. It is hard to be sanguine during that time because all that it presents to you are nothing but deaths and utter destruction. I have lost the ones I loved because of the evil Hsien clan and, then you are telling me not to seek revenge? I lose my family and friends, and you are telling me to enjoy my childhood and leave the matters to you, adults?" She scoffed in indignation. "Tell me, what have you, adults, done to prevent the carnage that happened in my village? Will it not be a bit hypocritical on my part to be so positive considering everything that has happened to me?"

Jinzhou Lu Wang Wei was momentarily struck speechless upon hearing what Tang Lao Fang had said. Truly, he never expected to hear such wisdom nor such biting accusations for one so young. "I apologize for your loss, Tang Lao Fang. But there are things, no matter how dark they may be, that should only be left to adults. Even if tragedy has came into your life, it does not mean that you let it embitter you. You are young and, life has so much to offer you."

"It is so easy for you to say because you are not in my position."

"Oh, trust me, Tang Lao Fang." Jinzhou Lu Wang Wei said with grave seriousness, a cloud of memory crossed his eyes. "I understand you but that still won't change my stance about denying you a slot to the Imperial army."

Yan Mei Ling looked at Jinzhou Lu Wang Wei for a moment before her shoulders slumped dejectedly. She looked into his eyes. She could sense that no amount of persuasion could change his mind but then, it would not hurt to try once more, "Is there nothing that I say or do that will make you change your mind and allow me to join the imperial army, Jinzhou?"

"No," Jinzhou Lu Wang Wei said resolutely. The firmness of his voice matched that of the serious glint of his dark eyes. His mouth pursed in a taut line.

"I respect your decision and your adherence to the law, Jinzhou. However, it doesn't mean that I am going to sit down and do nothing while the Hsien clan destroy everything in the empire. If you won't allow me to join the imperial army, then I don't need your permission to fight the evil Hsein clan nor your consent to exact revenge against them for all the things they did to my village." Yan Mei Ling said with bitter determination. She clenched her fists together; her body shaking with acrid disappointment. She wanted to fall on her knees and bury her face in her palms to cry but, at the same time, she would not.

Before Jinzhou Lu Wang Wei could see just how much his refusal terribly wounded her heart and pride, she hastily bowed respectfuly to him and started to walk away.

Upon hearing the graveness in the voice of Lao Fang, guilt and sympathy mingled in Jinzhou Lu Wang Wei's heart.

As if he was in a delusional trance, he remembered the girl in the market. He knew that what his mind seemed to conjure was insanity but he couldn't help but feel this insensible concern toward the Ninja boy. Was this because of his stark resemblance to the girl his mind couldn't help but remember? Before his sensible self took over him, he called the ninja boy, "Lao Fang!"

Yan Mei Ling turned her stare back to Jinzhou Lu Wang Wei. Hope and anticipation had filled her eyes. "Yes?"

Those eyes. His resolve was weakened. Now everything was too late.

His mouth uttered the words before he knew what those are:

"Go to Chou, the one who is in-charge of the imperial army registration and have your name listed. He will tell you what to do next." Jinzhou Lu Wang Wei said stoically before he turned his back and took his leave.

Upon hearing the Jinzhou's words, joy had came into Yan Mei Ling's heart was too much that she seemed dazed for a moment. She looked at the pinkish silver sky and uttered a silent prayer of thanks to her ancestors.

Chapter 13

The moon soared high up the dark sky, thinly cloaked by ghostly clouds. The wind was moderately chilly but the men gathered around the fire barely felt it.

"The emotional pain cuts deeper than what is physical," Tongjun Linghua said in a grave voice to his fellow officials. "With that simple guiding thought, we know where to attack Chixian Shenzhou."

The men around the fire were murmurring something among themselves while the others stayed silent.

"What exactly is your plan?" One of the officers asked with curiosity.

A slow malevolent smile made its way to Tongjun Linghua's thin lips.

"We will be attacking the village of the Imperial officials instead of just any random village. We will set fire upon their lands - reducing them into ashes; kill their pathetic men; satisfy our carnal desires with their women before killing those bitches; crush their useless children." Tongjun Linghua answered. "And, ultimately, enrich ourselves with the loots."

"Do you know what official to attack first?"

"Yes, of course," Tongjun Linghua smirked confidently, crossing his arms on his chest. "We will attack the Imperial Unit Commander's village instead of advancing further. All we need to do is take the other path of the village that we have just razed; from there, we will advance to the Imperial Unit Commander's village."

"Will it not be hard for us to penetrate the Unit Commander's village considering that we need to climb the perilous Mountain of Dark Skull?" the doubtful officer continued to fire another question.

"Where is your brain residing, Baron Xun Yun?" Tongjun Linghua mocked the officer who questioned him. He had grown irritated of Baron Xun Yun who always try to find an opportunity to oppugn each of his plans. Just because Baron Xun Yun was born with a silver spoon, it did not give him the privilege to act condescendingly towards him. He had to know his place; after all, he was still the Tongjun of this army. "The mountain of Dark Skull is not solely the way to the Unit Commander's village. We can traverse the back of the mountain, follow the river. There is an underground pathway, an abandoned mining site, that will lead us to our target. The Imperial spies will not expect us to go there considering that it is fraught with unimaginable dangers. It was fabled to be the dead miners' ghosts residence - utterly and completely inhabitable."

"Are you insane? Your plan is sublime foolishness - you are sending us straight to our graves!" Baron Xun Yun's eyes flared in indignation at Tongjun Linghua's mordacious words.

Tongjun Linghua sneered contemptuously at Baron Xun Yun before molding his face into an apathetic mask. "Are you afraid of the ghosts, Baron Xun Yun?"

"What kind of foolish question is that?"

Tongjun Linghua ignored Baron Xun Yun and explained his plan further, "Another thing, if we successfully wreck the Unit Commander's village, his attention will be diverted from his Imperial duties to his own personal predicament." His eyes took a darker sinister hue; he said, "I heard he has a daughter, a beautiful girl, maybe we can enjoy her before sending her pretty little head to her worthless father."

"You are brilliant, Tongjun," another officer, named Niu, said in amazement at Tongjun Linghua's plan.

Baron Xun Yun briefly clamped his lips together in disagreement to Niu's flattering words to Tongjun Linghua. He resumed his interrogation, "What exactly is the path that we are going to tread? How feasible is your plan? Are you sure that you are not sending us straight to an ambush?"

"Oh my, Oh my, our Baron Xun Yun is burning with curiosity." Tongjun Linghua said sarcastically with an aloof face before cracking up a false humorous smile. He lightly touched his chin, raising his other brow. "I wonder why."

"I need to know everything so that we can make sure that there are no loopholes! We only have one mission and that is to abduct the princess. The sooner we get the princess and give her to Lord Hsien Mao Dong, the better." Baron Xun Yun raised his voice in irritation, eyeing Tongjun Linghua intensely.

Tongjun Linghua shrugged his shoulders carelessly. He gave Baron Xun Yun an ironic smile. "That is exactly the purpose of this meeting, Baron Xun Yun."

The air between the two officials suddenly became charged as an invisible war rolled between the two.

"Here," Tongjun Linghua said frigidly after mentally battling with Baron Xun Yun. He unrolled a scroll and discussed the path that they would take to arrive to the Unit Commander's village and possible escape routes should the Imperial army try to ambush them and other military tactics.

All of the officers clapped in appreciation except for Baron Xun Yun who still appeared skeptical.

Tongjun Linghua eyed Baron Xun Yun and smiled at him meaningfully. "Oh, seeing that we have laid and discussed the plans, the meeting is adjourned. Let us rest, we have a long way ahead of us."

Baron Xun Yun tried to keep a blank face as he hurriedly scampered to his tent.

Tongjun Linghua silently observed Baron Xun Yun who was shaking with extreme ire as he entered his tent. He clucked his tongue in amusement before smirking. He eyed the dark sky and seriously contemplated against the darkness for a moment. He need to find a way to subdue that irking Baron.

"Niu," Tongjun Linghua called his subordinate who remained beside him.

"Yes, Tongjun?"

"I have noticed someone unusual," Tongjun Linghua started before pausing thoughtfully. He clamped his nosebridge with his fingers and continued, "It bothers me to no end, making my soul feel restless."

"What do you mean, Tongjun? What is it that you notice that bothers you?"

Tongjun Linghua's eyes turned into sharp slits and whispered to Niu, "I want you to kill Baron Xun Yun and, make it appear that he betrayed and left the army."

Niu's eyes widened in surprise. "But he is one of our comrades!"

Tongjun Linghua laughed in amusement before his gaze turned harsh again. "Don't be so naive, Niu. He betrayed his own Emperor! Do you think he can't do the same to Lord Hsien Mao Dong?"

Niu became silent, reflecting on Tongjun Linghua's words. His face creased in bafflement.

"Once a traitor, always a traitor!" Tongjun Linghua tried to persuade the confused Niu. "There is something you need to know - how do you think the Imperial armies know that we will be attacking this village? Aren't you a bit curious at there hasty response? Tell me, Niu! Tell me!" He angrily demanded, his face flustered with anger.

When Niu remained unresponsive, Tongjun Linghua grabbed him by the collar and hissed, "Baron Xun Yun betrayed us! He sent a message to the Imperial armies so that we would all die. If I had not intercepted some of his messages to the Imperial army, you would have not been breathing this air, seeing the moon shone bright against the murky sky nor stood with all your senses intact!"

Niu was flabbergasted by Tongjun Linghua's revelation but contemplated heavily on what the Tongjun told him. There was a great spectacle inside his mind but ultimately, he sighed wearily and stood for what was right to him. "I cannot let that deceitful bastard betray us." His eyes were serious as he held Tongjun Linghua's gaze with his. "I will do as you say and end the traitor Baron Xun Yun's pathetic life"

"Good," Tongjun Lingjua patted Niu patronizingly, seemingly pleased with the latter. "Remember, we are doing this for the glory of Hsien army. What profits our Lord Hsien Mao Dong, profits us, Niu. Never forget that."

My dearest Li Lei Shuang,

I am writing this letter to inform you that we will not be seeing each other for sometime as my father forbids me to leave our house for my safety. I may not have personally delivered this letter or informed you but I hope that you won't think that I don't value your presence nor our friendship. I assure you, you will always remain my dearest and beloved best friend.

Don't fear for my safety for I shall very well take care of myself so as not to vex you. I may or may not write letters to you during the time of my absence but I promise you, once the war is over, I shall not write you a letter but personally visit you.

Please don't think anymore of nonsense such as compelling yourself to a marriage to a man like Lord Hsien Mao Dong. You are of pure heart and he is evil; you both just don't complement each other, he will only bring misery not only to you but to the Empire as well.

Stay safe for me and, I will do my best to stay safe and alive for you. I shall see you hopefully soon. Please keep me near your heart as you have always been to my heart.

By the way, with this letter is a silver necklace that looks like a moon, I hope you'll wear it as I have always carried the precious dagger you'd given me.

Your bestfriend,

Yan Mei Ling

Far from what Yan Mei Ling's letter seemed to imply, Li Lei Shuang did not feel any real sense of assurance. What she felt instead was an unusual coldness creeping to her and an inexplicable fear she could not fathom out.

When she held the necklace to her gaze, she saw its pendant took ceaseless turns as the gentle autumn breeze played with it. With every turn of the silver pendant, it created an illusion of light reflected from that of the lanterns hanging from her room's ceiling.

True, the necklace reminded her of the luminous moon as what Yan Mei Ling said in her letter. But the moon only gave out light when it reigned on the night sky; for when the dark wispy clouds began to hover on the vast cimmerian sky, the moon often got shrouded and imprisoned with no light to give during the dead of the night. No matter what her thoughts seemed to tread to, she still wore the necklace around her neck with the pendant placed near her heart; feeling Yan Mei Ling's presence in it.

She took another look at Yan Mei Ling's letter; though the characters were wonderfully written and the words full of exuberance, she felt a dark sense of foreboding. Tears of anguish began to fall from her eyes and, in her heart, she felt a vacancy that was sooner occupied with fear.

She did not want to nor dare to think but it seemed that letter she received from Yan Mei Ling tell her nothing but goodbye.

As the bright afternoon sky faded into grey, a solitary nightingale gracefully perched upon the birch tree's thin trunk in the outer courtyard of the Yans. When the feathery clouds thinly cloaked the crescent moon and silence began to sing, the bird began to hum its sweet melody.

Just in time that the garden frogs' voices joined that of the nightingale in the nocturnal hymn, Yan Mei Ling arrived and called for Yeng who immediately assisted her in changing her clothes.

"Yeng?" Yan Mei Ling called her maidservant's attention as soon as she was done changing into her sleeping robe.

Everything was bathed in darkness but for the table where the lamp lay burning.

"Yes, my lady?"

"I want you to listen very carefully to me," Yan Mei Ling seriously said as she looked into Yeng's eyes. "I have heard that the Hsein clan did not only headed East but in every part of the Empire, at any time, his army will possibly arrive in our village."

"My lady!" Yeng exclaimed in fear. Tears began to form in her eyes.

"Don't cry, Yeng," Yan Mei Ling held her maidservant's hands with that of hers in comfort. "Listen, my father has not returned nor sent me any letter but we cannot wait for his signal. For the safety of the people in the village, we must immediately act before it is too late. Now, go to the village and tell them that my father, the Unit Commander, commands all of them to go to the mountain. You know where Master Tang Jiao Quon is, take them there. Make sure that you bring enough food. Bring everything that is needed."

"What if they won't believe me, my lady?"

"Don't worry, I will be writing a letter with my father's seal, that would be enough to convince all of them."

"But what about you, my lady? Are you not going with us to the mountain?"

Yan Mei Ling smiled but her eyes were blurry. "Don't worry about me, Yeng. I already enlisted myself in the army as Tang Lao Fang, 'The Ninja boy'."

"Oh, my lady," Yeng sobbed frantically. "That is dangerous! What if something bad happens to you? What if your father returns and finds out that everyone in the village are gone, including you?"

"Don't worry about my father's reaction, I have already taken cared of that." Yan Mei Ling paused for a moment, mentally cringing for that small lie, before continuing. "Don't worry about me. I assure you, I will be safe and, I promise to come back to get you and the villagers once the war is over."

"My lady, why can't you just go with us to the mountain?" Yeng tearfully pleaded as she covered her face with her hands.

"I can't," Mei Ling said sadly. "I need to do what is right. It may not be the safest but it is the only sensible thing to do. Oh, Yeng, I have just made the most important decision in my life."

Chapter 14

"The Journey towards the Uncanny."

When Unit Commander Yan Bao Rong received a message from one of the imperial spies that the Hsien clan planned to attack the Northern border under the Empire's dominion, he immediately sent his troops to tell the villagers to vacate their village for a safer haven.

When the village was cleared of the civilians, he had the imperial army, under his command, stationed there with its reinforcements ready thereby taking the Hsien army by surprise the moment that they arrived.

A bloody combat ensued between the two forces for several days. Monstrous roars of the cannons were heard and numerous arrows from crossbows were hurled at each other. Some soldiers from both armies were even brave enough to engage in hand to hand combats using spears and swords.

Soon the abandoned village were filled with lifeless bodies; some incinerated with arrows and spears, and the others where either headless or body parts were brutally torn and splattered at every corner.

As days passed by, the unbearable stench of decaying corpses and dwindling resources had taken there toils between the fighting armies. But the Hsien clan being the foreign force was soon suppressed as their reinforcements had became meager or took to long to arrive. When the remaining Hsien armies retreated, Unit Commander Yan Bao Rong , atop his muscled stallion rode around the village, declaring victory to his cheering subordinates.

On the third day since Unit Commander Yan Bao Rong 's victorious feat at the Northern border, his troops remained to clear the cadavers from the land while other villagers came back to help or start rebuilding their houses.

In the huge tent that was set-up on the village, Unit Commander Yan Bao Rong had a meeting with the other ranked army officials to plan their next move against the Hsien army. Amidst the seriousness of what they'd been discussing, an imperial herald dared to intrude and insisted to talk to the Unit Commander.

"Can't you see that we are discussing a very important affair? If you want to talk to me, then you wait outside and I'll talk to you after we are finished." Unit Commander Yan Bao Rong snapped, irritated at the herald's audacity to intrude.

"But, my lord, you need to hear what I say," the herald persisted and then he added gravely, "It's about your village."

Unit Commander Yan Bao Rong turned pale upon hearing the herald's word. For the second time in his life since his wife's death, he felt utterly afraid.

"Men, please excuse me," he implacably said to the other officials who bowed their consent, and then he motioned the herald outside of the tent. "Speak now"

The messenger though he tried to appear unaffected had noticeably swallowed the lump in his throat as if the news that he brought was too much he could handle lest speak. "The Hsien army had reached your village two days ago, my lord."

The Unit Commander's eyes grew wide with what he heard. He started to brace himself for whatever he was about to hear although a flicker of hope remained in his heart.

"The entire village was burned to the ground and there were no survivors. No corpses were recovered but ashes."

"But my daughter?" Unit Commander Yan Bao Rong asked in disbelief refusing to accept the conclusion that dawned in his mind.

"I am sorry, my lord, but there were no survivors." The herald said with remorse.

Unit Commander Yan Bao Rong silently fell to his knees after hearing the herald's tragic words. He tightly closed his eyes as he curled his fists painfully together. A chill seeped to the bones of his body as unbearable anguish and loss contained the very core of his heart.

'Stay safe for me and, I will do my best to stay safe and alive for you.'

"Oh, Yan Mei Ling," Li Lei Shuang whispered in an agonized voice as she read and re-read Yan Mei Ling's letter that promised that they would be together someday through teary haze. But then, that day would never happen for Yan Mei Ling, her beloved treasure, was stolen by Death forever. "Oh, Yan Mei

Ling," she sobbed once again as immeasurable pain gripped her heart which even made breathing a very difficult thing to do.

"Princess," Li Lei Shuang's head attendant said worriedly while the others stayed behind for they didn't know how to ease the sadness that the princess felt due to her loss.

"Please," Li Lei Shuang softly said. "Leave me alone. I want to be alone."

The attendants seemed hesitant at leaving the princess alone but they did as she told them but a few moments later, the Empress arrived, her beautiful face full of worry.

"My daughter," the Empress said with concern and then she enveloped her daughter in the warmth of her embrace.

Although her mother's embrace felt comforting, it barely eased the hollow pain that was agonizing her heart. "Mother, the news is not true, isn't it? Yan Mei Ling didn't die, right? She. . She. . She is still alive. . She promised me; look at the letter, read it. . She promised me she'll be safe and alive. The news is nothing but a lie. She isn't dead. Oh, my best friend, isn't dead!"

The Empress held her grieving daughter tightly in her embrace. She couldn't seem to find the right words to say for everything just seemed inappropriate. "My daughter, some things just happen because they are way out of our control."

"But if I only married Lord Hsein Mao Dong, this won't happen," Li Lei Shuang heart-brokenly said. "No, that's not right - Yan Mei Ling won't want me to even think of that.. But, mother, tell me, Yan Mei Ling is still alive. . She is strong. She can protect herself.. Oh, oh, it can't be. She can't be dead. It just can't be.."

Tears began to fall from the Empress eyes for she couldn't seem to comfort her own daughter. Although, it was hard to accept, it seemed that the light and sanity seemed to fade from Li Lei Shuang's eyes.

Chapter 15

The grimness of the night had been manifested in the darkness of the starless sky. The strong gust of the wind had seemingly intensified despite the receding leaves on the forest trees.

Yan Mei Ling snuggled deeper into the cotton cloth she had draped herself into. She felt the chill biting into her sensitive skin like sharp needles. She sat near the crackling fire, silently watching the other men who were talking to each other.

Winter had not came yet but the coldness that was creeping into her did not only form a melancholic ice around her body but to her restless heart as well.

She thought at first that she could stand being away from her from the ones that she loved but she was mistaken. The homesickness that endlessly plagued her was utter torture.

How is her father? How is Lei Shuang? What about Yeng and the villagers, have they had been faring well? Have she made the right decision of joining the imperial army?

She could not stop but ask herself with those questions several times as the feeling of loneliness continuously tugged at her. She felt like a small pebble on the beach thrown into the waves of uncertainty.

"The Hsien clan ought to die!" Someone exclaimed angrily as he added another wood to the dwindling fire.

"Certainly, they are the harbingers of evil," another one agreed. "Why, Lord Hsien Mao Dong resembled the Tiangou himself and his armies are the mógu□; they ought to rot in deepest chasm of Di Yu!"

"They do not have any mercy. Unluckily, the Si Xiong had seemed to be with them for they had captured several villages."

"They are all wicked mógu□!"

Yan Mei Ling just stayed where she was. She diverted her loneliness by listening to the men who were cursing and damning the Hsien clan. Although she longed for companionship, she felt utterly out of place among the imperial army soldiers.

"Hey, boy!" Someone called Yan Mei Ling's attention.

"Yes?" Yan Mei Ling answered timidly.

"How is it that you are silent there? Won't you join us?"

"We heard that you are the ninja boy. Is that true?" another chimed in.

"We heard your family died along with the people in your village."

'Insufferable men! Why can't they just leave me be.'

"I do not wish to talk," Yan Mei Ling answered rigidly and she stood to walk away from the nosy men.

"Oh, boy, does it hurt?" Someone mocked. "Isn't what we, adults, are talking too much for you? Our apologies, we have failed to forget that you are a still a boy. Poor baby."

The other men in the camp started laughing at Yan Mei Ling. As she listened to their jeering laughs, she remembered the people who had doubted her ability as a warrior. Each insulting word they threw at her had only served to make her strive to win each fight. She had disproven their doubts until the championship.

She curbed her fists together in anger. The ropes of her patience were straining to break.

Kick them! Make them eat their words! You are the ninja boy - they would not dare!

Before she lose her temper and gave in to the urge of wiping the arrogant jeers of the nosy men in the camp, Jinzhou Lu Wang Wei rushed and said, "Cease your nonsense chattering, men. You proclaimed yourself adults but then you are behaving like toddlers. You would have set yourselves as good examples to our young charge but then you started prattling like senseless hens. Now, shall I answer your unanswered question? This boy you are teasing is indeed the ninja boy; and all of you, very well, know how skillful a fighter he is."

The men in the camp looked nonplussed upon hearing Jinzhou Lu Wang Wei's words. They stared at Yan Mei Ling with fascination and a hint of wariness.

"You, Tang Lao Fang," Jinzhou Lu Wang Wei motioned to Yan Mei Ling. "Go back to your tent."

"I intend to," Yan Mei Ling answered stiffly, feeling a little affronted when the Jinzhou told the soldiers that she was the Ninja boy. Even if pretending to be the Ninja boy was one of the best things she had done, she did not relish the attention that she received from being him.

She could never claim the credit due to the fictitious warrior. Ninja boy was nothing but a lie. A big sham of a character!

"Good," Jinzhou Lu Wang Wei said. "Because if you don't, you will eventually draw fire. Save it for the war."

Yan Mei Ling was confused with the jinzhou's words. She absentmindedly watched him walked to his tent.

Could that he sensed her anger or her desire to throttle the men who dared mock her?

The Hsien herald nervously walked to the carpeted hall of the spacious Hsien palace.

The place was enormous. The walls were lavished with beautiful mosaics and tapestries obtained through trading with the Dashi.

There were also several decorative weapons attached to the wall. Large beautiful vases were aplenty - both made of fine porcelain and clay, the latter obtained through bartering with the Malayu, Mai and other farther Islands in the Southern seas.

He stopped in front of the great wonderfully-crafted sturdy wooden doors guarded by well armored soldiers. It was the chamber of the Harem of Lord Hsien Mao Dong.

The guards recognized and greeted him politely. They immediately opened the heavy and huge doors for him.

"Thank you," the Hsien herald said gratefully. One of the guards accompanied him inside the harem.

The moment he stepped inside, the sheer beauty of the chamber never failed to sweep him off his feet.

Plants were aplenty, making the room looked like an oasis of heaven. Silk curtains were hanging aesthetically, giving it a majestic flair. The walls were extravagantly decorated and the sound of beautiful music wafted through the air like the heavenly voices of the angels.

He looked around and could see some of Lord Hsien Mao Dong's women talking and enjoying themselves with the mouthwatering food served by female servants on platter. Some women were reading poetry at the other side as the room had plenty of scrolls containing literary masterpieces as Lord Hsien Mao Dong himself enjoyed reading.

The Harem's chamber might had a suggestion of exuberant flair, however, it was not hard to spot the sadness underneath the thick make-up of some of the beautiful women in the Harem. Most of the women inside were forced to become Lord Hsien Mao Dong's concubines after their lands were conquered. They were carefully selected - the daughters and unmarried women of the nobility automatically became part of the harem. As for the most beautiful maidens of the captured villages, the ones not born in nobility, were chosen as well. Refusing was never an option for these women because they would only end up being beaten, raped and then put to death.

They further walked into the room until they reached in front of an elegant four-postered canopied bed covered in opaque silk curtains. Beside the bed were female musicians playing strings and flutes for the enjoyment of Lord Hsien Mao Dong. At the side of the humongous bed, a maidservant stood straight beside a table full of scrumptious food and wine.

Despite the music being played, the mingled moans of Lord Hsien Mao Dong and his concubine was clearly audible.

Being a eunuch just like the guards who were assigned to guard the royal harem, the amorous acts of his lord never failed to make the herald blush furiously.

The guard who accompanied the herald gently walked to the maidservant and said, "Tell Lord Hsien Mao Dong that his herald has arrived."

The maidservant nodded and slightly opened the curtain of the four-posted bed. She whispered something and a moment later, stepped away from the bed to get the elegant red robe embossed with gold that was hung nearby.

Lord Hsien Mao Dong stepped out from the bed naked and the maidservant immediately assisted him in dressing up.

"It is a surprise to see you, Fa Peizhu. Are you here to tell me exactly what I want to hear?" Lord Hsien Mao Dong said with an enthusiastic smile after donning himself in his fabulous robe.

Despite his old age, Lord Hsien Mao Dong looked healthy and utterly formidable. He was a very skilled fighter and a brilliant strategist. Those were the reasons why he conquered several places not only limited to Chixian Shenzhou but also to what went beyond its borders.

The herald, Fa Peizhu, swallowed the lump in his throat in nervousness and said, "The news that I bring is quite delicate and it can only be said in your presence."

Lord Hsien Mao Dong jovial countenance suddenly became grim. He immediately motioned the female musicians to stop and leave along with the maidservant and the concubine he had sexual intercourse with. He walked to the table and poured himself a cup of wine.

"What is it that you want to tell me that it requires only my attention?" Lord Hsien Mao Dong demanded in a very intimidating voice.

Fa Peizhu could feel himself getting cold with fear but he tried his best to compose himself. "My lord, Unit Commander Yan Bao Rong and his men have suppressed your army at the Northern border"

Lord Hsien Mao Dong's eyes narrowed contemptuously and, then he angrily threw his golden cup to the floor, spilling its contents on the carpeted floor. "Bastard! Jiangjun Sui Xhiaolun was indeed a foolish weakling. Why, I should have personally mutilated his body and fed it to the dogs!"

The herald's head remained bowed though the tremor that ran to his body was unmistakeable due to his master's wrath.

"Have you brought news about Tang Jiao Quon whereabouts?"

The herald swallowed his throat and, answered as calmly as he could, "Tang Jiao Quon, according to the rumors, is dead."

"Rumors?!" Lord Hsien Mao Dong shouted with wrath, his voice resounding angrily within the walls of the harem. "Why, incompetent bastard, you better not tell me rumors. For if I find out that Tang Jiao Quon is still alive, I will severe both of your heads from your bodies and put them on display at the gates of my palace. Do you understand?"

"Yes, my lord," the herald's voice stammered with fear.

"Good," Lord Hsien Mao Dong said with satisfaction. He paced briskly on the floor and asked, "Now, what about his Imperial Majesty's decision to marry his daughter to me?"

"His Imperial Majesty remained hardheaded and refused to succumb to your amiable request, my lord."

"He is indeed trying my patience. Well, I will let him suffer." Lord Hsien muttered darkly, clenching his other fist. "Send Jiangjun Han Li to me immediately!"

"As you wish, my lord," the herald nervously answered and immediately took his leave when Lord Hsien Mao Dong flicked his wrist dismissively indicating that the he should go.

Chapter 16

The sky was overcast but the sun had almost claimed its throne as hinted by the streaks of silver, pink and orange above. The autumn air felt cool and comforting but it was the orchestrated voices of the birds that beckoned Yan Mei Ling to slip early from her tent into the deep forest.

As she walked on the damp ground where the grasses were bathed with nature's dew, she noticed a bird. It was a hawk or a falcon but she was not sure. The bird was flying swiftly ahead of her to a farther place.

'Does it feel trapped just like the way I do?' Yan Mei Ling silently mused.

She had spotted a huge fallen tree in front of her, blocking the way. But she opted to jump over it instead of taking another route to avoid it. The action was seemingly impulsive and dangerous but she delighted in throwing the caution to the wind, every now and then. Whenever she jumped, she loved the feeling of being suspended on the air though ephemeral the feeling might seemed to be.

Her feet had picked up another pace and urged herself faster, away from the camp that gave her nothing but the feeling of emptiness and desolation. It was somehow ironic how the urge to get as far as away from the camp could be so intense, considering that she had wished and envisioned this kind of life as a child.

Nothing stayed constant in this world. Human emotions were so fickle. What you wished for, might not be the one that you wanted when it was already given to you.

As of this moment, she could not discern what she wanted for the loneliness that had continuously gnawed at her heart. Her depression played havoc with her thoughts and emotions. She did not want to think of her pain nor did she want to drown herself in the ocean of sadness but neither was evitable.

All she wanted right now was to extricate herself from all the gloomy thoughts even for a brief moment in time. She wanted to go back home now. But somehow, she derived a certain kind of peace from running.

Running or moving her body had its means of liberating herself for she seemed to forget all worries as the swift breeze was whipped into her face. Every time she ran, she felt as if she was racing against something - she did not know what but she wished to out-win it. She loved to push herself to the limit. Push herself beyond the bounds of her physical strength. Fight the imaginary opponents that her active mind would conjure.

While she was running or jumping from tree to another tree, her mind had wandered to the people she loved.

'Are they safe?' Her heart could only hope.

'Are they thinking of me like what I have been doing now?'

'Have I caused them distress when I left without any further notice?' Yan Mei Ling thought guiltily and as if she was lost in her thoughts. She stumbled upon a small rock unto the soft forest ground.

She lay still for a moment, listening desperately to the sounds of her struggled breathing against the silence of the forest. She stood up even though a sharp pain shot through her knees. It was only too late that she realize why she had stumbled. Tears had blinded her vision and worries had dulled her perception.

She slowly touched her lips when she tasted something metallic from her tongue. When she looked at her forearms, she was stunned to see her bruises decorating them. It would have been normal for her to feel hurt as what the irritating pain of her wounds had implied but the physical pain she felt right now seemed pale in comparison to the pain she felt in her heart.

True, emotional pain most of the time ran deeper than the physical for it could hurt you in many ways you would imagine. It seemed unrealistic but when the pain was too much your heart could possibly handle, it would thwart with your sanity and torture your already baffled mind. And what would physical pain say to that? Absolutely, nothing.

Physical pain could exist only for a short period of time but emotional pain could be eternal.

Desolation and worry had terribly fractured Yan Mei Ling's heart. She was going insane; she couldn't stop but thought about her loved ones and the things she regretted doing. But, unfortunately, when she thought, all she could see was uncertainty.

How could she be at peace when she was a thousand miles away from the people she cherished? What would she feel but anguished when she was not provided any assurance of their well-beings?

Yan Mei Ling desperately tried to wipe the tears that streamed down her eyes. But, aghastly, as she wiped the tears from her eyes, the more incessant they seemed to be.

Oh, she missed all of the people she loved - her father, Yeng, Master, the villagers, and Lei Shuang. Especially Li Lei Shuang.

She took something from her chest and stared at the exquisite containment that bore the beautiful pearl and jade encrusted knife. It was her best friend's gift to her when they strolled the town to buy sweetmeats, two summers ago. She had always brought it and placed it near her heart wherever she go. It was her link to Li Lei Shuang every time they were away from each other. She cried harder as the pounding thing inside her chest tightened.

'Your handwriting is improving, Yan Mei Ling,' Lei Shuang told Mei Ling proudly.

'Truthfully?' Yan Mei Ling dubiously asked as she stared at her own crude handwriting. She took a quick peek at Li Lei Shuang's calligraphy and blushed in deep shame. Her best friend's handwriting was a work of art whereas hers was worthy of being called a duck's muddy steps than calligraphy.

'Truthfully,' Li Lei Shuang said with sincerity shining in her beautiful eyes. 'And the more you will be better if you give more time to calligraphy than martial arts.'

'Hmmp,' Yan Mei Ling snorted with displeasure in reference to the time she spent training martial arts with Master Tang Jiao Quon at the mountain. But, after a moment, an enthusiastic gleam came to her eyes. 'Before I forget, Li Lei Shuang, may I remind you of your promise to give me sweatmeats every time you notice a progress in my handwriting?'

'Certainly, my sweet, I will give you aplenty as soon as we are done with our calligraphy lesson.' Li Lei Shuang tenderly said as she caressed Yan Mei Ling's healthy pink cheeks.

'Oh, thank you, Li Lei Shuang,' Yan Mei Ling exclaimed excitedly. 'You certainly are the best of all friends I ever have.'

"Oh, Li Lei Shuang," Yan Mei Ling sobbed brokenly as she tenderly kissed the knife's containment. It was inevitable, she allowed sadness and misery to swallow her being for she could not take it anymore. She felt that if she would try to ignore the pain, she would die for her heart could not hold it. She had to let it go and stop pretending that she was tough for she truly was not - her heart was not made of stone.

"It is perfectly fine to cry even if it is away from the eyes of other people, Tang Lao Fang," someone said behind Mei Ling.

Yan Mei Ling was startled that she stopped crying.

How come he is here?

She looked back to confirm the identity of the person who was behind her.

It is indeed him.

She felt displeasure coursing through her veins at being robbed the privacy to be alone with the tumultuous feeling she was trying to sort out.

"What are you doing here, jinzhou?" Yan Mei Ling demanded with irritation. "Are you spying on me?"

"No," Jinzhou Lu Wang Wei shook his head. "I assure you, Tang Lao Fang, our paths have crossed today only because of chance not because I am spying on you."

Yan Mei Ling roughly wiped the tears on her eyes and scowled at him. "I don't care if you are my jinzhou or if you are a better warrior than I but I am immensely ired of your intrusion of my privacy. I doubt if our paths have crossed only because of chance. Obviously, you are spying on me for the truth is you don't trust me. I can sense it. Within your heart, you think that I can be a spy for the enemy and you might have only admitted me into the army to investigate on me and my motives. Am I not correct?"

Jinzhou Lu Wang Wei was stupefied by Tang Lao Fang's accusations for they were partly true. But, honestly, he never doubted the boy's motives for he could detect sincerity eventhough it was eclipsed with words or even actions. He only wanted to know why Tang Lao Fang went to the forest and, he was only concerned for him for what if the Hsien army arrived here and caught Tang Lao Fang. "No, I am not doubting your motives. I just want to make sure you are safe for you seem lonely at the camp."

"So are you following me?" Yan Mei Ling snapped indignantly.

Jinzhou Lu Wang Wei stared at her for a moment but the look on his face revealed no hint of emotion. Instead, he quietly answered, "I only want to make sure you are safe, Lao Fang."

"I can take care of myself," Yan Mei Ling said with less anger when she realized that the Jinzhou was only concerned for her well-being. Her childish outburst and harsh accusations were totally unaccounted for, and the realization had made her feel ashamed of her actions.

"I know you can for I trust in your abilities but, as a leader, it is my duty to protect all of my subordinates even if they are self-sufficient. For if I lose even just one of them, then I am lacking as a leader."

"I just want to be alone even for a moment, jinzhou," Yan Mei Ling said softly after a moment, her eyes downcast.

"I understand and I admit, I must have been too overprotective that I forget that everyone need some time to be alone. Please forgive me for my lapses, Lao Fang."

Yan Mei Ling looked at Jinzhou Lu Wang Wei whose face remained stoic, and nervously swallowed the lump in her throat. What was in him that made her feel ashamed and conscious of her actions? His nearness seemed to disturb her in a way that she could not define. "I apologize as well for my outburst, jinzhou. It is totally childish of me."

"Apology accepted," Jinzhou Lu Wang Wei said with a ghost of a smile. "Anyway, don't wander too far in the forest and return to the camp as soon as the sun rose completely for we are going to start a military exercise to prepare ourselves against the Hsein clan. Do you follow, Lao Fang?"

"Yes, jinzhou," Yan Mei Ling said though she was confused whether she would smile or not but she chose the latter for it seemed safer.

"Good," Jinzhou Lu Wang Wei said. He immediately left without looking back.

As soon as Jinzhou Lu Wang Wei left, Yan Mei Ling had almost forgotten the reason why she came to the forest. In a way, the jinzhou's enigmatic presence had felt more comforting than being alone in the forest with nothing but her misery to accompany her. Surprisingly, she did not know why she seemed to think so.

The feeling that the jinzhou evoked in her seemed baffling for she wondered what it really was. One thing she was sure of was whenever he was near her, she felt two opposite emotions at the same time. One she could easily define and the other she would not wish to acknowledge. It was hysterical for it seemed impossible to feel such nor for someone to make you feel such way.

Yan Mei Ling sighed wearily then she spotted the bird who had flew ahead of her in the forest once again - up to this moment, she still was not sure if it was a hawk or falcon - but this time, she was surprised for it was heading swiftly to the direction of their camp.

CHAPTER 17

He was confused and totally uncertain. His mind hanging precariously at the edge of sanity.

He was not sure how he got himself tangled into this hazy web of confusion but there was one thing that he wanted to happen, that he would be emancipated from the insanity that had shackled him. An insanity that started when he met Lao Fang.

Lao Fang.

He didn't know what had drawn him to the boy but he felt like a moth near a flame. He just couldn't determine whether the flame would burn or warm him.

Well, call it curiosity but deemed only at the start for he'd be damned if he call this inexplicable emotion he was feeling as such. And, if he gauge what it truly was, it would most likely be called an obsession. An obsession that was akin to a festering wound that no medicine could ever heal for the boy was too adamant in feeding his curiosity with scraps called information. True, he had known some information about the boy based from what he said - if they were indeed true - and, of course, by secretly observing him when he was unaware but what little information Jinzhou Lu Wang Wei had and known had even encourage him to seek for more or was he hoping to discover something else?

Jinzhou Wang Wei touched his nosebridge as he was in a reflective trance. This wasn't good. His curiosity had turned insatiable to the point it could almost be called insane for nothing could appease it. Lao Fang was a puzzle - a mysterious puzzle that could never be solved.

He slowly walked on the forest ground following an invisible spiral path. He straightened his body, slowly raised both his arms away from each other, palms turned down and fingers bent pointing rigidly to the ground. Slowly, after he felt an otherworldly force seeped to his body, he raised his left knee, and did a dexterous somersault. He then ran towards a tree, kicked the trunk with both his feet and did another somersault. He then jumped high from the ground, released a series of swift kicks while he was in the air. When he finally landed on the ground, he panted heavily from exertion.

He breathed in deeply and closed his eyes. He waited for his mind to be cleared from the thing that bothered him but the exercise he performed had barely emancipated his mind. He was still confused - thoroughly confused.

What was with the ninja boy that made him curious? Why did he feel that he trust the boy but remained skeptical to his identity? What kind of madness had possessed him to feel so uncertain? What kind of insanity that had taken hold of his mind that conjured the fiery girl from the market every time he looked at the ninja boy?

Of course, Lao Fang could not be the girl in the market! The girl was too feminine; he could still remember how her strolling robe clung wonderfully to her body. How the intricate patterns of the rich royal blue silk enhanced her beautiful white and pink complexion whereas Lao Fang. He looked pale in the black imperial army cotton robe which size was obviously too big for his small built. They weren't one despite the similarity of their faces. Possibly, they could be related to each other. If that was the case, then the girl. . She could. . No, he didn't like where his thoughts lead him to.

He breathed deeply again as his heart beat became steadier and looked at the sky. It was still dawn and here he was in the forest, plagued by the boy who occupied the other side of the forest and the girl whose identity he had yet to discover.

He clenched his jaws together and howled in frustration as he took the javelin he had left to lean on the tree trunk and strike imaginary enemies with it.

One. Two. Three. Four. Five. Six. Seven. Eight. Nine. Ten. Until he lost track of the number of strikes and hits he did with his javelin.

He should think of the war; it was the war and the enemies that should had bothered him. But unfortunately, it wasn't the war that bothered him but the emotion that was slowly flowering in his heart. He shook his head. He couldn't allow this certain madness to overcome him for it went against his nature and what he was used to.

One. Two. Three. . .

When his muscles felt numb after what seemed to be an infinite number of wind clashes he did using his javelin, he raised it with its sharp tip pointing to the ground, and then buried it to the hilt. He breathed heavily with desperation but even if he was panting for breath, his mind was filled with disquiet. He still had extreme difficulty deviating from the thought that disturbed him. If at any rate there had been any effect, it had became worst.

"Aggh!" He cried angrily in frustration and then with his fists clenched, he punched the rough trunk of a huge forest tree until his hands turned bloody raw and felt searingly painful.

What was this madness that possessed him?

He went down his knees and absentmindedly studied his severely wounded knuckles. He could see his blood trickling and small wooden debris protruding on the shallow part of his flesh.

He breathed heavily. He should not be confused, his mind reiterated. In fact, he should not feel at all.

Emotions always had adverse effect on him which was the reason why he'd became too detached and aloof. Every time things ran deeper than he preferred it to be, he automatically shut himself out. It made things simple that way - uncomplicated. It served pretty well throughout the years. Until now.

He violently shook his head and stood. He had more important things to think of and it would highly inconvenient of him to be bothered by what seemed to be futile. No one should bother him. No one could bother him. Not the unknown fiery girl who had stolen his heart. And, most especially, not the Ninja boy who reminded him of the girl.

CHAPTER 18

"Good day, Jiangjun Han Li. I, your humble subordinate, ask for your permission to speak to you," a soldier announced when the jiangjun's serving boy led him inside a big tent set-up solely for the highest ranking official in the camp.

Even if there were no extravagant amenities inside, but if compared to the other tents in the camp where several soldiers slept like bundled twigs on a small box, it was by far the most comfortable. There were animal skins and silks decorating the floor, a low table, and a cabinet where the jiangjun's things were kept.

"Speak," Jiangjun Han Li motioned to the soldier.

Despite the simplicity of the tent as compared to the grand quarter, the jiangjun was accustomed to back at Lord Hsein's domain, he never failed to flaunt his position nor to hide how well endowed he was. He was wearing a fine bright orange silk woven with beautiful geometric patterns. His wonderful steel armor never failed to boast power with the heavy and detailed design indicating the Hsien symbol which is the Red Hawk.

"Thank you, my lord Jiangjun. I come to tell you that the hawk is back; it is carrying something on it's beak."

"Good, I'll go outside," the jiangjun said as he leisurely exhaled opium smoke from his mouth. The haze had filled the tent that it lent a grim flair. "Now, you can go."

"Yes, Jiangjun Han Li," the soldier bowed respectfully and bode his leave.

The jiangjun took one last, slow wisp from the opium before coming out of his tent.

When he was outside, he whistled with his fingers and, with the beckoning sound, the hawk swiftly landed on his outstretched forearm. The jiangjun smiled as he took the thing that the hawk carried on its beak. He slowly examined it and something came to his mind.

"Duizhu Gang Bingwen," he called the man standing at his right side.

Duizhu Gang Bingwen immediately came nearer to the jiangjun and bowed respectfully, "Yes, Jiangjun Han Li?"

"I want you to prepare all of our men. The enemies are not far from south of us. Wonderful, for I feel overly generous to surprise them." The jiangjun said sarcastically. A sinister smile tugged on his mouth.

"Yes, Jiangjun Han Li," Duizhu Gang Wen said and hastily announced to the men in the camp to assemble themselves.

"Ho!"

A small, wiry boy immediately came and bowed lowly to Jiangjun Han Li as if was a god. "Yes, my lord Jiangjun?"

"Prepare my armor and weapons. Be fast or I will cut your head off your body, do you understand?"

"Yes, Jiangjun Han Li," the boy's voice shook with fear and then he immediately scurried to the jiangjun's tent.

Jiangjun Han Li watched as his men prepared themselves for the surprise attack on the Imperial Majesty's army who were camping not far from where they were. His camp had remained undiscovered by the imperial army for multitude of thick and leafy trees had conveniently obscured it; even noises were shrouded which prevented the other camp from hearing their activities - stealthy, that would best describe his camp if it was a man.

His men had prepared the horses, cannons, different kind of weapons and ammunitions. Several of his men had started to assemble after arming themselves with weapons and armors. Some soldiers were assigned to remain in the camp to guard the their tents and reinforcements while they were away. None of the tents were kept for he was certain his force can easily crush the imperial army. He smiled cruelly when he felt a sudden rush of blood lust seized him.

Defeat was not an option to Jiangjun Han Li. It would never be for a man as mighty as he.

His gaze turned toward the wide stretch of dusky sky tainted with streaks of pink - dawn it might have been but today was fated. He could tell that this day would obviously be another mark to the list of his victorious feats. He was extremely certain that Lord Hsein Mao Dong would be pleased with him enough to elevate his rank to that of a grand nobleman once Lord Hsein Mao Dong became an Emperor.

"I could not believe that the Emperor of Chixian Shenzhou is very stupid; how dare he sent someone not fit enough to face me on the battlefield. This will be an easy ambush." Jiangjun Han Li muttered menacingly as he walked toward his tent.

A bird's cry.

Yan Mei Ling frowned as she watched the bird flying swiftly from the camp to the opposite side. Strange. Something came to her that she couldn't quite put a finger on.

The bird reminded her of something but not of wonderful reminiscent but of grimer ones.

Was the bird a harbinger of an unfortunate thing to come? Oh, she hope it wasn't.

But the birds were creatures looking for permanent shelter in the bounty of the dense forest or they could be migratory, seeking shelter when the harsh and unforgiving winter invaded the season. But that bird couldn't be migratory, that bird could not be hunting either especially at this time of day when there were little chances of catching a prey.

'A bird, such a wonderful and useful creature. It could bring life to the dead night through its music or it could pronounced that the day is promised. Harmless it might seem to be but it could be an instrument of deception. Some armies trained and used it as a spy on its enemies or heralds of secret messages. Better know the difference between a bird trained by nature and a bird exploited by the scheming minds of men.'

Of course that could be a possibility and she always put to heart all the things that her Master Tang Jiao Quon had taught her.

In the time of war, all small things had their meanings. Small things couldn't simply be ignored though they seemed harmless at the moment; for sometimes they could create the biggest of all damage.

Yan Mei Ling stood for a moment taking time to reflect on the thing that came to her. She shook her head. She might have gone crazy. The time she spent in the imperial army camp, the loneliness she was experiencing of being away from the people she loved and, also the unwarranted feelings that Jinzhou Lu Wang Wei invoked in her heart had all twisted her mind.

She breathed in deeply as she tried to collect her thoughts. She slowly closed her eyes and spread her arms, savoring the pristine air and comfort only nature could provide. And for that moment, she allowed herself to forget all the worries that were imposed upon her shoulders.

She allowed herself to be a part of nature, not a separate entity. In a very magical moment, she could feel the soft rustle of the forest grass, the gentle swaying of leaves from the thick and big trees, the steady sound of a water current from a distant, and the orchestrated voices of the animals inhabiting the forest.

Everything seemed in so perfect and peaceful. It felt as if she was floating on the air with no weight sitting upon her. Could the empire be as peaceful as the forest? Life would have been better.

She allowed herself to be relaxed even in that imagined magical moment. But as wonderful as the notion to feel that way for all time, a sudden sense of foreboding came into her diminishing the magic. Where she felt the creatures of the forest, she could hear the ground vibrated which didn't seem natural at all.

Boom. Cluck.

Footsteps. Numerous footsteps!

In panic, Mei Ling opened her eyes as the sound became more pronounced especially when she could hear sounds.

Sounds not from that of the animals living in the forest. It felt unnatural as that of a furious stampede.

She paused and realized. It was as if that her heart just stopped beating.

This was catastrophe! And time was dwindling rapidly. She had to return to the camp!

She needs to go in haste!

Chapter 19

She hurriedly ran back to the imperial army camp when she gave up on trying to find where Jinzhou Lu Wang Wei was in the forest.

While she was running, she could hear her heart colliding violently against her chest. Her legs felt wobbly and about to gave up due to constant running.

It seemed hysterical but all of the trees in the forest looked as if they had transformed into evil giant soldiers garbed in heavy lamellar armors engraved with the demon warlord's seal. Impossible, but even the branches resembled like swords and javelins poised to attack her.

Yan Mei Ling paused for a moment as she struggled to catch her breath. What was happening to her? It seemed that her fear had taunted her vision creating illusions that served only to magnify her already frightened senses. Was this the feeling that the soldiers felt during a skirmish?

She had no time to know the answers to her questions. She had to go back to the camp and tell everyone what she had discovered. Despite her exhaustion, she urged herself to continue running. Her pace kept on increasing as if she was being pursued by the enemies.

'Oh, please keep them safe. Please, please.'

Her mind had suddenly wandered to Jinzhou Lu Wang Wei. Tears started falling from her eyes as a great sadness struck the very core of her heart. Was this how mingled guilt and sadness felt?

If something happened to him, then she would blame herself for he was merely following her to make sure she'd be safe even leaving the camp behind. But she drove him away. .What if he was caught by the enemies or possibly ambushed? Despite the animosity she felt for him, she did not wish for him to be harmed.

She would never forgive herself if something happened to him.

A battle cry.

Dark clouds still canopied the sky making it looked funereal but war did not choose what time it would happen.

The Hsein armies had furtively surrounded the imperial army's camp and began their surprise ambush on the soldiers who were still lethargic from sleep. When Jinzhou Lu Wang Wei had arrived from the forest, he was shocked to see a lot of the soldiers in his command were killed and those who fought weren't even donned in their combat attires just like him but that never deterred him from joining his soldiers in fighting the enemies. He only hoped that it was not too late.

Multiple arrows were hurled at every direction. The chances of dodging away from its fatal pointed end seemed thinner than a javelin's deadly tip.

Steel met steel, the loud clashes of metals sounding sharp and shrill against the ears. Numerous horses' hooves furiously shook the ground, cries of pain and taunting shouts caused a frenzied uproar in the camp.

Boom!

Boom!

Thugsh!

Cannons were fired and as they burst, dilapidated bodies were thrown in all four directions of the wind. Fires were set on the tents spreading rapidly on the others like a wildfire.

The sky continued to weep blood. Dark red blood. Thick crimson blood. Repugnant blood. Raining down like an incessant and raging storm.

'Where is he?' Jinzhou Lu Wang Wei worriedly thought as he fought his opponent when he realized that someone was still missing. His heart was beating rapidly and adrenaline was pumping vigorously in his vein.

He ducked from the deadly steel that would have divided his head from his body and, swiftly, countered by kicking his opponent's hip when he reached his side. When his opponent's knees gave in due to pain, he immediately took the opportunity to stab him on the head. He could feel the skull being drilled and its soft brain being twisted as he urged to go deeper. Blood bathed his opponent's body as it lifelessly fell on the ground the moment that he pulled out his sword.

Unfortunately, the war was not over yet; as soon as he killed one, another came running to him in hopes of stabbing him at the back for he was not wearing any armor making him look like a vulnerable target. But his magnified senses warned him of the impending danger so he somersaulted and was transported to the enemy's back instead. He pivoted to his side and immediately plunged his sword at the exposed part of the enemy, the one unshielded by the lamellar armor. As he pushed his sword, he could feel that its blade had encountered a chain of bones and flesh. He thrusted deeper until the blood furiously flow from the fatal wound. Another down but the enemies seemed both inexhaustible and interminable.

Jinzhou Lu Wang Wei pulled back his sword drom the enemy's body - the sound of broken bones and the splashing of blood was audible. His breathing became labored due to exertion as he desperately scanned the camp to look for Lao Fang amidst the clamor of the war.

'Where is Tang Lao Fang?'

His heart furiously drummed against his chest as he ran in every direction of the camp while dispatching the enemies who unfortunately dared cross his path.

He continued to scan the surroundings, running through the men who were clashing to death.

When he could not find Tang Lao Fang among the soldiers, dread had instantaneously came into his heart, momentarily freezing his senses. A different kind of coldness came into his being and, surprisingly, his vision suddenly became a blur.

This could not be.

Was Tang Lao Fang cornered by the enemies when he left the boy alone in the forest?

A Hsien soldier tried to attack Jinzhou Lu Wang Wei with a sword but he immediately parried the attack. He bent his knees and swept the Hsien soldier with his feet. When the Hsien soldier lose his balance, Jinzhou Lu Wang Wei stabbed him on the heart. The dark red blood of the enemy splattered all over his shirt.

This could not be, his mind repeated. Tang Lao Fang could not be dead. The thought seemed unacceptable that his mind went strongly against it.

"Aggh!" Jinzhou Lu Wang Wei let out an enraged cry as he angrily charged toward a group of enemy soldiers who came to swarm around him. He immediately killed them all by rapidly turning himself around like a tornado, striking them brutally with his sword's blade. Different body parts were torn and thrown - heads, limbs and tendons. He apathetically watched as blood burst from the lifeless bodies like a lava that was spluttered carelessly from the volcano's mouth during a dangerous eruption.

Jinzhou Lu Wang Wei killed several more soldiers - splitting their bodies into half and decapitating their heads. Someone tried to engage him in a melee but he quickly dispatch the foolish person by leaping above the latter's head and ultimately landing on the shoulders. He quickly grip the enemy's neck with his boots and turned himself around, breaking the spine in the process as indicated by the ominous crack.

Despite the violence nor the simmering action in the battlefield, he surprisingly felt numb. It seemed that his heart had stopped pumping blood into his veins and it felt more like an empty dead vessel. Even time seemed to stop for a brief moment; even the people who were fighting each other in the camp.

This could not be.

He shook his head - profound disbelief was clearly etched in his face. He swallowed the painful lump in his throat and held tighter to the handle on his sword. Blood covered its steel like a snake slithering upon a tree branch.

He could feel that his body started to seethe with so much ire that his heart would burst if he couldn't spend it.

"Hsien armies, I swear to the Son of Heaven and my ancestors that you will all die!" He shouted at the top of his lungs as he furiously attack the Hsien army soldiers.

Chapter 20

Jiangjun Han Li was watching the ongoing war between his men and the imperial army from a cautious distance atop his armored stallion but he could feel that his anger was starting to build up. No, anger was too mild an emotion for it did not even describe half of what he felt right now. He was extremely livid!

He angrily clenched his fists on the bridle of his horse. His jaws were hardening with extreme displeasure and shame as he watched his men, one by one or even in groups, extinguished by a certain mad man in black.

"Duizhu Gang Bingwen!" Jiangjun Han Li angrily called.

Duizhu Gang Bingwen immediately rode his horse to the jiangjun's side. "You called for me, Jiangjun Han Li?"

"Exactly," Jiangjun Han Li sarcastically hissed, his small eyes narrowing into furious slits. "Who is that man in black and why can't any of our men kill him? You told me that we can ambush the Imperial army with just a hundred men but I should not have listened to your stupid suggestion."

Duizhu Bingwen momentarily shook on his saddle, confusion was clearly etched on his brows. "I did not tell you. ."

"Insolent fool!" Jiangjun Hang Li shouted menacingly at Duizhu Bingwen. He immediately aimed the tip of his sword on the latter's neck - interrupting whatever Duizhu Gang Bingwen was about to say. "Your excuses will not be tolerated! I even doubt if your unspoken apology will appease the utter humiliation that I am feeling right now. How could I, a man of supreme intelligence, even consider to listen to the advice of a man whose brain obviously resembled that of a lowly worm?"

Duizhu Bingwen mouth went agape making him look like a fool as what the jiangjun ranted he was. His shame began to flare as a lot of his men had witnessed him minimized to the means of a lowly scum by the deceitful Jiangjun Han Li. How could the Jiangjun deflect his mistake to him?

Now, to the eyes of his men, he was a stupid and incapable fool. His flesh seemed prickled by millions of needles as he felt some of his men laughed at his back and, worst, regarded him with pity. But the shame he felt right now seemed pale in comparison to the fear he felt as the sharp end of the sword delved even deeper into his flesh - possibly drawing blood.

An unspoken threat and command was clearly visible on Jiangjun Han Li's evil eyes.

Duizhu Gang Bingwen had no choice but to swallow his pride and allow the jiangjun to degrade him further; the need for self-preservation held more weight as of the moment. Against his heart, he said, "I greatly apologize for not seeking your golden counsel and mindlessly asserted my worthless battle tactics instead. I will join the men and vow to bring you the head of the man in black. I will rectify the grave mistake I have made, Jiangjun Han Li."

Jiangjun Han Li raised his brows in approval and sarcastically smirked, his sword still pointed on Duizhu Gang Bingwen's neck. "Just make sure to bring his head to me; for if you fail, ohh, it is still fine with me. Anyway, that man in black will save me the expense of doing such a menial task of personally cutting your brainless head off your body. Remember, bring more men with you. With your incompetence, I doubt if you can take that man down yourself."

"As you wish, Jiangjun Han Li," Duizhu Gang Bingwen said in an apathetic voice despite the resentment and shame that shook the very core of his being. Now was not the time to give in to his tumultuous emotions. He would have to deal with it later after this battle. Revenge could not be done if you were already an ice cold corpse.

When Jiangjun Han Li finally removed the tip of his sword from Duizhu Gang Bingwen, the latter hastily urged his horse to the direction of the man in black.He could not stomach looking at the repulsive face of the cowardly and deceitful general.

'I will make sure to kill that man in black. After I'm done with him and this war, I will vow to make you eat all of your words and, shame you as what you did to me in front of my men before I finish you off, Jiangjun Han Li.'

The angry shouts of the cannons had intensified as Yan Mei Ling came nearer to the camp. She could see a thick haze of smoke damning the still-not-yet-bright sky to eternal darkness. A pandemonium of cries and shouts had assaulted her ears which made her knees even weaker.

'I am too late,' Yan Mei Ling said to herself as she stifled the urge to cry.

She sprinted faster and her senses ran amok as she found several lifeless bodies on the ground. Some were incinerated with sharp weapons, others could not be distinguished for they were thoroughly dilapidated like butchered meat.

Arrows were thrown in a projectile motion, cannons roared worst than a pack of lions and people were fighting each other despite the smog.

Tears furiously ran down Yan Mei Ling's cheeks as she scanned the fighting people. Where is Jinzhou Lu Wang Wei?

"Ahh!" someone shouted behind Yan Mei Ling. When she turned to the direction of the voice, she saw an enemy running towards her with his javelin poised to stab her.

Now, I'll be dead.

"Agh!" the enemy suddenly fell dead to the ground as several arrows hit his back.

"Boy, run retrieve the man's javelin. You can't fight with your bare hands!" The man who had saved Yan Mei Ling shouted to her before he resumed to fighting the other enemies.

Yan Mei Ling sighed in relief before she ran towards the fallen enemy and retrieved his javelin.

The moment that she held the javelin in her hands, a huge gleaming jian almost sliced her body into half but her well-trained body had avoided it by laying on the ground and swiftly turned to the other side.

"Die, kid!" The enemy said with malevolence as he attempted to assault Yan Mei Ling again with his jian. She managed to roll on the ground thus avoiding the deadly attack again.

With the other edge of the enemy's jian still embedded to the ground, Yan Mei Ling took the opportunity to stand quickly kicked the enemy far from his weapon. The enemy tried to stand up but she immediately stabbed him with the sharp end of her javelin.

The enemy's eyes dilated in shock as Yan Mei Ling urged deeper. Every inch deeper, she could feel the sharp javelin boring into the thick flesh of the enemy.

An unusual feeling came to her making her stomach queasy. The feel of incinerated flesh and blood flowing off from a man's body were more than enough to repulse her. She could not take it. This was utterly disgusting. She let go of the javelin and went down her knees.

Her body began to quiver violently as she desperately threw up the bitter contents of her stomach on the ground. She had just killed someone!

"Boy, what is happening to you? Now is not the right time to get sick. Keep yourself together. We need to fight and kill our enemies or else, it will be the death of us." The man who saved her came back to her. Both concern and apprehension were shown on his face.

Yan Mei Ling looked at him weakly and whispered, "I've never killed anyone in my life, sir. The sight of blood repulses me."

The man's brows creased then an understanding dawned upon him. "I understand you. This is the first time you have joined a war. All of us feel the same way on our very first battle but if we don't bleed our enemies, they will bleed us. We can't let them take over the empire and hurt the ones we care for, right? Think of the reason why you join the war. Now, stand up and fight. We should not let our enemies defeat us."

Yan Mei Ling looked at the man again and could feel a distinctive warmness crept on her cheeks as she took in his features. His small almond eyes were deep set; his nose straight and long; his beautiful lips curled into a kind brotherly smile. He reminded her of Jinzhou Lu Wang Wei if not for his hair. The latter's hair was long yet tied into a neat ponytail while the former has a short unruly hair barely reaching his nape. But he was not Jinzhou Lu Wang Wei.

Her heart was filled worry and fear when she remembered Jinzhou Lu Wang Wei. Where is he?

"I. . I" Yan Mei Ling muttered incoherrently as she tried to control the mounting fear in her heart. "Yes, Sir, I need to stand so I may fight the enemies."

The man smiled at Mei Ling again. "Good. Anyway, don't call me Sir. My name is Lu Jinhai."

Lu Jinhai stood to take the jian of the man whom Yan Mei Ling had killed and gave it to her. "Take this jian, Tang Lao Fang. You need this."

Yan Mei Ling's mouth went agape in wonder when she realized that he knew her alias.

"I know you, Tang Lao Fang. I have seen you fight with Jinzhou Lu Wang Wei. You are an exceptional fighter despite the fact that you've never been to war before. Now, take this jian and prove to this filthy Hsien pigs that you are the greatest warrior of Chixian Shenzhou."

Yan Mei Ling hesitated for a moment but despite the fact that the whole event had traumatized her, she accepted the jian. "Thank you, Lu Jinhai."

Lu Jinhai nodded to Yan Mei Ling and said, "Do your best to stay alive. I will see you after this battle, Lao Fang."

Chapter 21

The war was relentless and it seemed that the enemies had increased exponentially. But none of those could extinguish the burning flame within Jinzhou Lu Wang Wei's raging heart. As if caught under a manic spell of destruction, he killed the enemies in a way only a madman would do.

When another group of Hsien soldiers encircled around him, instead of being suppressed, he had effectively slain them all by swiftly juggling himself and his sword alternately at the enemies. The enemies were shocked at his unhuman speed that it seemed too late for them to realize that their arms and legs were gashed. When the enemies collapsed, Jinzhou Lu Wang Wei stabbed each of them to death.

After killing the enemies, Jinzhou Lu Wang Wei's robe became heavily smeared with the enemies' blood. His hands were coated in both dried and wet blood.

"You!" Someone shouted to him. "I challenge you to a fight!"

Jinzhou Lu Wang Wei looked to the direction of the voice and saw a heavily armored man with the Hsien army emblem atop a muscled stallion. He narrowed his eyes but his shoulders remained rigid and his sword's sharp tip was still pointed to the ground.

"Who is going to fight me - you or your horse?" Jinzhou Lu Wang Wei asked with an aloof face although his tone was clearly mocking.

The armored man's eyes flared angrily at the insult. His face reddened with barely suppressed wrath.

"Bastard!" The man spat and then he hastily urged his horse to the direction of Jinzhou Lu Wang Wei. He raised his sword in a stance to cut the latter into half.

When the armored man and his horse came nearer, Jinzhou Lu Wang Wei knelt rapidly and gracefully slid beneath the galloping horse. He quickly cleaved its hocks and knees in the process. Before the horse's great body staggered upon him, he already reached a safe distance away from it.

The armored man however had swiftly jumped off his horse before its body crushed him to death. His eyes widened in stunned bewilderment and when reality set in, his blood was boiling with irrepressible wrath at seeing his favorite horse incapacitated and bleeding to death.

"You have killed Huimie! I swear to the gods and my ancestors that you will pay for this!" The armored man shouted furiously.

"You have killed a lot of my men and destroyed our cavalry units. You can't expect me to be merciful."

"How dare you, good-for-nothing peasant! Nobody dares to mock me. Don't you know who I am?"

"I believe this is the first time we have met so no." Jinzhou Lu Wang Wei said tightly. "And, just to correct your assumption of me, I am not a peasant."

The armored man's eyes narrowed at the answer but, after a while, he began to smirk. Something came to him. Unbelievable but it seemed that an inexplicable kind of excitement had seeped into his veins.

All his life, Duizhu Gang Bingwen had ate, slept, breathed and lived war but never had he witnessed a warrior as good as the arrogant man who stood in front of him. Finally, he had found his match. He mentally took note to thank the Jiangjun Han Li for giving him the opportunity to fight this great warrior. Before finishing that undeserving and deceitful Jiangjun.

"You have a bizaare sense of humor, do you know it? By the way, I believe introductions are in order. I am Duizhu Gang Bingwen of the Hsien army Hong se unit and you are?"

Jinzhou Lu Wang Wei was surprised at the sudden change of the armored man's mood but he remained wary. "I am Jinzhou Lu Wang Wei of the Imperial Army who serves the real and only Emperor of Chixian Shenzhou."

"Oh," Duizhu Gang Bingwen exclaimed in a daze. "I know you, Jinzhou Lu Wang Wei. I have heard that you are the greatest warrior of the Imperial Army. And, of course, if I am not mistaken, you have just recently won the annual Imperial tournament."

Jinzhou Lu Wang Wei was surprised at what he had heard. How does he know and how much does he know?

Duizhu Gang Bingwen chuckled humorously at the stunned look on Jinzhou Lu Wang Wei's face. "I know what is on your mind. Just to answer your unspoken question, we have spies in your empire-lots of them." He continued looking at Jinzhou Lu Wang Wei from head to foot as if scaling the latter before smiling that malevolent smile of his.

"This is very exciting. I am extremely happy to be given the opportunity to face you in the battle today. You just can't imagine how much I look forward for this day. But then again, my happiness of having to fight you is not enough for me to spare your life. It is such an unfortunate waste that you are one of the enemies."

"We will see about it then." Jinzhou Lu Wang Wei said aloofly.

"You are one confident warrior but I cannot blame you." Duizhu Gang Bingwen said, the evil smile never left his mouth. "I hate to thwart your confidence but I have to warn you, my face is the last face that you will ever see."

Jinzhou Lu Wang Wei stared blankly at Duizhu Gang Bingwen for a moment. Without warning, he made a quick turn and aimed a flying kick accurately to the duizhu's chest.

Duizhu Gang Bingwen staggered at the intensity of the attack. He was so astonished that he was immobilized for a moment. Before he could react, Jinzhou Lu Wang Wei, did another follow up attack by stamping his foot on Duizhu Bingwen's stomach.

"All talk and no action will put you in grave danger," Jinzhou Lu Wang Wei said to the enemy while he was groaning in pain. He waited for the duizhu to recover from his attack.

"You are indeed legendary as they say." Duizhu Gang Bingwen exclaimed as he wiped the mixture of spit and blood from his mouth with the back of his hand. He stood and haughtily scrutinized Jinzhou Lu Wang Wei.

"I don't think we need any weapon," He announced as he quickly discarded his weapons. "You and I should use brute strength."

"If that's what you want," Jinzhou Lu Wang Wei obliged and discarded the weapons from his body too.

"You are unfortunately armorless which works well to your advantage a while ago," Duizhu Gang Bingwen commented before he took off his body armor leaving the orange cotton tunic and dark green trousers behind. "I think I might follow suit."

Jinzhou Lu Wang Wei smiled but, in a heartbeat, the devious Gang Bingwen, attacked him by flying to his back before throwing him down with a fatal kick. The latter continued by grabbing Jinzhou Lu Wang Wei by the neck and kicked him on the stomach with his knee.

Jinzhou Lu Wang Wei doubled in pain. His vision darkened due to the unspeakable pang. But the assault didn't end there. He received another stomp to the stomach, a series of kicks to the ribs and chest.

"A bitter taste of your own medicine?" Duizhu Gang Bingwen sarcastically laughed as he continued his relentless thrashing to the supine Jinzhou Lu Wang Wei.

Jinzhou Lu Wang Wei closed his eyes as the assault continued on him. His body was swimming in immeasurable pain but his mind more alive as ever. 'I can't die. The empire needs me. I need to defeat the Hsein army.'

With a strength Duizhu Lu Wang Wei thought he didn't possess considering his current state, he was able to grab Jinzhou Gang Bingwen's foot as it was about to aim another stamp upon his chest. With supreme effort, he twisted it. He could hear the satisfying crack of the latter's broken ligament before he shoved his opponent backwards.

"Ugh!" Duizhu Gang Bingwen groaned in pain as he fell down. "You, bastard!"

"You are a bastard too." Jinzhou Lu Wang Wei replied weakly as he struggled to stand up. He could feel that some of his bones might possibly be broken and his body shaking violently. He gasped as he swallowed a handful of air to ease the sharp pain in his body. Slowly, he walked towards Duizhu Gang Bingwen.

"You think you can defeat me now that my other foot is injured? Ha! You're wrong!" Duizhu Gang Bingwen snarled angrily and launched himself to connect his fist to Jinzhou Lu Wang Wei.

Jinzhou Lu Wang Wei was able to avoid the attack. But he was surprised, he swore he had broken Duizhu Gang Bingwen's other foot but the latter seemed uninjured.

Duizhu Gang Bingwen jumped by striking his uninjured foot to the ground and then made a turning kick to Jinzhou Lu Wang Wei's face.

Jinzhou Lu Wang Wei used his forearms to shield himself from the attack before striking back.

The two fought with all their might like two powerful celestial beings struggling to outdo each other. It seemed that the two of them were the only people fighting in the war for each of their armies refused to interfere; both of their forces were too occupied in prevailing each other.

Cannons had shook the ground, burning several tents and trees while creating a massive inferno; shouts of rage and taunts had intensified the clamor; arrows and javelin had created a deadly deluge in the camp but the two mighty warriors remained oblivious-too immersed in their battle and too proud to give up.

"This is the best fight that I have ever had." Duizhu Gang Bingwen exclaimed in awe despite his broken and bloody face. His breathing ragged.

"Same here," Jinzhou Lu Wang Wei replied. His face equally torn and bloodied.

"But I guess one of us must die," Duizhu Gang Bingwen said with a hint of regret. He genuinely smiled at Jinzhou Lu Wang Wei before he made a run for one of his discarded weapons. He quickly picked his javelin and then threw it on Jinzhou Lu Wang Wei's heart.

"Jinzhou Lu Wang Wei, be careful!" A familiar voice shouted in warning.

Jinzhou Lu Wang Wei looked to the direction of the voice. Extreme relief and gratitude flooded his senses. Lao Fang is alive and safe. With unnatural speed, he caught the javelin with his hand and adroitly threw it back to Duizhu Gang Bingwen. His aim perfect as the sharp end penetrated his opponent's chest and back.

A froth of blood flooded Duizhu Gang Bingwen's mouth. His eyes wide with unbelievable shock before he stumbled on his back.

Jinzhou Lu Wang Wei immediately ran to the lying Duizhu Gang Bingwen. His opponent's blood quickly spread from the deeply incinerated flesh, creating a dark crimson pool.

"You are indeed legendary, Jinzhou Lu Wang Wei." Duizhu Gang Bingwen struggled to speak. His breathing came in shortly; his face ghastly pale and the blood in his mouth threatened to drown him. "I am lucky to die in your hands. I have no regrets even if you had defeated me. It is worth it. But please do me a favor."

Jinzhou Lu Wang Wei frowned warily at what Duizhu Gang Bingwen said but then he asked, "What will that be?"

"Please kill Jiangjun Han Li for me." He whispered weakly.

"I will. You can count on me to do that."

Duizhu Gang Bingwen smiled before closing his eyes, finally succumbing to eternal sleep to which he could never wake up from.

Chapter 22

The sun had set high on the sky searing the wide span of land with its vehement temperature; the clouds were sparse and thin, like that of a fine spider web. The sun and its ray looked like a pole that had a tip made of a circular molten gold. The day indicated that it was already the peak of the afternoon.

The combat with Hsien army Hong se Unit had remained an unfinished business since its jiangjun along with its remaining troops had fled the camp like spineless cowards. They eventually realized that they stood no chance of crushing the imperial army.

True to his vow to the deceased Duizhu Gang Bingwen's request, Jinzhou Lu Wang Wei had attempted to chase after them in hopes of killing Jiangjun Han Li but his weakened and wounded state had impeded him. He past out even before he could ran after the enemies.

He woke up to what seemed to be prisms of sun rays that passed through the multitude of holes on his torn tent and the sounds of men working outside. He struggled to sit down but when he did, he could feel a sharp stab of pain torturing every muscle and bone in his body. What surprised him even more were the bandages on his wounds and the tiny needles on his flesh. A torn cloth was placed upon him to cover him from any chill. However, despite the fact that it was already Autumn, it seemed unnecessary considering the current weather. He tasted something bitter and unfamiliar on his tongue and he remembered that someone had tried to feed him something in his unsteady state of consciousness.

His head turned when he heard that the door of his tent was being lifted. Someone entered his quarter. His eyes widened when he saw Tang Lao Fang carrying a bowl that emanated a strong and pungent. It was so strong that it irritated his nose.

"You are awake now, Jinzhou," Tang Lao Fang observed, relief was evident in his voice.

Jinzhou Lu Wang Wei was about to stand and approach him but then the boy had stopped him from doing so.

"Don't stand, Jinzhou, or else the needles might fall from your flesh or worst, they might go deeper making it hard to remove them."

Jinzhou Lu Wang Wei's forehead wrinkled in confusion. "Who had done this to me, Lao Fang?"

"He is Lee Sui Song, one of your soldiers; he is a village doctor's apprentice who lived East of the Imperial Palace. He is also the one who made the concoctions that were fed to you while you are unconscious. I merely assisted him. Ah... I have brought something for you, Jinzhou."

Tang Lao Fang went near him and handed him a bowl full of dull greenish-brownish liquid.

Jinzhou Lu Wang Wei wrinkled his nose in disapproval and eyed it skeptically. "What is it?"

"It is a fortifying broth. It will help you recover fast, Jinzhou."

"I don't need that - I think I am fine now, Lao Fang.I need to stand and go after the Hsein Army Hong se Unit." Jinzhou Lu Wang said with determination despite the nettling pain in his body. "I am certain that they are not far from us."

Yan Mei Ling secretly looked heavenward in frustration. She was not pleased with what she heard from Jinzhou Lu Wang Wei.

Why must he pretend that he is fine when, in fact, he seemed to wince even with simple body movement? Men and their twisted masculine notions are, most of the time, absurd and stupid.

"Go on. Stand up, Jinzhou, and let's see if you go after them and fight them considering your current state right now."

"I can't waste my time lying down doing nothing, Lao Fang. The Empire's safety lie in our hands. Any delay will endanger all of us."

"I know but stop being stubborn and listen to me!" Yan Mei Ling blurted out in frustration. She paused when she realized what she had just said. It was very ironic of her to tell those words when she, herself, was as stubborn as the Jinzhou Lu Wang Wei she was speaking with right now.

"Yan Mei Ling, don't be stubborn. Please listen to me."

She could very well remember Li Lei Shuang saying those words but only in a much gentle and calm way. Her best friend never raised a voice on her. A certain kind of sadness suddenly enveloped her eyes and she felt that she was being strangled.

Tears were threatening to expose her vulnerability in front of the man who she never wanted to witness it.

"Tang Lao Fang," Jinzhou Lu Wang Wei inquired gently, interrupting Yan Mei Ling's thoughts. "Is something amiss?"

Yan Mei Ling silently counted in her mind before she breathed noisily through her nose. She forced a counterfeit smile on her mouth. "A debris has stuck in my eyes." She lied guiltily before she furiously wiped her eyes with the back of her hand.

"What I actually mean, Jinzhou, is that most of us are still too weak to fight and are salvaging whatever is left from the encounter with Hsien Army Hong se unit. All of us must rest and recover. If we go after the enemies right now, they might kill all of us. Who knows if they have reinforcements waiting to lull us to their trap."

Jinzhou Lu Wang Wei remained silent for a moment and looked at Tang Lao Fang seriously in a different light. He noticed that the boy's cheeks had turned bright red either due to embarrassment or anger. He heard Lao Fang deliberately cough as if telling him to stop inspecting the latter as if he was someone of no consequence.

A smile tugged Jinzhou Lu Wang Wei's mouth then he said, "Your wisdom is astounding considering your age. I know that you will be an asset to the Imperial Army. You have indeed proven me right, Lao Fang."

"Thank you for your kind opinion of me, Jinzhou," Yan Mei Ling said shyly. "Ahm.. Can you please take and drink this broth?"

Jinzhou Lu Wang Wei accepted the bowl though with less enthusiasm. "This does not smell good at all, and it looks different. Is it also Lee Sui Song who made this one?"

Yan Mei Ling nodded cheerfully. "Yes, he is although it smells and looks bad; it doesn't taste bad as compared to the first concoction we had force-fed you, Jinzhou."

"So you have drank this too, Lao Fang?"

"Yes, all of us who have survived had drank it, Jinzhou."

Jinzhou Lu Wang Wei smiled grimly at Tang Lao Fang's words. It pained him greatly to know that a lot of his men died due to his neglect and improper planning. He had never anticipated that his enemies would attack on dawn where light was scarce. He took a sip of the broth and asked, "By chance, is there someone who knows how to cook other than broth?"

"Of course, there is, he is Lim Hok Se. He is the one who has made Lee Sui Song's fortifying broth tolerable. Isn't it amazing, Jinzhou? There is someone who knows how to heal, cook or possibly more. You should take time to know what your subordinates skills are other than their ability to hold a sword and fight. You will be surprised if you do."

Jinzhou Lu Wang Wei smiled and teased Tang Lao Fang. "And I thought that you can't get along with the others."

"Hmmp," Yan Mei Ling exclaimed. "I am not totally the brat that you might have possibly think of me. My previous unpleasant encounter with the your other subordinates does not define my attitude to those who are treating me with kindness and are offering me their friendship."

"Good"

"Good," Yan Mei Ling replied to Jinzhou Lu Wang Wei's statement. "Now, if you will be so kind to think of recovering fast so we can pursue the remaining Hsien Army Hong se unit by finishing the entire broth."

Jinzhou Lu Wang Wei smiled as he continued to sip the warm broth. The boy was indeed a paradox; he couldn't quite get the latter. The boy seemed to him as someone who thought maturely but acted with a youthful exuberance that would never mistake his juvenile age.

When Tang Lao Fang bode his leave and was about to go out of the tent, Jinzhou Lu Wang Wei felt a different sense of emptiness that had urged him to call after the boy. "Tang Lao Fang!"

Yan Mei Ling swiveled to the supine Jinzhou Lu Wang Wei and looked at him with wonder. "Yes, Jinzhou?"

There was a pregnant pause and a indescribable feeling that had surrounded the tent. This was kindred perhaps.

"I am glad that you are safe, Tang Lao Fang."

A blush crept to Yan Mei Ling cheeks as if they had been set afire. "I am glad that you are safe too, Jinzhou Lu Wang Wei."

Inside of the fortified walls of the Imperial Palace, the war was a relentless shadow of a fearsome behemoth threatening to destroy. The peace within seemed to veil the dangers of the war like an invisible shield. But it was only a sham for the news brought by the harbingers and spies of the Empire had narrated the most gruesome and twisted things that had truly happened in the war.

Within the intricate and protected walls of the Imperial palace was a duplicate of what seemed a heavenly oasis, the imperial garden. The bamboos,ferns and different kinds of flowers continued to dance merrily along with the Autumn breeze; the birds continued to sing like heaven's choir; and varied insects danced around, seemingly oblivious to the war.

It was night time but the cloudless sky was dark and moonless. It wasn't completely dark though because of the palace torches and hanging lanterns. But their unnatural light didn't reach half of the sheer beauty illuminated by the moon. The beauty of the surroundings was still solemn that it seemed a mockery of the war that was progressing outside.

Li Lei Shuang sat beside the pond and stared absentmindedly on the twirling lotuses. The light illuminated by the lantern and torches reflected white beams on the dark green water. It had been several weeks since the tragic news of what happened to Yan Mei Ling's village. No one survived not even the villagers' ashes; everything crumbled into dust as if there was no people who used to inhabit it.

The thought created a painful hole in Li Lei Shuang heart. It was as if she was being strangled slowly and surely with every recollection of the days she had with her best friend. She could very well remember Yan Mei Ling's childlike laughter resonating in her mind, and she struggled to conjure her living image but, to no avail, just like the houses in Mei Ling's village; her best friend's face crumbled into dust.. Into nothingness..

"Oh, Yan Mei Ling," Lei Shuang choked and, once again, a stream of tears fell from her heavily swollen eyes. Her throat constricted by the cumbersome lump in it. Her heart in extreme desolation. "Oh, Yan Mei Ling, why do you have to leave me? You made a promise."

Through the painful blur in her eyes, she struggled to recall the happier memories of the past.

'Li Lei Shuang, look, I caught a beautiful butterfly!'

'Oh, it is indeed beautiful. Can I held it in my palm, Yan Mei Ling?'

'Sure,' Yan Mei Ling said as she gently transferred the colorful butterfly into Li Lei Shuang's open palms.

'It is truly beautiful!' Li Lei Shuang gasped in awe but her reaction had startled the butterfly that it flew away from her palm.

'Oh, no, you scared it, Li Lei Shuang!' Mei Ling cried in disappointment.

'I am so sorry, Yan Mei Ling,' Lei Shuang apologized and, then, gently placed her hand on Yan Mei Ling's slumped shoulders. 'Don't worry, my sweet, I have something to show you. I am sure you will like it.'

'Really?' Yan Mei Ling exclaimed excitedly; her disappointment over the butterfly forgotten.

'Yes,' Li Lei Shuang nodded happily and led Mei Ling to the most beautiful part of the garden.

'Wonderful! All the butterflies are here!' Yan Mei Ling gasped in admiration as her eyes hovered in delight on the butterflies and other colorful insects feasting on the beautiful plants in the garden.

"Yes, they are all beautiful but none compared to you, my sweet Yan Mei Ling."

Li Lei Shuang sobbed tearfully as the memory faded. She couldn't believe that Mei Ling would now be forever gone. How she wished the news was nothing but a nightmare. When she woke up, Mei Ling, just as her best friend always did, would come and visit her in the palace.

Li Lei Shuang seemed so absorbed in recollecting all her memories of her best friend that she was oblivious to the sinister beings observing her from a distance. She did not notice that someone from the dark and hidden part of the garden had been bidding his time.

Now was the perfect timing! Like a stealth predator, he furtively walked and, with lightning speed, he got hold of Li Lei Shuang. Before she could scream for help to alarm the Imperial Palace guards, she past out as a dizzying substance was stuck in her nose and mouth.

"TongJun Linghua," the kidnapper called in a low voice. "I got the princess!"

Another person came out from his hiding place in the garden.

He was more formiddable and more dangerous. An evil smirk formed in his mouth as he said in a low silky voice laced with danger, "Perfect. Now, we need to get out of the palace and bring her to Lord Hsien Mao Dong."

Chapter 23

The sky was already dark when Jinzhou Lu Wang Wei went out of his tent. He dozed for several hours after drinking the broth that Tang Lao Fang brought to him. Amazingly, his body felt light and energized- ready to fight the Hsien enemies again.

As with the previous nights, the sky remained moonless and starless that you would lost your direction if you did not have a lantern or a lamp in your hand. He walked into the camp and saw his subordinates warming themselves by the fire. They greeted him as he passed which he too returned.

As he looked around the camp, his heart was filled with remorse and regret upon seeing the damage and loss his command had had after the encounter with Hsien Army Hong se unit. A lot of his men had died and their reinforcements were almost useless; the bodies were buried in a mass grave to prevent the smell of the decaying bodies from spreading any disease among the remaining men in the camp. How would they survive with their meager number and resources?

Some of his men even picked and piled all the weapons that were left after the skirmish, be it from theirs or that of the Hsein army Hong se unit.

He pondered deeply upon his and his men's situation. He needed more men. He badly needed them if he wished to survive the next encounter with the Hsien army. Although, he was a skilled warrior, he had doubts of surviving the campaign to the enemies base with just a few men.

He whistled through his fingers and, in a few seconds, a falcon swiftly appeared and landed on his outstretched arm.

"Shan de Tiangkong," he cooed to the bird. He tied a little parchment on its talon and whistled an odd tune before sending the bird drifting back to the wide dark sky. He greatly hoped that it would hastily send the message to the Imperial Palace.

Jinzhou Lu Wang Wei was staring at his falcon as it flew away when someone called him.

"Lu Wang Wei"

Lu Wang Wei stared to the direction of the voice and acknowledged the one who called him. "Lu Jinhai"

"I wish to speak to you-in private."

"About what?"

"I'll tell you but can we go to a more secluded place where no one from the camp can hear us?" Lu Jinhai suggested. There was something about the tone of his voice that indicated that they would be talking about a serious matter.

"Of course," Jinzhou Lu Wang Wei nodded and followed Lu Jinhai who led him outside of the camp to a secluded area in the forest.

When they were away from the camp, Lu Jinhai started to attack Wang Wei with questions and words, "Where had been during the start of the encounter with the Hsein Army? Why did you come in late? Did you see the damage those Hsien armies done to us? You are assigned as the Jinzhou of this campaign but it seems you are being lenient about it."

"I have to do something important." Jinzhou Lu Wang Wei merely replied in a voice devoid of emotion.

Lu Jinhai stared at Jinzhou Lu Wang Wei disbelievingly. "Important? You are not in the Imperial Palace; what other important thing should you attend than to lead us during the war? Instead of leading us to the war, you only came into action when a lot of our men had died. What kind of leader are you?"

"That is none of your business, Lu Jinhai," Jinzhou Lu Wang Wei said dismissively and started to walk away.

"None of my business," Lu Jinhai muttered with indignation. "How come it is none of my business when the success of this campaign means the safety the Empire and the people - including me? Do you think me a fool? Merely joining the war without any thoughts of our people's welfare? Oh, come on, Lu Wang Wei, admit it you are being lenient which resulted to the loss of our men and most of our resources. Who knows if we all died during the war while you are away. Stop being all superior and perfect. Admit your mistake."

Lu Jinhai's words hit a mark in Jinzhou Lu Wang Wei that his aloof features had finally showed the emotion that was brewing inside him. His eyes glittering with regret and suppressed tears. "You are right, Lu Jinhai. I became lenient and because of that i had placed our army in jeopardy. I admit my mistake. I swear to our ancestors that if I could bring back the time, this disaster that came upon us will never happen."

Lu Jinhai was taken aback by the placating attitude of the usually aloof Jinzhou. It took him a few moments to respond.

"Where had you been when the war started, Wang Wei?" Lu Jinhai asked in a calmer voice.

"I have to sort myself, Lu Jinhai," Jinzhou Lu Wang Wei said, still not wanting to disclose the reason. "I have my apprehensions. I promise you though that this will be last time that I will commit such grave mistake."

"You have always been a secretive person, Wang Wei; no one can really get information out of you unless you want to give it. No wonder you gained favor from the Son of Heaven," Lu Jinhai commented reflectively. "Anyway, I'll owe up to your promise, cousin."

The sky looked like a wide canvas; it was as if a black ink was splashed onto it and, then created a flurry of dark colors in varying hues. Though several trees surrounded the camp, the air felt still - utterly still that it seemed that she had attended a wake of the dead with the absence of mourning ladies.

Yan Mei Ling opted to stay at a secluded part of the camp in solitude. She could not sleep. She had been thinking and reflecting the whole day.

She had this sense of foreboding that was nettling her ever since the encounter with the Hsien army - it was as if that something dark and dangerous was about to happen but whatever it was; it was unknown to her. She felt like a prey being pursued in a wide and thick forest that was full of predators hiding within, bidding their time until they could find the perfect moment to catch her unaware and, ultimately, go for the kill. She placed her hand on her chest and could feel the intense and nervous vibrations of her heart.

A momentary gust of the wind had landed on the place which made the trees swayed violently. But then just like a passing dark force or magic, it was gone.

She felt kind of hysterical about how the her thoughts go to or how her mind seemed to imagine bad events in comparison to what just happened to her just like the fleeting gust of the wind. In fact, she felt that the wind was an enemy and its suddeness seemed like that it had took someone or something important away from her life. She felt frightened and, fervently prayed that it was just her imagination that was running wild. She could not bear losing something or someone important right now. It was most unthinkable. Her heart could not handle it. She thought that her training with her master and joining the imperial tournament had made her tough and ready for the war but she was very wrong. She had overestimated herself and had impulsively followed her heart not caring for the consequences.

War was totally different story for it could break you in many ruthless ways. It could affect your thinking and emotion, and would warp your previous views about life. Somehow, she had regretted her decision for she missed her best friend, father and the villagers.

"Oh, baba," she mumbled in remorse as she understood the real reason behind her father's extreme objection of her joining the Imperial army.

It was not just because she was a female. He might have been very strict but he never clip her wings. She realized that her father was just protecting her from the terrible things that happened during the war.

For a war was no vacation. It was a very dangerous mission with only two outcomes: either you live victorious or die as an unnamed casualty.

Another wave of agony and fear hit her again, she would not want to think about any negative things but it seemed that they would not refrain from entering her mind. She was tempted to slam her head to the thick old tree where she was leaning her back on if that could only make her forget the things that had been bothering her.

Thud. Thud. Thud. Thud.

There went the nervous beat of her heart. Sleep was still evasive yet her thoughts were still scattered. She could not fathom what was happening to her or where the fear in her heart had taken its roots. She just felt utterly and unnaturally afraid. She took a deep breath to calm herself but, unfortunately, it did nothing. In the end, she went back to the camp and, desperately wished that she could sleep her fears and sadness away.

Chapter 24

The imperial palace had became a haven of chaos and grief the moment that Princess Lei Shuang was discovered missing. A lot of the members of the Imperial palace guards and servants were under investigation and inquisition. Several of those who were not able to give satisfactory answers were immediately executed and those who might possibly provide information, little or big, were thrown in the dungeons.

Worst happened to those who were assigned to guard the palace and serve the princess around the time she was missing because they were tortured in the most unimaginable ways after denouncing them as traitors. All of them were ordered to be killed after being brutally tortured.

People outside the palace heard of what happened and the fear inside their hearts had further intensified. The fear had first taken root due to the news of the Hsien army campaign against the ruling imperial army to invade the empire. More so since the Emperor had became so vindictive that anyone who was suspected to have possibly connived with the Hsein army would be imediately be brought and then tortured into giving information before being ordered to death. Several imperial armies were sent to check on all the people under the Empire's domain, more imperial spies were paid to obtain more information from the enemies and several campaign units were made to be sent to the enemy's base.

In a bleak morning in the Empire, Emperor Li Huang Di sat on his throne as he aloofly stared at one of the palace guards who attempt to plead for his life while bowing on his knees. At this moment, he didn't feel like listening to any pathetic pleas and would rather plan his next move against the Hsein army with his officials however this situation required his presence because only him could give the orders to spare someone's life.

"Heaven's appointed, oh, Son of Heaven, Bixia, I never connived with the enemies. By the time that the princess was gone, I was not at the palace and was being cured by our village doctor. I have not yet been fully healed by my affliction but I come to prove that I am innocent as to the princess's disappearance. If Son of Heaven will permit me, I will help in searching for the princess. Please have mercy, oh, son of Heaven, merciful Emperor, and spare my life."

Emperor Li Huang Di stared at the palace guard so cold that if he had mystical powers upon him, the latter would be frozen to death. The palace guard felt the coldness of the emperor s gaze that he turned pale and visibly trembled in fright. He reverently touched his head to the cold marble tiled floor and tears rained from his eyes.

Emperor Li Huang Di directed his implacable gaze at the javelins displayed ornately on his palace's magnificent columns and thought deeply, his mind diverted. He was worried for his only child, Princess Lei Shuang, and could not accept the fact that she was kidnapped inside his palace after strengthening and increasing the imperial security. He suspected that someone inside the Imperial Palace had spied for the Hsein army and vowed to find that someone. Once he found him or possibly them, he would make sure to make him feel his wrath. He would not show any mercy since he could not and never tolerate traitors.

He did not feel a sliver of regret nor sympathy for those long-time servants, guards and officials he had ordered to be tortured or executed for they had miserably failed to do their duties. All he had wanted them to do was to ensure the safety of the princess but then they had not taken their duties with serious gravity. As for Hsien Mao Dong, that despicable swine, he would have his head and display it outside of the palace gates to tell everyone that traitors would never be treated with dignity. He clenched and unclenched ond of his fists, seemingly impatient.

While the Emperor was still in deep thoughts, a herald arrived and announced his presence to the Emperor.

The herald kowtowed to the Emperor and respectfully said, "May I have the permission to speak to the most radiant Son of Heaven, Lord of Ten Thousand Years?"

"Speak," the Emperor ordered commandingly. The tearful palace guard was momentarily given a reprieve.

"Thank you for giving me the permission to speak to Son of Heaven, Lord of Ten Thousand Years. The reason why I wished to speak to his most radiant Son of Heaven is because of a letter that comes from Captain Lu Wang Wei. May I have the permission to read its content to his Imperial Majesty?"

"Read it," the Emperor said aloofly yet his voice echoed powerfully through the huge palace hall.

"Thank you, son of Heaven, Lord of Ten Thousand Years," the herald reverently said. "The letter says,

Heaven's annointed Most High Emperor:

I, Jinzhou Lu Wang Wei, Son of Heaven's humble appointed servant of the Phoenix unit, humbly beseech your permission to ask for additional men and reinforcements for the war against the Hsein army. We have engaged one of their units in the battle and, eventhough, we win against them, we have lost a lot of men and our reinforcements are destroyed. We are currently heading south of the enemies base which is the shortest yet most dangerous path and should we engage with another Hsein army unit in another battle, we will possibly be outnumbered.

Have mercy, Son of Heaven, I assure you that we will win this battle and totally crush the Hsein armies.

Son of Heaven's humble servant,

Jinzhou Lu Wang Wei"

Emperor Li Huang Di thought for a moment. At the mention of the word 'Hsien,' his blood boiled with supreme wrath that his desperation to obliterate the entire Hsein army had increased tenfold. He would make sure to not spare even just one Hsein soldier. Oh, he might do something worst than what he had originally intend to do to the traitorous snake's head, Hsein Mao Dong. Whatever it might be, he would make sure that it could mark an impression to anybody who planned to betray him.

"Write a message and send it to Jinzhou Lu Wang Wei that he would receive reinforcements and additional men in the soonest possible time. You may leave now." Emperor Li Huang Di dismissed the herald and beckoned for one of his high military officials. "Jiangjun Yu Hui Cheng, come near."

Jiangjun Yu Hui Cheng hastily came near the Emperor and kowtowed. "All of your commands even at the cost of my life I shall heed, Son of Heaven. May I know what Son of Heaven wants me to do?"

"Assemble an army of 20000 men, let each of them carry weapons and reinforments good for two people enough for a month and send them to the Hsein army's base. Let them take the route to the south. They will be additional forces to Jinzhou Lu Wang Wei's and I want you to lead them so make haste."

Jiangjun Yu Hui Cheng visibly shivered at the Emperor's command. He bowed down his head and suggested, "The path to the south is the most perilous one when going to the Hsein's base, may we take another path instead, Son of Heaven, Lord of Ten Thousand Years?"

"Are you refusing my command, General Yu Hui Cheng?" Emperor Li Huang Di said to the jiangjun in a menacingly low voice. His eyes turned into hard slits and his jaws clenched with barely suppressed irritation and disapproval.

Dread seeped to the jiangjun's bones instaneously that he immediately placated himself, "Oh, no, never. My humblest apologies for my worthless suggestion. I shall gather 20000 men with enough weapons and reinforcements that will last a month; each of them shall carry enough for 2 people. We will, most assuredly take the path going south to reach the enemies' base, Son of Heaven."

"Good, remember, Jinzhou Lu Wang Wei has already headed south, should his unit be killed by the Hsein armies before you reached and aided him, I will have your head. Do you understand me?"

"I understand you, Son of Heaven, Lord of Ten Thousand Years," Jiangjun Yu Hui Cheng said ingratiatingly while bowing his head.

"Good to know that we have an understanding. One more thing before I you go about what I have commanded you, Jiangjun Yu Hui Cheng."

"What is that, Son of Heaven? I assure his radiant Imperial Majesty that I will follow his command even if it costs my life."

"Nothing too grand at the moment, Jiangjun Yu Hui Cheng," Emperor Li Huang Di said drily as he meaningfully looked at the kneeling and teary-eyed palace guard. "I want you to get that pathetic man off my sight and send him to prison. I will have to decide later if I will either spare or end his life."

"As you wish, Son of Heaven, Lord of Ten Thousand Years," Jiangjun Yu Hui Cheng kowtowed to the Emperor before dragging the tearful man who felt immensely thankful for being ordered to be sent to prison instead of being executed.

It was still dawn and the coldness of the temperature felt as if that the bleak winter had finally reigned the season.

Mei Ling sneaked out of the camp when everyone was still asleep. She had barely slept last night. She thought that forcing herself to sleep would shut the thoughts that taunted her to no end but it seemed that she became more emotionally distressed.

Lately, she seemed swimming in the ocean of hysteria; not knowing what she was really feeling as she felt that different waves of emotions were being slapped at her face. Ever since she left her village to join the war, she could barely recognize herself. It was as if the she had morphed into an entirely different person- someone who was always lonely and utterly pessimistic. She became emotionally unstable and trauma was playing mind tricks on her; she even thought that she had gone insane.

'Get a grip of yourself, Mei Ling,' she told herself. 'Remember why you have joined the war in the first place. There is no use regretting something that you have done and no chance of backing up.'

Mei Ling continued walking not knowing where she was heading. She just wanted to walk. The forest was too silent. There were no birds singing; possibly the chill had been too much for them to bear. Even the branches of the thick forest trees looked wimpy. She heard several faint animal shrieks, probably mammals on a hunt. She was somehow amazed; despite the little sleep she had last night, her senses were still sharp. Maybe the encounter with the Hsein army the other day had made her senses more conscious or possibly it was her fear that magnified them.

Mei Ling turned to the direction of the sound of a running water and followed it. She felt relieved when she found a creek and, the need to dip in its cool water seemed like an irresistible temptation. She followed her instincts but before she extricated herself from her clothes, she took a long final look around her to make sure that she was alone.

When she was certain that the place was devoid of any human but for her, she immediately removed her clothes and unbind the silk gauze that tightly bound her breasts. Practically naked, she plunged herself into the creek and relished its gentle waves that seemed to massage her sore muscles. A hot water would have done her better but knowing that she didn't have such luxury in the war, the cool brook water was a bliss. She also felt her hands on the creek's bed and rejoiced when she found a smooth stone. She began rubbing herself of the grime in her body until her skin looked red. Despite her toughness or as she assumed she was tough, she loathed the sweat and grime on her skin unlike her fellow soldiers who didn't give a damn about personal hygiene. Oh, probably not all of them, there were a few exceptions but she really didn't want to dwell on the thought in the fear of provoking an emotion she had somehow suppressed or she believed she had.

'Ah, war, you make practically make me feel and think of different things in a span of time. First, I am depressed now, I am sighing in bliss.'

It seemed like an eternity when Mei Ling stayed in the comforting coolness of the water when she heard a twig that had been snapped into two. Disrupted and panicked, she immediately hid herself behind a huge stone, most of the part of her naked body was still submerged in the water. "Who is there? Show yourself."

She waited for a moment. Her body was extremely tensed and her heart was beating with fear for being discovered of what her identity really was or worst, the person might have been one of the Hsein army soldiers. Now, the last one would be the most tragic and she would rather commit suicide than being captured by the Hsein army. When no one still emerged and the place remained silent, she sighed in relief and went back to the land. She hastily dressed herself. Once she was done, she searched every corner, bushes and even the tree branches just to make sure that she was indeed alone. After a thorough search in the area, Mei Ling sighed again in relief, the sound might have just been her imagination. It was nothing.

She started to traced her steps back to the camp. Despite the momentary panic that she had experienced a while ago, she felt a bit energized.

Abducting the princess from the formiddable walls of the Imperial Palace had been both dangerous and delightful for TongJun Linghua. Dangerous because if they were caught, the were as good as headless; delightful because the princess was a true beauty to behold.

When he first saw her under the moonless sky, sitting by the pond with the palace lanterns' lights playing wonderfully with the beautiful contours of her face, he was struck breathless. He had never seen any maiden in the entire vast land as beautiful as her, not even those pretty maidens he had raped and paid could match her face. No wonder Lord Hsein Mao Dong wanted the princess so bad, he was willing to go on war with the Emperor. But, perhaps, she was a means to get the empire. Her incomparable beauty was just an incentive in getting the empire.

TongJun Linghua mentally laughed. The princess was worth it. Had he been in Lord Hsien Mao Dong's place, he would do exactly as what his lord had done. In fact, with the princess sleeping just within distance, he had been tempted beyond imagination. Too bad, he couldn't have her. And, if he forced himself upon her, Lord Hsein Mao Dong would not only castrate him but chop his head as well. Now, he wouldn't risk his balls nor head for a taste of the delightful princess no matter how sweet she seemed to be. Perhaps he could have a taste of her, after his lord had had his fill of her. Now, that was something worth anticipating.

Oh, the princess was one hell of a fighter. How she had goaded him into forcing his strength upon her when she scratched his eyes and that of his companion when they struggled to get her out of the palace to their camp. But, thankfully, the drug he had pressed upon her nose and mouth had effectively silenced her. He just hoped that he would return to Lord Hsein Mao Dong's palace so that he would get his bounty and, perhaps, he would sneak into his lord's harem to enjoy himself as what he had secretly done in the past. Oh, he couldn't wait to be in paradise again after campaigning in hell.

CHAPTER 25

Yan Mei Ling was still a bit wary on her way back to the camp. When she heard one of her fellow soldiers shouting hysterically like a lunatic, her anxiety increased tenfold.

"I saw a girl! I saw a girl! I saw a girl!"

His screams had disrupted everyone in the camp. Sneers, curses and taunts had filled the camp as many soldiers had been disturbed from their slumber. Those who were awake were vastly irritated.

"I swear I will smother the life out of that lunatic for irritating my ears early in the morning!"

"I should have killed him in his sleep." Another muttered in frustration.

"If that bastard will not stop, I will surely gag his mouth!"

As Yan Mei Ling entered the camp, her heart somersaulted anxiously. Her entire frame was shaking with alarm. 'Could he be the one in the forest?'

The raving soldier, known to everyone as Chen Fu was running around the camp as if he was chased by a monstrous yaomo. The moment he spotted Mei Ling, he came near her.

He looked at her with unfocused eyes - eclipsed with insanity. What happened next made her swallow the lump in her throat so hard that it almost choke her. He was staring at Yan Mei Ling knowingly despite the lunacy that befuddled his mind and, very softly, he whispered to her, "I saw a girl."

"Where?" Yan Mei Ling managed to croaked a question despite the elevated nervousness in her heart. She could hardly breathe and sweat began to form profusely at both sides of her temple. The camp's surrounding turned even more colder, giving her gooseflesh. It was as if that it was already winter.

Chen Fu paused for some time but as moments passed, his expression dumber. His brows furrowed which indicated that he did not comprehend Yan Mei Ling's question at all. He merely repeated stupidly, "I saw a girl. I saw a girl."

After saying those words, he then ran away as if he was possessed by some evil spirit while continuing to wreak havoc in the camp. Yan Mei Ling, on the other hand was still trembling from intense perturbation.

"Do not mind Chen Fu. He has been shouting, 'I saw a girl' ever since our encounter with the Hsein Army." A cheerful and familiar voice materialized behind Mei Ling's back; disrupting her from her thoughts and, at the same time, startling her.

"I am sorry if I have startled you, Lao Fang. It is not a usual habit of mine to speak to people unannounced and who are deep in their thoughts."

"It is fine, Lu Jinhai," Yan Mei Ling said softly as she could to somehow hide the alarm emanating from her heart. "I am just concern about what has happened to Chen Fu - that's all"

"Hmmm, well, you do not need to concern yourself about these kind of things happening during a war. In fact, they are all normal occurences. War does a lot of things to any person. The consequences may be too much for the heart and mind to handle thereby making anyone insane as what has happened to poor Chen Fu. But, anyway, his lunacy is not a thing in question, for it runs in his family." Lu Jinhai sighed wearily. He continued speaking while stroking his chin, "I sometimes wonder how the imperial army just accept anyone including those whose identities are questionable. Are they that desperate? What are your thoughts about that, Tang Lao Fang?"

Yan Mei Ling's heart took another frantic dive at Lu Jinhai's words. She did not know if they were merely expressed opinions or veiled double meanings. Her thoughts were in a chaotic muddle. She could not form a coherent thought in her mind anymore. She was rendered speechless until a light tap at her shoulder brought her back to her senses.

"Are you fine, Tang Lao Fang? You look pale as a paper." Lu Jinhai asked with genuine concern. He gently touched the back of his hand on her forehead to check if she was afflicted by fever.

Yan Mei Ling breathed in deeply to somehow relieve herself of tension but still her voice stuttered, "I am fine. I am just tired, Lu Jinhai."

"It must have been the war." Lu Jinhai commented thoughtfully. "Unfortunately, you cannot rest. Jinzhou Lu Wang Wei is back from the forest. In a while, we are about to start a military exercise. Cheer up and be strong, Tang Lao Fang."

Yan Mei Ling took in a sharp intake of breath as she saw Jinzhou Lu Wang Wei emerged from the forest to the direction of the camp. Their gazes held each other for a moment: hers with nervousness and his was full of question or was it suspicion?

If her encounter with Chen Fu and Lu Jinhai had alarmed her, seeing Jinzhou Lu Wang Wei emerged from the very same forest where she took a bath almost struck her dead with fear. Surprisingly, except for the brief questioning gaze, Jinzhou Lu Wang Wei had immediately and effectively masked any emotions on his face.

Could it be that he was the one who had startled her from her bath at the forest? Could it be that be that he was bidding his time before he confront her?

Yan Mei Ling had not felt so nervous and uncertain in her life until this very moment. Not even what she felt during the encounter with the Hsien army could equal to the intensity of what she was feeling right now.

How she wished that the earth would just open and swallow her into its deathly chasm. The though seemed preferable than for her identity to be exposed.

Unit Commander Yan Bao Rong seemed to have lived his life in limbo since he learned about what happened to his village. What was even more devastating was the death of his only child, his treasure, Yan Mei Ling.

He was all alone now - no wife, no child and family. He found it utterly ironic how he had dedicated his life protecting the empire but could not even keep his own family from harm's reach.

His heart seemed twisted painfully as he strolled around his village - everything was a mess. Nothing was left of what he had worked hard for. What used to be a vibrant village had been diminised to ashes.

The vast and bountiful rice fields were gone; the trees were burned. The thatched houses that used to fill the village had became coals. Gone were the laughing villagers who were busy with their daily chores or the laughing children who used to run around. Gone was the house where the most cherished moments in his life happened. But, what truly caused a great searing pain in his heart was the thought of not seeing or hearing her daughter for the remaining days of his life.

Oh, he would give his life if only he could see his daughter. He was not even there to protect her. What had they done to her? Had she been crying out for his help? What a useless father he was, he thought bitterly.

He looked at the graying sky, only to fall down on his knees. His shoulders shook violently and his tears fall down his eyes. He punched his knuckles on the ground, fighting an enemy that was not even there until they bleed.

He was frustrated and angry. Frustrated - because he could not find the person who had destroyed his village. Angry - because of his incapacity.

He had promised his wife on her deathbed to protect her daughter but he was not able to do that. He had thought that his village was the safest place for his daughter but he never expected that this is also the place where his daughter would die. He had never anticipated for tragedy to struck his village even if he was one of the empire's best strategists for being able to anticipate several outcomes which had made him victorious in all of his campaign.

"Unit Commander," someone called his attention.

Unit Commander Yan Bao Rong did not bother looking at the person behind him but he asked in a grave voice, "What do you want?"

"The Son of Heaven asks for your presence in the court."

Upon hearing the words, Unit Commander Yan Bao Rong stood to face the man, who was one of the imperial heralds, and grabbed him roughly by the shirt, "You and the Son of Heaven are both bastards! I am grieving for the destruction of my village and the death of my daughter; and you dare to ask for my presence?"

"Unit Commander," the herald said in tremulous voice. "My condolence for you loss; I understand that time has been rough for you but -"

"Rough is an understatement!" Unit Commander Yan Bao Rong interrupted the herald's words. "I have lost everything - my village and my child; my only remaining family; my own flesh and blood! You do not know even half of the pain that I am feeling right now, insensitive fool! I am even tempted to kill you but not even your death could pacify me." He roughly pushed the herald to the ground. "Tell the insensitive Son of Heaven to get lost and never to contact me again."

"But, Unit Commander, it is most urgent and important -"

"Shut up!" Unit Commander Yan Bao Rong shouted angrily and grabbed the herald again. "Nothing is important to me now. I have lose everything. I am good as dead. Do you understand or shall I make you understand?"

"I hope that you will calm down and listen to what I am going to say, general," the herald said calmly; trying to appear unruffled despite the fear that had shook his heart. "The Son of Heaven's daughter was abducted. She is your daughter's best friend - surely, you also care for her. The Hsien army had kidnapped her several days ago inside the palace and up to this moment, there are still no news about her. The emperor needs you - you are the best military official that he has and you are the only one who could save the princess."

"Damn you! It is also because of the princess why I have lost my daughter!"

"I am sorry," the herald said sadly. "If not for the Son of Heaven, why not do it for your daughter? Your daughter has been overprotective of the princess ever since and the princess to your daughter. If something happens to the princess, your daughter will not be happy. Please, unit commander, please do it for the memory of your daughter."

"My daughter is gone. I am alone now. Nothing matters to me."

"There still one thing that matters, unit commander," the herald said with serious gravity. "It is revenge."

Unit Commander Yan Bao Rong's jaw hardened upon hearing the word but he remained silent.

"Think of it, are you just going to waste yourself, mourning for your loss, when you could have done something about it? Take a look around you." The herald motioned his hand around emphasizing on the terrible destruction that had happened in the general's village. "Look at what those filthy animals did to your village. They had made a vast wasteland out of it. They had destroyed it, your people and, of course, your daughter. They had suffered in ways that only the gods know how and what. However, judging from what your village has become, it is definitely terrible. Are you just going to let those animals get away with it? Grieving and wasting yourself means passivity. Being passive will not bring your village nor daughter back."

"You are a fool." The Unit Commander hissed as his grip on the herald tightened. "Do you not realize that revenge will not bring them back either?"

"Yes, it will not." The herald answered unflinchingly. "However, it will bring justice to everything that you have lost. I may not be in your position but if this happens to me, I will turn the earth upside down to kill those who do me wrong."

"You are still a fool if you think you can sway me with your words." The Unit Commander hissed angrily. His eyes turned into slits with barely suppressed rage.

"Call me a fool but look at yourself, unit commander. What you are doing right now will be construed as apathy. Are you apathetic to their deaths? Do you not care about what had happened? If think you can get an ounce of honor or even a sliver of comfort by grieving silently like a pathetic hermit, you are wrong. Now, who is making a bigger fool out of himself?"

Unit Commander Yan Bao Rong remained silent but his grip on the herald loosened which made the latter continue. "Look around again and try to see beyond the superficial, unit commander. Try to imagine the pain all of your people had been through. The fearful screams of your daughter as she cried for help when those barbarians destroyed and burned everything into ashes." The herald clucked his tongue and looked at the general with pity. Surprisingly, it did not made the Unit Commander angry. "Those filthy animals are not even so kind as to leave any corpses for you to somehow build a monument on. This is pillage and murder at its worst - how despicable. You need to do something about it other than wallowing yourself in self-pity; it does not suit you at all. The Hsien armies massacred and razed what is yours. You need to do the same, Unit Commander Yan Bao Rong. Blood for blood."

The herald's words struck note within the Unit Commander's hardened heart that he let go of former. Tears fell rapidly from his weary eyes. He looked at the graying sky and the mountain a few distance from his village, seemingly contemplating.

An onslaught of memories came into him, crumbling his defenses.

He remembered his loving wife's beautiful face as he built their courtly house; he remembered his daughter as a child running in the rice fields along with the villagers' children; and, most of all, he remembered them alive. His face became more determined.

"I will get my revenge - mark my words. I will kill all of them and I will not give that swine, Hsien Mao Dong, the satisfaction of getting the princess. Tell the Son of Heaven that I will soon go to the Imperial Palace."

"That is right, Unit Commander. Kill all of those fools who did this to you; save the princess so that she may not fall in the hands of Hsien Mao Dong. They have taken everything from you, it is only right that you kill all of them."

****

Dear readers,

Thank you for the tremendous support you have given me. Although, I am a bit slow in my update as I am very busy with my work which had me rendering extended amount of overtime and offer time. I beseech for your understanding and; I also need you votes and comments to keep my story's rating afloat. Thank you once again and God bless each one of you.

==============================

THIS CHAPTER IS ALREADY FINISHED BUT NEEDS TO BE EDITED.

Chapter 26

Paranoia.

That was exactly what Yan Mei Ling was experiencing right now. It was somehow insane but every strange stares or even simple gestures from her fellow soldiers made the entire skin jump off from her muscles. Relaxing and focusing had been both grueling for her even as the military exercises - this was somewhat strange because this was her most favorite part in being in the camp.

It was highly unusual at her but she could not seem to perfect the execution of each exercise. Her mind was a complete mess and her body seemed to rebel against her will. In fact, she had stumbled several times and her attention had been detached from what was supposed to be done. Her entire senses was clouded due to the fear and guilt that had been gnawing inside her.

She feared that her real identity would be exposed and the consequence of being ostracized. She also feared that instead of bringing honor to her family's name, she would bring shame.

But what she truly feared was that she couldn't protect her best friend, Li Lei Shuang, from the clutches of the evil warlord Hsien Mao Dong.

"Tang Lao Fang, are you sure that you are fine? You look paler." Lu Jinhai called behind her, his voice sounded worried.

"I am fine, Lu Jinhai. I am just," she paused and forced herself to breathed in deeply to calm her frantic nerves. "I am really just tired. This is nothing."

"I can talk to Jinzhou Lu Wang Wei so that he can let you rest, if you want me to."

"No, please don't. I can manage."

Lu Jinhai looked at her skeptically. "Are you sure?"

"Yes, I am."

"If you say so," Lu Jinhai said though there was still a hint of doubt in his voice. "But, please, tell me if you are truly not feeling well and, I will be in haste to help you."

"Yes, I will."

"Now, everyone, please pay attention." Jinzhou Lu Wang Wei's voice sounded authoritative and firm. "Even if this is a military exercise or a mere simulation of what we will be doing in the actual war, we still need to treat this one with seriousness. Our numbers are dwindling and each one of us should act like we are more than one person to make up for those who are gone. Keep your focus and you will be alive after the war."

He then looked at Yan Mei Ling. His eyes looked at her with a different level of intensity as if he was reading through her soul, unraveling all of her secrets one by one. His eyes, the way they pierced through Yan Mei Ling, made her shudder both with fear and with an emotion that was something entirely different. It provoked a feeling that made her stomach flutter yet in a bizarrely sublime way. It was something that created a sensational jolt that went straight into her heart - touching its deepest emotion, making it feel more alive.

Yan Mei Ling silently swallowed the lump in her throat, feeling the heat creeping into her cheeks.

"Tang Lao Fang, you are out of focus." He said then he walked to the line where Yan Mei Ling stood.

Yan Mei Ling almost dropped in panicked when he was in front of her but she did her best to control herself. If she would only be exposed, then she would act the firm and brave not the guilty one. It would only make her more pathetic.

"I... I.." Yan Mei Ling stuttered. She couldn't answer. She was completely rendered speechless.

"You look pale," Jinzhou Lu Wang Wei said firmly but there was also gentleness and concern in his voice.

"I have the same sentiment, Jinzhou Lu Wang Wei," Lu Jinhai said.

Jinzhou Lu Wang Wei looked at Lu Jinhai and said, "I am talking to Tang Lao Fang not you, Lu Jinhai."

"Of course," Lu Jinhai chuckled sarcastically. "Who am I to merit such right to speak to my superior? Am I not just a lowly soldier who cares about what is happening in the camp and my fellow soldiers?"

A pulse beat at the temple of Jinzhou Lu Wang Wei as he struggled to control his temper. His cousin was deliberately making him lose his control but he wouldn't allow that to happen. With supreme effort, he put a stoic face on. "You will do best to remember that: I am your superior."

Frustration flickered on Lu Jinhai's eyes before he smirked and enunciated every word sarcastically, "Of course, Jinzhou"

"Good," Jinzhou Lu Wang Wei said in an unemotional voice. He then turned his attention back to Yan Mei Ling and stared at her as if assessing her condition. For a brief moment, Yan Mei Ling had caught a glimpse of concern glazing through his eyes before he immediately put back his impassive mask.

"One more round of exercise then we will rest and, to those who still have the energy, you can accompany me to hunt for food so we won't die of starvation. Do we all understand?"

"Yes, jinzhou!" all of the soldiers responded.

Jinzhou Lu Wang Wei looked at Yan Mei Ling one last time, in a fleeting manner, before he went in front to lead the military exercise.

Yan Mei Ling, on the other hand, trembled with dread. But, surprisingly, he did not say anything. Perhaps he was bidding his time, she thought.

When the exercise was finished, a bird's cry was heard. Jinzhou Lu Wang Wei then extended his arm and the bird landed swiftly on it. "Shan de Tiangkong"

He took the rolled parchment from the falcon's talons and placed the bird on his other shoulder. He hastily unrolled the parchment and silently read. His eyes widened a bit before he turned his aloof masked on. He turned his gaze to all the soldiers in front if him. All of them were curious as to what contained in the letter.

"Help, weapons and food are coming soon," He announced, his voice echoed strongly in the camp. The soldiers cheered happily at the news but then he waved his hand as if to silence them. "This is not a time to celebrate as our task has became even more harder."

The soldiers became silent and suddenly everything seemed tense.

"The princess is abducted in the palace and we need to reach the Hsien clan's domain before her abductors do."

Upon hearing the words, Yan Mei Ling's body froze with dread and the entire muscles of her body stiffened. She couldn't breathed as if someone was choking her. Tears began to form in her eyes and without warning they fell. She wanted to rage and shout but her voice was gone. She was shocked - extremely shocked.

'Li Lei Shuang!' she screamed in her thoughts. Her blood was boiling with both rage and dread. She was hysterical. 'They couldn't take her. She is not kidnapped. The news may have been a misinformation. It has to be.'

She tried to open her mouth to swallow some air but the moment she did, her vision darkened and her knees became weightless. As she was about to succumbed to darkness, the last voice that she heard was Jinzhou Lu Wang Wei who desperately tried to call her name.

"Tang Lao Fang!"

Jinzhou Lu Wang Wei's bravery, intelligence and skills were just one of the few things that made the Son of Heaven choose him as one of his trusted officials. True, he was a nobleman - a minister-diplomat's son - but unlike those other noblemen, with the exception of the Duke Unit Commander Yan Bao Rong, he never lived his life in debauchery and luxury. He was a warrior just like his mother's father. He abide by all the imperial rules and his loyalty to the Son of Heaven was unquestionable.

As an only child, he lived his life in solitude ever since his father, an imperial peace minister, was assassinated on his way to the Chou clan's domain - the Son of Heaven's half brother clan who threatened to seized the empire yet failed. After that incident, he became a lonely child ever since. It even took many years before he talked to other people. Some of the children his age would not even play with him because of his aloof attitude.

His mother was so worried about him that she brought him to the village where she was born. His mother did not come from a rich family unlike his father, in fact, her family were simply farmer-warriors living in a secluded mountain where population was rather small. She brought her under the care of her father to teach him everything - literature and, most importantly, martial arts.

Master Ming Liao or simply grandpa taught him everything he needed to know. He had taught him about the Dragon warrior; the techniques he used; his unbelievable strength; and his heroic acts of saving the empire.

He aspired to be like the Dragon warrior - strong and fearless. Nothing and no one frightened him - not even death. When both of his grandfather and mother died, his world crushed. Anger and vengeance fueled his heart and determination when he learned of the cause of his family's death: Lord Hsien Mao Dong.

He was sent back to his father noble relatives only to receive cold reception but that did not deter him from being what he was today. He joined the military for the purpose of getting his revenge but after many years and wars, he realized that revenge was futile.

It was loyalty to the Emperor that made him want to win every war. The emperor had been like father to him. Where his relatives were cold, the emperor was warm. He worshiped the very ground that Son of Heaven tread upon and would do his best to protect him and all that matters to him.

As he steadily rose into ranks, he was known for being fearless. He would unquestioningly accept dangerous campaigns and emerged victorious. He fear nothing. He fear no one. For was death was of no importance to a man with no real family. But, surprisingly, as he stood outside a small, dilapidated tent, he was restlessly pacing. His heart was beating worriedly, and his mind was almost blank. He was worried - very worried.

He did not understand but he felt this need - the assurance - that Lao Fang was fine. He realized that he was afraid of losing him. The realization had dawned to him that he was not totally immune to the feeling of fear - more aptly, the fear of losing someone.

The boy was more than a subordinate. He was important. He did not know why he felt that way towards the boy but his feelings for the boy was at a different level. Inexplicable but there certainly was.

Lee Sui Song, a doctor, came outside, and Jinzhou Lu Wang Wei almost leapt upon him in anticipation. "Is he?"

Lee Sui Song breathed deeply as if relieving himself out of tension. "The boy is fine."

A large amount of weight seemed to be carried off Jinzhou Lu Wang Wei's shoulders. "Thank you, doctor." He hastily went to the door of the tent but the doctor, despite his small frame, blocked him from entering the tent.

"Please do not go inside yet, Jinzhou. The boy is over-fatigued. He needs his rest. Visiting him might only stress him further thus delaying his recovery. I have given him some medicine. With the heaven's grace, tomorrow, he will be fine."

Jinzhou Lu Wang Wei looked at him with doubt but then he did as the seemingly nervous doctor said.

"The boy will be awake in the morning but he specifically requested me not to be disturbed while he is resting. He will be fine tomorrow - that I can assure you."

"I will take your word on it, doctor."

"Thank you, jinzhou."

When Lee Sui Song left, Lu Jinhai walked towards Jinzhou Lu Wang Wei.

"How is the boy, Jinzhou Lu Wang Wei?"

"Why are you interested in his condition?"

"Why won't I be? He is a friend of mine." Lu Jinhai said with a hint of irritation. "But, the big question is, why are you outside the boy's tent pacing like a nervous mother hen?"

Jinzhou Lu Wang Wei was tempted to punch Lu Jinhai but he controlled himself. He merely squeezed his fist tightly. He said in menacing voice, "He is my subordinate therefore it is my duty to know what will happen to him."

"Really?" Lu Jinhai scoffed incredulously. "Did my words to you the other day made some real sense in you? If that is the case, then that is already too late. A lot of men had already died and all because of your self-centeredness and carelessness."

"I regret that day and I am doing my best to make up for all things that I lack as a leader. You do not have to slap my face for that one every now and then."

"I am merely doing it to make you remember your duties. You may have served the emperor but, right now, he is not your only concern. It is all of us. Put that in your mind, cousin."

Lu Jinhai tried to shove Jinzhou Lu Wang Wei away from tent's entrance but the latter stalled him. "No one is allowed to get inside the tent, the doctor instructed. Lao Fang is over-fatigued. He needs his rest."

Lu Jinhai's eyes widened - concern was evident in them. "What has happened to him? He is not going to -"

"Tang Lao Fang will survive. He is the ninja boy, remember? He is a tough one." Lu Wang Wei said aloofly.

Lu Jinhai visibly looked relieved then he seriously stared at Jinzhou Lu Wang Wei for a moment. "I will visit Lao Fang tomorrow. Until then, cousin."

Lu Wang Wei looked at his cousin as he left then he turned his gaze back to the tent where the boy was resting. He silently prayed to his ancestors and the heavens that Lao Fang would be fine.

"My father will catch you." Princess Li Lei Shuang told TongJun LingHua. She appeared undaunted despite the fact that her wrists were tied which had rendered her helpless, completely at the mercy of the enemy. She did not even know where she was right now since she was blindfolded when the Hsien army abducted her. However, she could tell that she was in the wilderness, even if she was confined in the tent, because outside seemed eerily silent but for the angry sound of the chilly wind.

"Oh, really, princess?" Tongjun LingHua mocked the princess who looked at him with daggers in her eyes. Her used-to-be perfectly styled hair was in disarray and the jade pins were hanging askew after being carried like an insignificant baggage on a horseback. The yellow ruqun that she wore was torn at the hem though her banbi remained firmly tucked. But despite those, the princess remained enchantingly beautiful and her disheveled state had almost tempted him beyond reason. "Where is the Son of Heaven's army? Is he able to protect you from us?"

"Do you know that serving Lord Hsien Mao Dong will not bring you any honor? He is not mandated by the heaven to rule nor will he be fit to rule. He is a cruel man who has no feelings for his subordinates. You could have done well serving the empire."

"What do you know of honor?" Tongjun Linghua spat angrily at the princess, his face just a few inches closer to Princess Li Lei Shuang's. "Did you know that if not for Lord Hsien Mao Dong, I would have remained a lowly peasant? I am what I am now if not for him!"

Princess Li Lei Shuang turned her head away from Tongjun Linghua not only because of the intolerable stench coming from his mouth but also because the intensity of the emotions in his face had awakened a guilt within her. Guilt at her incapacity to help uplift her people's lives. "True, you are a general but you have tainted your hands with that of the innocents."

Tongjun Linghua took a few steps away from the princess, his shoulders shaking with mirth. "Tainted my hands with the lives of the innocents? Really? What about the Son of Heaven? Do you think that his divinity has overshadowed his cruelty? The

Son of Heaven has already fallen out of favor from the heaven. If you look beyond your lavished and beautiful palace, then you will see that people need someone who can rule them better. He is a cruel man! He keeps on taking without giving. He only cares about power but does not care about the people whom he gets his power from!"

"You are lying!"

"I am not, princess." Tongjun Linghua snickered ominously. "Your life has been too sheltered from all the wickedness that the Son of Heaven has done. You know nothing of the truth."

"My people have always been contented!"

"Hmmp, wrong." He cackled humorlessly before his eyes turned hard and full of contempt. "They are hungry and cold and tired - those are the truths."

Helpless tears streamed from Princess Li Lei Shuang's eyes then she stared at Tongjun Linghua for a long time. She wanted to asked him about something — something that she wanted to avoid yet she wished to know. She needed to know it even if it seemed a self-inflicted torture. "Tongjun Linghua, may I ask you a question?"

"You may but it is also possible that I do not have the answer."

"Thank you," Princess Li Lei Shuang said politely even if she was bracing herself from the magnitude of the pain that the answer might possibly bring her. "Are you the one who attacked the village located at the east of the empire?"

"Yes"

"What have you done to the people?" Princess Li Lei Shuang asked, her voice never trembled despite the unspeakable pain that had stabbed her heart.

"Oh, the usual thing that happens during a pillage. Honestly, princess, I do not want to sully your innocent ears with wicked things."

"Please. I want to know." She insisted with indomitable calmness despite the tears that glazed her eyes.

"Well, if you insist," Tongjun Linghua shrugged nonchalantly. "We went to the village, set everything afire, rained our cannons, killed the men, tossed the children to burn in the flame, and, of course, raped all the women before ending their lives."

"You are evil. You are evil.." Princess Li Lei Shuang said as calmly as she could even if her shoulders were shaking with un-containable grief. Her eyes looked at him with extreme hatred. He was the one who killed her beloved best friend, her sweet Yan Mei Ling.

"At least, I never assumed to be good." Tongjun Linghua said cryptically before he left the princess.

When he was gone, Princess Li Lei Shuang broke down and wept all the pain inside her heart. She could not accept the fact that Yan Mei Ling's death had been very brutal even to imagine. She was not even there to protect her. She felt utterly helpless and useless.

'I swear I will protect you, Li Lei Shuang... I will be the greatest warrior in Chixian Shenzhou, I promise.'

"Oh, my sweet, Yan Mei Ling... My beloved.."

Chapter 27

It was pure torture - excruciatingly painful. It felt like the inside of her abdomen was being ripped apart. Why in the world would this monthly torture visit her in this very inopportune time?

Yan Mei ling was torn between physical and emotional pain. It was very hysterical to the point that she seemed driven to madness. She hugged herself tighter as the pain stabbed her again.

Someone she knew in the camp had already known her secret and he was the doctor, Lee Sui Song. He was only doing his duty as the camp doctor but when he saw the blood stains on her back, he already knew.

"You are a girl!" Lee Sui Song gasped in shock.

"I beg you - please do not expose me."

"I... I do not know what to do but you shouldn't have joined the military - you are a female!"

"Are you men all like that?" Yan Mei ling asked in hurt indignation.

"What do you mean?" Lee Sui Song stammered, unable to get what she meant.

"Bunch of prejudiced snobs!"

Lee Sui Song opened his mouth, as if hurt by Yan Mei Ling's opinion, then he shut it again contemplating before answering. After a moment, he slowly shook his head. "You are wrong about your opinion."

"Then why do you judge me for my sex in joining the military?"

"It is not like that, Tang Lao Fang," Lee Sui Song gently and calmly said. "I am just surprised why a female join a war - please do not react yet - it is not a usual thing. I do not know if it is allowed but whatever your motive for joining the military is then that will be your own."

"Women are not allowed to join the military. We are looked upon as the weaker sex and tasked to be incarcerated in domesticity." Yan Mei ling said bitterly.

"Then why did you break the rules and join the military?"

"I want to save my friend - joining the military is the only way that I can save her." Yan Mei Ling said with tears in her eyes. "But I guess joining the war didn't help her either."

"Why?"

"She is abducted by the Hsein armies." Yan Mei Ling hiccuped violently - tears fell from her eyes like a violent deluge.

Lee Sui Song looked at her with sympathy and tried to comfort her. "I am sorry. War is very unpredictable - we do not know what will happen. It is like a devious and sneaky thief who comes to your house and then takes away the most precious things that belongs to you without any warning. But you should not lose hope, we can still save your friend and defeat those Hsien armies who abducted her."

"It is so easy to say."

"You are right; it is so easy to say." Lee Sui Song mumbled in dejected agreement. "Anyway, who is your friend?"

"The princess."

"You mean Princess Li Lei Shuang?" Lee Sui Song eyes went agape in surprise. "You know her?"

"Yes, we are best friends."

"Who exactly are you,Tang Lao Fang?" Lee Sui Song asked, his face frowning in curiosity.

Yan Mei Ling breathed in deeply and said, "I am Yan Mei Ling, the daughter of Unit Commander Yan Bao Rong."

"Your father is the highest ranked military official and he is a duke which makes you a noble!" Lee Sui Song exclaimed as she looked at Yan Mei ling as if she was someone way beyond him - like heaven to earth. He felt unworthy of conversing with her, a noble, considering that he was a mere peasant practicing to be a doctor.

"I am but I do not feel like one - please do not look at me as if I am someone higher than you, Sui Song."

"But you are..." Lee Sui Song bowed his head timidly.

"I am your friend." Yan Mei Ling said gently then suddenly, her face looked contorted as she felt a sharp pang of pain attacking her.

"Lao Fang... I mean, Yan Mei Ling, are you fine?" Lee Sui Song asked in panic.

"Please call me Tang Lao Fang lest someone may know who I really am. I can trust you to keep my secret, can I?"

"Yes, of course." Lee Sui Song nodded swiftly. "Ah, I think today is your moon cycle. I have a lot of sisters and all of them experience the same thing. I will make something that will relieve you of your pain though temporary it may be."

"Please do."

"I will."

"Thank you very much... Oh, Lee Sui Song?"

"Yes?"

"I know that Jinzhou Lu Wang Wei is outside. Please tell him that I am not feeling well as of the moment and I need my rest. Tell him I will be fine tomorrow."

"Good thing that you told me that. The Jinzhou is very worried about you. It is the first time that we ever seen him like that. He is normally aloof - very unemotional - but now he seems to be cracking just a bit."

"Maybe he is showing that he is a human just like us." Yan Mei Ling said in a jest though she blushed lightly at what Lee Sui Song said. A wonderful feeling touched her - grazing her heart with the smoothness of silk.

It flattered and somehow warmed her that Jinzhou Lu Wang Wei actually cared for her. She never imagine, despite the fact that she felt an initial animosity towards him, that he could actually make the table turn and made her like his person. Like him more than enough that his face surfaced in her dreams; like him well enough that the mere thought of losing him left a lonely void in her life; and like him more than enough to the point that it almost reached the depth of the feeling she thought that she would only feel for her best friend, Li Lei Shuang.

Yan Mei Ling gingerly took a sip from Lee Sui Song's concoction after reminiscing what had transpired a few minutes ago. Though she is inside her tent, she could feel that someone was guarding her outside - she could hear the anxious footsteps pacing back and forth. She was certain that it was Jinzhou Lu Wang Wei. She had heard him talked to Lee Sui Song from the outside as he was about to make his entrance to the tent where she was recovering. She had even heard the faint sound of his voice as he argued with Lu Jinhai. Now, despite the silence, she could hear his worried sighs as his shadow walked past the entrance of her tent - how she wanted to talk and assure him that she was just fine.

She also wanted to get well and get outside of the tent because she felt that her affliction had stalled everyone. They would have planned on their next move against the Hsein armies - either to attack the Hsien's base or, possibly, retrieve the princess. How she wished they would be planning more on saving the princess, her best friend, as the fear in her heart would never be subdued unless she knew that Li Lei Shuang was safe.

The moment that Unit Commander Yan Bao Rong arrived at the imperial court, he had asked the Emperor's permission to have all the highest officials summoned to the military hall. The Emperor hastily agreed and even let his momentarily prodigal Unit Commander to spearhead the meeting as he had other pressing matters to attend to.

All the highest military officials had arrived to the military hall where the Unit Commander was already waiting. Even if the military meeting hall wasn't as extravagant as the main imperial meeting hall, it couldn't be dubbed as simple either. Its roof was made of sturdy red ceramic tiles and, its stone-and-wooden walls were decorated with beautiful geometric patterns. Inside, several sturdy wooden pillars mounted the ceiling and roof closer to the clouds of heaven. The strong wooden beams had miniature dragons sculpted on them in honor of the imperial dynastic symbol. Several beautiful paper lanterns were hanging majestically, creating a wonderful glow inside and, blue wall papers decorated the entire interior walls. The gargantuan lattice windows were firmly shut to provide privacy. The floor was made of marble and ceramic tiles which lent a flair of subtle extravagance. In the middle of the hall was a huge heavy wooden table where the officials immersed in a serious discussion.

"They cannot go further to the South - they will be stuck in the wilderness. With the ferocious howls of the wind, they won't risk travelling nor will they take another detour considering that they perfectly know that we have huge camps stationed everywhere other than the South." Unit Commander Yan Bao Rong said in an impassive voice, his eyes glinted like a newly sharpened steel - perfect for murder.

"Then that will be a massacre," one of his high ranked subordinates said with satisfaction.

"Yes, that is the plan, Jiangjun Chonglin Da," Unit Commander Yan Bao Rong answered aloofly. Despite the fact that he had barely shown any reaction or emotion on his face, inside his heart, he was burning with a festering ire which could only be assuaged by the death of the entire Hsien army. He had worn his heavy dragon-embossed lamellar armor though with less gumption as he had before - merely for formality or, aptly, for survival's sake.

"Should we make our move now?" Jiangjun Chonglin Da tentatively asked.

"Yes. I want you to divide the army into four units with the majority on horseback - assign one Tongjun and Jinzhou each. If we lack military officials, raise one of the most promising JunFu or Duizhu to the position - let it be known that I have the Emperor's word that I can do whatever I want with the military as long as it is not detrimental to his interest."

"As you wish, Unit Commander Yan Bao Rong."

"As for those who will go on foot, I want you to divide them into 5s and assign each group with a cannon. Do not forget to provide them with bows and arrows, jian, quiang and gun - do the same with the cavalry units."

"Yes, Unit Commander," Jiangjun Chonglin Da answered then he stared at his commander for a while - a look of sympathy clearly evident on his face. His commander had always been silent but now, he seemed different. Before the devastating tragedy in his village happened, Unit Commander Yan Bao Rong's eyes always had this zealous yet powerful blaze on his eyes but, now, there was nothing but an eerie calmness laced with an inexplicable gloomy light reflected on his seemingly apathetic eyes. He had felt his commander's painful loss, and it was something that anyone, even the bravest men, could barely handle. "My condolence for your loss"

Unit Commander Yan Bao Rong merely regarded Jiangjun Chonglin Da in long silence then he turned his back as if the jiangjun's words had finally registered in his mind and, felt its searingly painful impact upon him. Everyone in the room suddenly became eerily silent.

"I will go ahead, Unit Commander," Jiangjun Chonglin Da told his silent and brooding commander to go about the task that was assigned to him.

Yan Mei Ling's legs still felt a little wobbly from traversing for several hours since yesterday was the last day of her moon cycle. The troop had resumed their journey towards the Hsein domain while tracking the Hong Se unit who escaped after their previous encounter. All of them had to walk afoot considering that their entire cavalry horses were extirpated.

They were already four days behind as Jinzhou Lu Wang Wei had decided to let everyone stay in the camp because they need to recuperate and prepare themselves against the Hsien army but Yan Mei Ling knew that it was her that caused the delay. It was highly uncharacteristic for Jinzhou Lu Wang Wei to camp for a few days considering his burning desire to go after the Hsien army Hong Se Unit after the war. It made Yan Mei Ling guilty because the delay had made the odds of saving her best friend, Li Lei Shuang, low. But despite her guilt, she was somehow touched that Jinzhou Lu Wang Wei albeit in his own bizarre way had actually cared about her.

"The doctor, Lee Sui Song, said that I can now visit you so I - I come here to visit you." Jinzhou Lu Wang Wei said in an impassive voice but there was a sign of timidity in his beautiful eyes - as if he was unsure of himself. "He told me that you can now go back to training but when you did not show up, I had him go to take a look at your condition and he said that you need a day more to rest so I decided to let the troop do the same thing."

"I apologize - "

"No, Tang Lao Fang" he immediately cut her off. "There is no need for you to apologize. You are right when you told me before that we need to rest considering the damage that has befell upon us after the fight with Hsien army Hong Se unit. I never realized the extent of my people's exhaustion until I saw you collapse during our military exercise; I never imagined that it will happen to you since I expect that you are the last person who will experience it."

There was a moment of silence and an awkward air filling the tent which made the surrounding romantically dim. All that Yan Mei Ling could hear was the erratic beat of her heart - she swore that it might actually burst from her chest. If seeing Lu Wang Wei made her heart beat in a different rhythm, being near him - with just a little space to close the gap - drowned her with sensations beyond her comprehension.

"Thank you, Jinzhou." It was all that Yan Mei Ling could say. Whatever was in Lu Wang Wei but he most certainly had this power of making her thoughts scatter into the wind.

"You are welcome, Tang Lao Fang," Lu Wang Wei said with a ghost of a smile - a smile Yan Mei Ling would only see when they were talking. "By the way, I just want to make sure of one thing, are you feeling fine now?"

"I think I am," Yan Mei Ling said with a smile. She noticed Lu Wang Wei's clenched his jaws as if he was controlling himself. She did not know what came into her but she suddenly felt the urge to touch and cradle his face in her hands until it was devoid of any tension. In many ways, the unbidden thought had flabbergasted her.

"We will stay here for one more day."

"But the princess - "

"We will save her. I had news that her abductors will have no choice but to head south which means that they might come across the new troops being sent by the Emperor to aid us or, possibly, our troops."

"I hope so - we really need to save the princess, Jinzhou Lu Wang Wei. If Hsien Mao Dong gets hold of her, then that will be the downfall of the empire. Everything that we fight for will be in vain if that happens."

"I will never let that happen, Lao Fang." Jinzhou Lu Wang Wei said with serious gravity - a steely determination reflected in his eyes. "We will crushed the Hsein army; we will all survive and emerge victorious. I am confident that if her abductors will indeed head our way, we will kill all of them and save the princess - that I can promise."

Yan Mei Ling put her heart in what Jinzhou Lu Wang Wei said. She had this great trust in him that they would succeed and save Li Lei Shuang. Her effort in joining the military will never be in vain. At this very moment, things had changed for her, everything had been illuminated and she found a new meaning that was worth taking the plunge in - she knew, it could never be denied, that she her feelings for Jinzhou Lu Wang Wei had reached to a different level.

She didn't want to succumb to it but her heart could not deny it anymore. As clear and as radiant as the moon light, a realization came to her: She likes Lu Wang Wei.

Chapter 28

"The imperial army are coming and they will attack your domain."

Baron Chao Bo looked at Jianjung Han Li with confusion and said, "I clearly do not understand the reason why The Son of Heaven will attack us when in fact we have lived peacefully in the forest and are never a threat to his empire."

"You do not know what goes into the insane mind of the Emperor. We have evidences that he is coming, in fact we can prove it; but worry no more, I am sent by Lord Hsein Mao Dong to offer you protection against the imperial army."

"I still do not understand - Lord Hsein Mao Dong, who is he?"

"He is your only hope and savior against the greedy and corrupt Emperor." Jiangjung Han Li said with conviction. "Oh, just to enlighten you as to the Emperor's motive; he has taken interest in your village when he realizes that your numbers are growing. He wants to suppress and make slaves out of all of you."

Baron Chao Bo, the village proclaimed leader thought hard about what Jiangjung Han Li said. His forehead wrinkled in deep thinking and worry.

"I am a living proof of the Emperor's cruelty. He had set afire on our village and corrupted all of our women. If you do not heed me, blood will soon spill the soil of your village."

"I will never let that happen." Baron Chao Bo said resolutely — anger evident in his eyes. A burning desire to protect his village fueled his heart. "If the Son of Heaven wants war, then I will give it to him."

"About my proposition?" Jiangjung Han Li asked, his other brow rose in question.

"Yes, of course," Baron Chao Bo nodded without a trace of hesitation. "I will let your army camp in my domain and give you additional forces in fighting against the Imperial army."

"Wonderful! You have made an excellent decision, Baron Chao Bo." Jiangjung Han Li smirked in triumph - Baron Chao Bo was a fool for easily believing that he offered protection when he had another plans for his village. Ah, some men are just so easy to deceived, he thought. "When will be the additional forces ready?"

"When do you need them?"

"The Imperial army's trail is not far behind as we have engaged them in a battle just a week ago; any time of the day, they will possibly arrive - I need the additional forces in the soonest possible time."

"I will have them assembled now."

"That's perfect."

"Wine, sir?" A maidservant approached the low table where Jiangjun Han Li and Baron Chao Bo were seated.

Jiangjun Han Li looked at the maidservant and eyed her with interest - she was a pretty little thing. A wicked thought came to his mind but he would have to take care of it a little longer after defeating the Imperial Army headed by Jinzhou Lu Wang Wei. He then took in the furnishings inside the huge tent of Baron Chao Bo. Despite the fact that his people had lived in a secluded area, away from the Central, they had not failed to procure wonderful and precious ornaments such as intricately crafted vases and silk adorning the walls. Artillery were not a problem as he had seen that the forest-village had acquired high-powered cannons and several bows and arrows.

"Yes, please," Jiangjun Han Li finally answered and smiled at the maidservant who had been standing awaiting for his reply.

As the maidservant poured wine into Jiangjun Han Li, he struggled to discreetly take a peek of what seemed to be amply hidden by her clothes. But another thing caught his attention - nah, it was quite an understatement - someone had captivated him.

"I see that my beloved daughter is here." Baron Chao Bo announced merrily.

"Bàba!" Chao Bo's daughter exclaimed happily and hugged her father before she warily looked at Jiangjun Han Li.

"Oh, excuse my manners," Baron Chao Bo apologized. "My daughter, this is Jiangjun Han Li of the Hsien army Hong Se unit, he is a new alliance of mine; Jiangjun Han Li, this is my wonderful daughter Chao Biming."

"Splendid to meet you, my lady," Jiangjun Han Li said with extreme interest. He stared at Chao Bao's daughter and reveled in her outstanding beauty. Her face was perfection as if sculpted by the heavenly Gods - her eyes sparkled with life, cheeks nary of rouge but rather glowed with health and, even if her figure was hidden by the silk dress, he could tell that beneath those layers of cloth was a body made to incite any living man to lust.

"I am sorry for interrupting you, bàba, I thought you are alone." Lady Chao Biming apologetically whispered to her father. "I apologized as well, Jiangjun Han Li."

"You are no interruption at all, my lady," Jiangjun Han Li replied courteously.

"Yes, my daughter, you are no interruption at all but what brings you here?"

"Uhm, I have seen a strange army in our camp."

"Well, they are not strangers anymore, daughter, they are our saviors."

"Savior?" Lady Chao Biming's beautiful brows rose in confusion. "Why do we need saviors when we do not have any enemies?"

Jiangjun Han Li cleared his throat. "The Imperial army has decided to make enemies of your village. The Emperor sends them to seize everything in your village and make slaves out of all of you."

"The Son of Heaven cannot be so cruel to do that - we are never a threat to his Empire, why now?"

Jiangjun beseechingly looked at Baron Chao Bo, uncomfortable with discussing war matters to a female.

"I see that my daughter is indeed mirror of my own mind - we have the same sentiment." Baron Chao Bo proudly commented.

"Should we discuss such sensitive matter where females are around?"

Lady Chao Biming was affronted with Jiangjun Han Li's statement that her face flushed with angry red but she chose to keep her mouth shut.

"The females in my village are treated as equals of the males -- after all, they carry our children and helped in building our village; without them, we are nothing." Baron Chao Bo explained to Jiangjun Han Li.

"That is surprising," Jiangjun Han Li commented with delight in his voice though the disdainful sneer on his mouth was unmistakable; he was strongly opposed to Baron Chao Bo's notion of male and female equality. He would have to deal with this one later. There would be a lot of things to change in Baron Chao Bo's village but those things would have to wait as defeating the imperial army was his imminent concern as of the moment. He would swallow his pride, pretend that he was the savior when he planned to add this village to the list Hsien army's casualties.

"It is surprising indeed for someone who has an aversion to the notion," Lady Chao Biming said sarcastically unable to contain her irritation.

"Daughter!" Baron Chao Bo exclaimed, a bit scandalized, though pride could be detected in his voice.

"Please excuse me, bàba, I am dying to take my leave." Lady Chao Biming said hastily, unable to stomach the overbearing Jiangjun Han Li who had first eyed her as if he would tear her clothes off before transforming into an abject snob. "Excuse me, Jiangjun Han Li." She hissed in indignation before taking her leave.

"Sure," Jiangjun Han Li replied at the retreating Lady Chao Biming. His eyes lasciviously followed her as she headed her exit to the tent's door. The chit was very beautiful yet fiery but he could easily handle the likes of her. 'Want to play fire, my lady? I will make you burn.'

==

Author's Note:

Hello, guys!

I am sorry for the delay in update. I have been busy due to training and this week, I will also have another one. As of the moment, I will be posting just half of Chapter 29 and next update will not be determined due to my busy schedule. Please do not forget to support my story by clicking the vote button or if you want to interact with me, you may comment and I will do my best to reply.

Thank you and I love you all!

-Midnight_Carousel

Chapter 29

Yan Mei Ling snuggled deeper into the torn and ragged cloth that she used to shield herself from the cold as the wind had gone increasingly colder as if autumn had been conquered by winter. She could hear the wind, sounding like that of a newly-stoked flame of a camp fire. The thinning foliage of the forest seemed a faint reminiscent of what had been a verdant summer. The trees' barks were covered with algae and other plants like tapestries to a wall. The dewy grass struggled to grow on the wide forest floor. It would have been terribly silent if not for the wind but the sound did not give any comfort - it sounded more like a warning.

The walked to Hsien's domain had proven taxing considering that they had lost their entire cavalry units and most of their provisions. All of the soldiers despite the few days reprieve from war looked more weary than rested; some of them even looked more afraid and uncertain – almost to the point of feeling utterly hopeless.

She took a quick peek at Jinzhou Lu Wang Wei who had remained silent and aloof throughout their journey. He greatly reminded her of a fire that had turned into a huge block of ice. Secretly, she longed to see the other side of him who was cheerful and passionate – the one he usually showed when they were both alone together.

'I should not have been thinking of him, should I?' She thought bitterly. 'I should think more of Li Lei Shuang and how to save her from those perverted Hsien pigs.'

She took a deep breath to compose herself. She felt hysterical; she could not even control her thoughts or how she should feel. 'Has my soul left my body to be independent? I think I am going crazy.'

"You seem to be in deep thoughts, Lao Fang." Someone tapped Yan Mei Ling's shoulder.

Yan Mei Ling shuddered in surprise before smiling. "It is of no importance, Lu Jinhai."

"Is it not so important that your brows seem to stick together to a frown like you are solving a rather difficult puzzle?" Lu Jinhai asked with humor in his voice.

Yan Mei Ling blushed slightly under his intense scrutiny. "I have this tendency to look strange sometimes."

"Hmmm," Lu Jinhai exclaimed while staring at her intently. "You do not look strange at all to me. In fact, you make me feel strange."

"What do you mean?" Yan Mei Ling blurted in panic.

Lu Jinhai laughed at her reaction and crumpled her hair in affection. "Little Lao Fang, you look so cute when you react like that."

"Why are you deflecting from the topic?"

"Hmmm?"

"I mean - what do you mean when you said that I make you feel strange?"

"Oh," Lu Jinhai smirked mischievously. "The innocence of a child - do you know that it is one of your endearing qualities?"

"Endearing qualities?" Yan Mei Ling frowned in confusion. She could not figure out what Lu Jinhai had been alluding. "Are you mad, Lu Jinhai?"

"Hmmm, maybe"

"You have not answered my question."

"I am not entitled to answer your question," Lu Jinhai chuckled in amusement.

"You are unfair!" Yan Mei Ling lightly punched his shoulder to which earned a laugh from Lu Jinhai. "I thought you are my friend."

"Of course, I am," Lu Jinhai solemnly said to Yan Mei Ling while placing his hand on the middle of his chest where his heart was residing.

"Hmmmp!" Yan Mei Ling snorted indelicately, disappointed at not getting an answer.

"I will forever be your friend, Lao Fang, and because of that, I will you protect even at the cost of my life."

Yan Mei Ling looked at Lu Jinhai and saw the sincerity of his beautiful eyes. Her heart took a few hops and she struggled to understand what was happening inside her - could that be that she felt something for Lu Jinhai too? She thought that she had gone hysterical. The war indeed would make any sane person mad just as what it did to her.

"Thank you, Lu Jinhai," Yan Mei Ling said timidly. "Rest assured, I will do the same thing for you."

"No, please do not," Lu Jinhai slowly shook his head. "I very much prefer that it is you who will survive should the time comes that only one between the two of us will live. I want you to live and be happy."

"Why are you talking like that?" Yan Mei Ling asked him – her voice tinged with sadness and confusion. "We will all survive the war and live happily, you shall see."

Lu Jinhai looked sadly at her before smiling. "Of course"

Yan Mei Ling looked at Lu Jinai and smiled at him. The breeze swayed his rumpled hair.

"I am glad that you are fine now, Lao Fang." Lu Jinhai said in a voice filled with raw emotion. "I thought that something happened to you. I was so worried for you. I..."

"Everyone!" Lu Wang Wei announced in a loud voice to get everybody's attention. "There is a village near. It could be Baron Chao Bo's domain – he is known as a kind and virtuous man. We can ask for his help so that he will allow us to camp inside his village and ask for provisions."

All of the soldiers' weary faces turned bright with hope. The enervated march had turned more energetic as they approached the forest-village.

"Stay right there!" One of the Chao's guards who seemed to be the head halted them from his watch when they were near the gates. "Who are you and where do you think are you going?"

Lu Wang Wei smiled and bowed his head respectfully to the guard before saying, "We are the soldiers of the good Emperor of Chang'an and I, in behalf of my troops, humbly request for an audience with your kind lord, Baron Chao Bo."

The one who talked to them smirked as if he did not believe Lu Wang Wei's words at all. "How humble and respectful of you to say that but, too bad, we already know the purpose of your coming."

He signaled the guards who immediately aimed their cross-bows at Lu Wang Wei and his soldiers. "Allow us to give you the warm welcome you rightfully deserve, deceitful scums!"

Chapter 30

Yan Mei Ling's shuddered with extreme fear as she saw the crossbows of the Chao's guards aimed at them but what made her heart froze was that Jinzhou Lu Wang Wei was in front. He would be the first to be hit by the arrows. Those crossbows were not just any ordinary crossbows but were Chukonu or repeating crossbows. How would they survive?

She remembered Lu Jinhai's words to her a while ago.

Did he have a premonition of what will happen to them? Is this the end of all their sacrifices?

Yan Mei Ling looked at the sky and saw storm clouds casting a dark ominous shadow. She never felt hopeless in her entire life.

'I am sorry, Li Lei Shuang... I am really sorry. I will not be the one to save you but I hope that even in my death that you will still be saved. I love you and good bye, my sweet best friend.'

She looked at Lu Wang Wei who remained calm despite facing certain death. His face remained unreadable – not one emotion flickered from him.

'Lu Wang Wei, I may not have the opportunity to tell you what I feel for you but thank you very much. You will always hold a very special place in my heart; and should we meet again, in a different place and lifetime, I hope that I can still remember what I feel for you.'

Jinzhou Lu Wang Wei briefly turned his head and stared at Yan Mei Ling. There were so much emotions on his face – so much uncertainty and, surprisingly, affection. In the silence that transpired between the two of them, he was trying to tell her something but Yan Mei Ling dreaded that this will be the last time that he would communicate with her.

"Shoot!" the head of the guards shouted and then multiple arrows began to fall like a deluge of a furious rain.

"Everyone, run and get away from here! Do not look back!" Lu Wang Wei shouted as he swiftly unsheathed his sword and began to attack the arrows.

"Jinzhou!" A hysterical cry escaped from Yan Mei Ling's throat.

"Let us get out of here, Lao Fang!" Lu Jinhai said with desperation as he dragged Yan Mei Ling with him while warding off the arrows being shot at them with his sword.

"No! No! What will happen to Jinzhou?" Yan Mei Ling said with tears in her eyes.

"If he is meant to survive, he will," Lu Jinhai blithely said. He forcefully carried Yan Mei Ling who was struggling with all of her might.

"Jinzhou! Jinzhou!"

Lu Wang Wei looked at Yan Mei Ling. A smile tugged his usually aloof lips and he gently waved his hand as if saying good bye to her.

'I will see you soon, Lao Fang. Please stay alive for me.'

Yan Mei Ling did not stop from struggling even if they were far from the Chao's gate. She could see that a lot of her fellow soldiers stumbled down after being hit by the arrows. And, of course, the memory that would forever haunt her for the rest of her lifetime was Jinzhou Lu Wang Wei who was slicing the arrows with supreme speed so that they would survive. This was his ultimate sacrifice -- his life.

She saw red before everything became a blur.

"Jinzhou Lu Wang Wei..." she sobbed heart-brokenly as she felt that this day would be the last time that she would see his precious face.

"Bastard!" TongJun Linghua spat angrily when he was roused from sleep when he sensed the angry sounds of the horses' hooves approaching the place where he and his army were camping. He did not recall asking additional forces or help from Lord Hsien Mao Dong which gave him the idea that the Imperial army had finally tracked him down.

He quickly went out of his tent to go to the tent where he confined the princess. He unceremoniously carried the slumbering princess on his shoulders and ran outside to fetch and saddle his horse.

"What do you think are you doing? Put me down!" Li Lei Shuang said in a protest as she struggled desperately to be freed from the TongJun Linghua's strong grip of her but failed miserably since her hands and feet were bound.

"Stop struggling, fiery princess, if you do not want me to do something that will make you regret being alive in this world!"

"You – you, impudent person! How dare you do this to me! How dare you manhandle women, do you have no respect?"

TongJun Linghua laughed as if he had just heard the funniest joke in his entire life. "Respect? To whom? Women? You are one funny person, princess."

"I am not being funny! Put me down, you are hurting me!"

"I only show respect to women when I keep them alive after raping them," TongJun Linghua threatened in a dangerous voice – his eyes dilating in extreme irritation. "You may consider yourself special since it happens that Lord Hsie Mao Dong wants you to be his wife and I cannot risk his wrath. But if you do not stop struggling, then I might just stuff my c0ck into your mouth to silence it!"

TongJun Linghua's words stopped Princess Li Lei Shuang from struggling and helpless tears streamed from her eyes.

"You are evil," she sobbed, feeling utterly pathetic and weak. "You are evil.."

"I never recalled saying or showing you otherwise, princess," TongJun Linghua sarcastically hissed as he carelessly dumped the princess at the back of his horse. He hastily tied the princess at the back of his horse, not caring if the rope would bruise her delicate skin. "Niu!"

One of his subordinates, the one who aided him in kidnapping the princess, ran at the sound of his voice.

"TongJun Linghua, I am here," Niu said in a breathless voice as he bowed his head to his superior.

"I can sense the Imperial armies coming and I need to bring the princess to Lord Hsein Mao Dong as soon as possible. As my second-in-command, I will entrust the entire army to you. Can I trust you with that, Niu?"

"With all my heart, TongJun Linghua," Niu bravely and solemnly said.

TongJun Linghua smiled affectionately at Niu and said, "I do not tolerate failures so make sure to crush the approaching Imperial army and stay alive. I will be waiting for you at the Hsien capital."

"Yes, TongJun Linghua"

"I shall not stay long here. Remember, I do not tolerate failures!" TongJun Linghua repeated before climbing his horse and kicked it to a run.

CHAPTER 31

The angry growls of the cannons were heard as they were fired shook the earth. Bodies buoyed above from the impact only to fall down into unrecognizable pieces. The arrows shot to the sky, falling down like the meteor stars on a beautiful night but with a death wish to whoever they would fall upon.

Blood flowed like crimson rain sprinkled by the sky, pooling like a red stream, only to be soaked by the ravenous and monstrous earth. Metals clashing against each other, horses' stampeding on dead and living bodies. Cries of despair and anger were forced to do a duet – singing a terrible song of war and massacre.

"Do you think that you are good enough to fight me?" A man said in an ominously low voice, his eyes sparkled dangerously like rubies, reminding anyone of a furious and hungry Yaoguai. He lightly touched the tip of his sword on the neck of his opponent while exerting more pressure on his boot that was placed on the latter's chest. "How do you want me to kill you?"

"You are a bastard! Do you think you will win? Our Tongjun already escaped with the princess to Hsien capital, and Lord

Hsien Mao Dong will wed her as soon as she arrive so you killing me is futile - you lose, we won." The fallen soldier laughed like a mad man despite the extreme fear that shook the very core of his heart.

The man ignored him and merely looked at him with bone-chilling coldness. "Do you want me to castrate you first before I proceed to cutting the other parts of your body?"

The fallen soldier convulsed with so much horror that his spit began to form a froth from his mouth. "Kill me right away, you bastard, cut my head!"

The man with the sword slowly shook his head and smirked, obviously enjoying the fear that emanated from the man who was entirely at his mercy. "I will do that if you beg me." He removed his boot from the man's chest as if to give him the opportunity to beg. "Go on, beg me, pathetic animal; I might pity you and give you a hasty death."

The man who was on his back immediately stood to spit on the man who held him down a while ago. "If you think that I will put myself down to you, despicable, imperial soldier, you are wrong!"

The man with the sword wiped the spit on his face with the back of his forearm. His face ghastly unreadable and a pulse angrily beat at the side of his temple. He clucked his tongue and then look at the man who had the audacity to spit at him. He swung his sword and severed the impudent man's knees.

"Aaahh!!! You are an animal!" The incapacitated man cried, tears rolled from his eyes while his body shook with terrible fright. Blood gushed violently and the veins hung like a messy spider web from his severed knees.

The man with the sword merely laughed sadistically before he slashed open the fallen man's trouser and cut the manhood.

"Animal! Animal!" The man shouted while groaning at the unspeakable pain.

"Don't you dare call me animal, you pathetic worm." The man with the sword muttered furiously. "My name is Jiangjun Chonglin Da!" He then kicked the man as if the latter was a mere pebble.

"Please kill me now!" The man beg with tears. Blood flowed from his body, his heart and resolve were both weakening. "Please, I beg you, kill me now."

"How late - you dumb animals prefer to be tortured first before you give in but I am feeling rather generous today so I will grant your wish." Jiangjun Chonglin Da carried the incapacitated man by the hair and sliced the head cleanly from the body with his sword. He carelessly threw the head to the ground and looked at his army who were currently in a hand-to-hand combat with the Hsien soldiers.

He saw the Unit Commander clashing sword with the most capable man in the Hsien army. Looking at his superior's face, certain sadness mingled with sympathy evoked within him.

He remembered the Unit Commander's daughter; the headstrong yet surprisingly sweet beautiful girl, Lady Yan Mei Ling. His heart clenched painfully at the thought of his superior's daughter. He would give her death a justice it rightfully deserved.

'I will help you avenge your daughter's death, Unit Commander. I will not show the Hsien pigs any mercy.'

A Hsien soldier tried to attack Jiangjun Chonglin Da but he quickly penetrated his sword on the attacker's chest.

"Weakling," he remarked in a bored tone when he plunged his sword upon the chest of another Hsien soldier. He pulled back his sword, blood trickling on the cold and dangerous metal.

Another Hsein one ran to Jiangjun Chonglin Da but he stalled him by throwing his spear on the enemy's forehead. The sharp spear's head turned around until it perforated into the enemy's skull, blood expelled like a wave while some of the mushy tissues of the brain were being spurted from the hole. He promptly pulled the spear from the dead enemy's skull and aimed it accurately on another attacker. He continued brutally killing Hsein soldiers with dexterity until he was near the Unit Commander who was holding the enemy by the collar.

"Where is the princess, you bastard?" Unit Commander Yan Bao Rong demanded with indomitable calmness. His eyes glaring frigidly.

"Ha! She is gone; probably wed to Lord Hsein Mao Dong by now." The man cackled humorously, he tried to look brave but the fear within his eyes was undeniable. He was also breathing in deep gasp due to the injuries he sustained from the fight with Unit Commander Yan Bao Rong.

"Perhaps, that pathetic worm prefers unorthodox ways of obtaining information; shall I castrate him, Unit Commander?"

Unit Commander Yan Bao Rong looked at Jiangjun Chonglin Da and arched his brow. Under his grip, the man he held started to piss in his trousers due to extreme trepidation.

Jiangjun Chonglin Da bowed his head to his superior and then said, "The man I just tortured told me that the TongJun of this army already escaped with the princess. If you allow me, I will go after that cowardly TongJun and save the Princess."

Unit Commander Yan Bao Rong paused for a moment, reflecting on Jiangjun Chonglin Da words. He remained aloof but the unmistakable aura of fury within him was felt. "No, I want to personally decapitate their TongJun. After all, it his army who had wreaked havoc upon my village."

"As you wish, Unit Commander,"Jiangjun Chonglin Da bowed his head respectfully. "By the way, what shall we do with that man?"

Unit Yan Bao Rong looked at the man whom he held by the collar and then slammed him in front of Jiangjun Chonglin Da. "I want you to torture him; toy with him. Give him a death that will continuously haunt him even if he is already in hell. Do the same with all the other Hsien soldiers – do not spare anyone nor show mercy. And, after this, I expect that you will catch up with me in no time." He then left and went back to the cavalry to get his horse.

"Of course, Unit Commander," Jiangjun Chonglin Da answered. He then smirked evilly and callously placed his boot at the head of the injured man who was thrown at his mercy. "Worm, do you have a name?"

"You, bastard; do not call me a worm!"

"I will call you whatever I want to unless you give me your name."

"I am Niu!" The man stuttered with fear; his heart was colliding with extreme frenzy in his chest. "I am one of the elite soldiers of the Hsien army, you have no right to treat me low!"

"Hmmm," Jiangjun Chonglin Da commented reflectively while stroking his chin. "If you are an elite soldier of the Hsien army, then I pity the Hsien army for recruiting weaklings like you."

"How dare you!" Niu stammered. This man, Jiangjun Chonglin Da, was more wicked than his superior. If the Imperial Army's Unit Commander had a trace of humanity in him, Jiangjun Chonglin Da had none. His eyes reflected a hellishly cold polar frost. He was a killing machine trajected into a human body.

"Tell me, Niu," Jiangjun Chonglin Da smiled dangerously while ignoring Niu's words. "How do you want to die?"

CHAPTER 32

Yan Mei Ling could still not grasp the reality - that Jinzhou Lu Wang Wei was ultimately dead. Just a few days ago, he was talking to her, promising her that they would end up victorious.

His words kept on resonating in her mind like a very distant memory she would not want to forget:

'We will crush the Hsein army; we will all survive and emerge victorious. I am confident that if her abductors will indeed head our way, we will kill all of them and save the princess - that I can promise.'

His words were like the air that she breathed in; the one that she needed to be alive. It just seemed tragic that the air that she needed was inadvertently cut off from her. She felt like she was being strangled to death - she could hardly breathe. Her heart was mortally wounded and the pain it caused had tormented her; pushing her to the brink of hysteria. It was not something that she could just ignore like a dull ache that momentarily irked her; it rather felt like an opened wound that was repeatedly salted thus the pang was amplified to a level that she could barely tolerate. It was way too much.

Lu Jinhai. She was very disappointed with him. She could not believe that he did not bother helping Jinzhou Lu Wang Wei. Moments after the escape, he had tried talk to her, comfort her but she did not want to speak to him. He did not know just how much his actions a while ago deeply hurt her - he was a huge disappointment. Too think, she almost fancied herself liking him. And just like a house with a poor foundation shaken by an earthquake, it crumbled into dust. She did not hate him. In fact, she understand that he was only after her safety but he did not know what she felt about Jinzhou Lu Wang Wei. It was unfair to treat him with coldness but, still, she could not help but feel disappointed.

"Tang Lao Fang," someone called Yan Mei Ling.

Yan Mei Ling did not bother looking or answering; she remained seated on a secluded place while leaning on a huge tree. She did not feel like talking to any person for the fear that her emotions would get the best out of her. Despite her sadness, she still had her pride to uphold - she did not want to appear vulnerable.

"You should eat, you know." Lee Sui Song said in a worried voice a bowl of soup was in his hands. "You have been so detached since the escape. I am beginning to think that something happens to you."

Yan Mei Ling continued to ignore Lee Sui Song even if she felt a bit guilty for doing it. He did not deserve her apathy but she could not bring herself to respond. A heavy lump in her throat had obstructed any voice from coming off her mouth.

"I am sure you are grieving because we have lose so many fellow soldiers right now and some of them are our friends but do not get yourself ill." Lee Sui Song continued to speak with concern. "I will not pressure you to talk to me right now but should you feel like talking to someone or sharing the pain that is in your heart, please do not hesitate to call me. I am your friend and I am willing to listen, Tang Lao Fang." He carefully placed the bowl of soup beside Yan Mei Ling and silently bode his leave.

"Lee Sui Song," Yan Mei Ling called in a tremulous voice.

Lee Sui Song turned to look at Yan Mei Ling.

"Thank you for your understanding."

"Not a problem, Tang Lao Fang," Lee Sui Song said with a smile then he nodded his head to signal that he would be leaving. Yan Mei Ling nodded back to him in confirmation.

Yan Mei Ling tended her watery sight above. The sky had already been conquered by the darkness; there were no glittery stars or beautiful light coming from the moonlight that she loved - it looked as gloomy as what she was feeling right now. The air felt damp and the chill soaked to her bones causing uncomfortable tingles within her body, her teeth were shattering from the coldness but she ignored it. Oh, it was an infirmity of the heart that truly affected her; it even eclipsed the physical affliction that her body was experiencing.

She swallowed the lump in her throat as the pain came washing over her again like the huge waves from the sea as it desperately tried to touch the shore. Every time the pain came, the throb magnified to a hundred.

She knew that she still had the mission to save her best friend Li Lei Shuang but a part of soul was lost; a part of her will triturated to tiny pieces and she doubted if it would still be mended. She was grieving for the love she thought she had but unfortunately lost. Like a solitary pebble on the shore, the waves carried it away to the sea only to be irrevocably vanished forever into the ocean of uncertainty.

The world was indeed a cruel and harsh place to live. Just when you thought that happiness was within the palm of your hand, things had gone astray and like a stealthy thief during a moonless night, circumstances took it away from you without any warning.

She sobbed while placing her hand in her chest. She lightly thump it repeated as if trying to ease the pain that was consuming her entire senses but to no avail, it stayed to continuously plague her. She closed her eyes, exerting more effort as she did so, to prevent the tears from escaping but they persisted like wayward criminals on the loose, falling incessantly like the rain.

Crack!

The sky sounded like it was whipped but then a few moments later, the rain started to fall. She welcomed the angry outpour coming from the clouds of heaven, she needed a distraction from the throb within her heart. She was suffocating with too much pain but still, just like the other things she tried doing, it barely washed the pain away.

The thunder roared even loudly like an incensed tiger but she remained unfazed by it. She cried even louder even as the relentless thunder overpowered the sound of her cries. Her frame was rocking with extreme dolor, convulsing like a vehement volcano erupting the lava from its mouth.

'Oh, why does it have to hurt?' She began to punch the ground in a blind rage ignoring the dirt and mud splattering over her.

'But I need to be strong for Li Lei Shuang. I need to - I have to kill all the Hsien.' She continued weeping until she felt someone put a cloth around her. 'I need to kill the Hsien...'

"You should not stay outside when it is raining, Tang Lao Fang. You might get sick again." A gentle voice gently chided her.

Yan Mei Ling froze in shock. Had she gone mad with so much sadness that she could clearly hear his voice and vividly felt his touch? She turned around and saw Jinzhou Lu Wang Wei smiling at her.

Was she hallucinating? She still could not speak. A hand touched her forehead as if checking if she had a fever. It felt so gentle like a soft feather caressing her.

"They have set-up tents on the camp, why are you not there?"

His voice sounded so gentle like a tender breeze during the spring. It felt like a dream and she did not want to wake up if this was indeed a dream - he felt so surreal.

"Jinzhou Lu Wang Wei?" Yan Mei Ling's voice sounded like a croak. Disbelief written all over her face. Was she imagining everything?

"Yes?"

"I thought you were..." Yan Mei Ling's voice trembled with so much emotion; her lips quivering both from sadness and the cold. "That you were..."

"Dead?" Jinzhou Lu Wang Wei clarified with a gentle chuckle while raising his brow in surprise.

Yan Mei Ling nodded weakly unable to speak. She was shaking inside. It was hard to contain whatever was inside her.

"Of course, not," Jinzhou Lu Wang Wei chuckled lightly then he gently rumpled Yan Mei Ling's hair in a brotherly way. "Did I not promise you that we will crush the Hsein armies and end up victorious? Besides, we need to save the princess and, hopefully, help will arrive in the soonest possible time before we reach the Hsein's base."

Yan Mei Ling smiled with so much relief and happiness. It felt like the pain in her heart was instantly gone. It was as if that a huge rock that had been dislodged from her chest. "Can I... can I..."

"Yes?"

"Can I hug you?" She blurted out awkwardly then suddenly heat rose in her cheeks due to embarrassment. Why did she say that? Where did it come from?

"Uhm, I hope you do not get the wrong idea, Jinzhou," Yan Mei Ling babbled incoherently as if she was chewing her words. "I.. I just want to make sure that it is truly you - that you are truly alive and not just a figment of my imagination.. Yes... It is --" before she could finish her words, Lu Wang Wei immediately enveloped her in a fierce hug.

"I am very alive, Tang Lao Fang." Jinzhou Lu Wang Wei whispered to her - his voice full of emotions. He embraced her as if trying to protect her - to assure and promise her that he would always be there for her. "I will always protect you."

"Jinzhou Lu Wang Wei..." Yan Mei Ling hugged him back and leaned further into his hard chest; she never felt so secured and relaxed. She could hear the steady beating of his heart. It was so unlike hers which was beating rapidly that she almost run out of breath but she did not mind.

Yan Mei Ling had so many happy memories in her life. But this one, being in the strong arms of Jinzhou Lu Wang Wei, was one of the happiest. It did not matter if she was drenched and freezing from the rain for as long as she knew that he was alive, everything would be fine.

CHAPTER 33

The rain halted and the sun reclaimed its glorious throne back in the vast sky. It endlessly bled cerulean. The air although a bit damp from the recollection of yesterday's outpour felt wonderful like a lover's blowing kisses. Everything smelled good; the distinctively tangy sweet scent emanating from the plants was unmistakable. It blended well with the musty yet fascinatingly vibrant and redolent aroma emitted by the earth bathed by the drying rain water.

The orange and green leaves swayed as they were caressed by the flirtatious zephyr. The birds sang a beautiful song fit for the ears of the celestial beings yet rewarded to men. The morning was truly beautiful and ethereal.

Yan Mei Ling woke up refreshed and vibrant as the morning despite the little sleep she had as she exited her ruined tent. Her heart was filled with happiness but a part of it was grieving for those friends she had lost due to the unexpected assault of the Chao's soldiers. She tended her stares to her side and saw her fellow soldiers looking grim. Perhaps, they too were grieving from the lost of their comrades and crumbled hope.

She walked around the camp to look for Jinzhou Lu Wang Wei. She just needed to assure herself that last night was not just a mere hallucination or an illusion playing tricks when her heart was at its direst state.

A few minutes passed and her heart began to delve downward. She swallowed a lungful of air to calm herself but then tears started to gather at the side of her eyes. She might have done something terrible that the celestial gods played dreadful tricks upon her.

"Tang Lao Fang," someone called her.

Yan Mei Ling turned but the gloomy expression of her face never left her. "Lu Jinhai"

Lu Jinhai's face looked a bit crestfallen at the sound of her aloof voice. He took a few steps forward until he was near. "When you left the camp last night, I was worried about you. I am still worried about you."

"There is nothing to worry about." Yan Mei Ling merely said then she turned her back at Lu Jinhai as if she could not bear looking at him. Yes, she was being unfair and foolish but she was still smarting from a heart ache. The dream she had last night had even made her feel worse as her expectations were trampled.

"You sound different," he said in observation. There was sadness in his voice that evoked guilt within Yan Mei Ling. "How could I not worry?"

"Really, Lu Jinhai, I am very fine and you do not need to worry." Yan Mei Ling said trying to sound a bit cheerful if that would make Lu Jinhai feel at ease and leave her alone.

"Look at me, Tang Lao Fang," he implored.

"What for?" Yan Mei Ling asked in a tremulous voice. There was bitterness in it.

"You said there is no need to worry about but you are not the Lao Fang that I know."

Yan Mei Ling began to lose her temper at Lu Jinhai's words that she turned around to face him. "Really? Who is that Tang Lao Fang that you know?"

"He is a happy person who always have a smile even if everything is breaking apart." Lu Jinhai said with tenderness.

"Are you mad?" Yan Mei Ling asked with incredulity. "We have lost a lot of men and also our Jinzhou. Do you actually expect me to be cheerful; are you really the Lu Jinhai that I know? As far as I believe that he is not callous and insensitive."

"Yes, I am still the Lu Jinhai that you know."

"No, you are not. I do not know you at all." Yan Mei Ling contradicted and began to walk away from him.

"Jinzhou Lu Wang Wei is alive."

Yan Mei Ling stopped in her tracks but her back was still presented to Lu Jinhai.

"He arrived last night and you were the very first person that he looked for. Did you not see him, Tang Lao Fang?"

Yan Mei Ling turned to face Lu Jinhai again. Her eyes full of skepticism. "I see him last night but he is not here; it is possible that what I see yesterday is just a figment of my imagination. Are you jesting me, Lu Jinhai?"

Lu Jinhai smiled lightly then he shook his head. "I am not jesting you. He is alive and is currently leading a group to hunt for food. The rest of us here will either mend what needs to be mended and, of course, recuperate."

"What I see yesterday is not a ghost?"

"No." Lu Jinhai replied. "What you see is Jinzhou Lu Wang in the flesh and very much alive."

Yan Mei ling looked at him for a moment, trying to see if lies had been spouted. She took a deep breath and warned him,

"You will not hate me but rather the opposite of that." Lu Jinhai chuckled light-heartedly. "Do you want to bet?"

"No, I am not a gambler." Yan Mei Ling said with a specter smile grazing her lips.

"Afraid that you will lose?"

"No, but I prefer not too. I can rely in the truthness of your words, can I?"

Lu Jinhai looked at Yan Mei Ling affectionately before answering her. "Of course, I am the most reliable person that you have ever met, Tang Lao Fang."

Yan Mei Ling smiled at him. "Oh, anyway, I have to look for Jinzhou Lu Wang Wei. I think I want to extend my help in hunting. I am fast and strong, you know."

"You wound me." Lu Jinhai said in disappointment before laughing in amusement. "Ah, you are just saying that because you are still doubting me."

"Of course not! I really just want to help, are you not going to?"

"I am just joking, Tang Lao Fang," Lu Jinhai exclaimed with mirth. "But as much as I want to help, I need to recuperate."

"Why? What?" Yan Mei Ling asked in confusion then to her surprise, she saw the bandage that was wrapped around Lu Jinhai's arms extending to his back underneath his torn shirt. Her heart shuddered with extreme guilt. She had been treating him in a deplorable manner a while ago that she did not notice that he was wounded. Those wounds were probably sustained while they were escaping from the Chao soldiers' assault and, to prick her conscience even more, he was carrying her at that time which might had limited his movements.

"I am so sorry. I did not notice that you are wounded, Lu Jinhai."

"It is fine. I feel good. What is important to me is that you are safe and unscathed. I cannot bear it if something happens to you, Tang Lao Fang."

Yan Mei Ling looked at him in wonderment before she got back her senses. Her heart was being difficult again. "Thank you for being such a good friend. I do not know how to repay you; I am very much indebted to you, Lu Jinhai."

"I do not ask for any payment or anything in return. I just want you to be happy."

"Thank you very much," Yan Mei ling timidly said.

"You are welcome." Lu Jinhai said gently looking at Yan Mei Ling as if in trance. "Oh, by the way, are you not going to hunt for food?"

"Ah, yes, of course"

"Stay safe and please greet jinzhou a good morning from me."

"Of course I will"

"Good," Lu Jinhai said before rumpling Yan Mei Ling's hair affectionately.

CHAPTER 34

It was too out of the world; too incredible.

How she came back from what seemingly a fantasy world. It felt like a dream when she stayed in the Sky Heaven's landing and; when she plunged into the death-inviting depths of the wide and gigantic bottomless waterfalls, the transition from the ethereal dimension to the world where she belong to was like getting herself sucked into a very powerful maelstrom. It was a very terrific and scary feeling, as if her skin was forcefully removed from her muscles.

'Kick to your right side!' Someone shouted a command in her head.

"Baba?" Yan Mei Ling gasped in surprise.

'Don't ask; just do as I say!'

She did a turn and snapped her leg quickly to the right. The ball of her foot connected to the side of her enemy's chin, catapulting him to the wall.

She made a rapid turn and realized that she was inside the Hsien's main wing as what Ryuu told her. The wall was painted brilliant blue; there were precious jade and porcelain humongous wares mounted on it. When she shifted to another direction, she could see several Hsien soldiers running, their spears were pointed at her.

'They will throw the spears at you; jump now!' Ryuu warned in her head.

She would have asked him why she could still hear his voice but he already had an answer before she could even utter her question, 'I'll answer your question later. Jump, my child!'

She hurdled above just in time that the spears sharp points came flying to her direction. She performed a quick aerial walk, somersaulted, caught one soaring spear and landed a few inches in front of the stunned soldiers. Without any further ado, she plunged the spear into the abdomen the of Hsien soldier who stood directly in front of her. She withdrew the spear and plunged it to the chest of another petrified soldier at the same time that her first victim fell on his knees; the fallen adversary held his perforated belly in an effort to abate the bleeding.

The second Hsien soldier lay flat dead on the floor with the blood oozing from his wound. With the shaft of the weapon still embedded to him, Yan Mei Ling brought her body up by pushing two of her fingers at the end of the spear. She did multiple butterfly kicks before descending on the head of her enemy; she swung her other leg to the far front and lowered it a bit before swinging it back. When the back of her heel connected with his nape, she was certain that his spine was broken considering the impact. She did a back tuck and reached for the sword in his waist before she fully stood upright. She immediately severed his head just to make sure that he could not retaliate. A huge amount of blood immediately gushed from his decapitated body.

The remaining soldiers gaped in front of her, immobilized by her skills.

"Who wants to be next?" Yan Mei Ling dared her enemies with a devilish smirk while brandishing her sword menacingly.

'Don't be so cocky, just kill them before they do.' Ryuu reprimanded her.

Yan Mei Ling frowned in disappointment before she pursued her enemies head on. She merely raised her jian and, to her astonishment, different parts of the body - head, limbs and legs - were flying around the place. When the murderous haze began to vanish, she saw thick blood coating and dripping from her sword; her suit was drenched too, as if she bathe in a red rain. How did she do it?

'How's my trick?' Her divine ancestor boasted smugly.

"Now who's being cocky?" Yan Mei Ling retorted under her breath.

Ryuu chuckled in her head.

'Why am I still able to communicate to you, baba?'

'Don't you want to?' Ryuu simply shrugged. 'Move now, run straight to the hallway.'

Yan Mei Ling did as the Dragon god said however she pushed her question again while running, 'Why am I still able to communicate with you?'

'Baba,' Ryuu reminded her.

'What?' Yan Mei Ling muttered cluelessly in irritation but then she conceded with a mental sigh when she remembered, 'Seriously? Okay, baba.'

'Your body is not totally healed. If I vacate your body right now, you will be drowned in pain.' Ryuu replied.

'Are you telling me that you are still inside my body?'

'Yes'

'I thought that I was already healed in the Sky Heaven's lan ding...'

'It was not totally healed there. You survive the explosion because I momentarily take charge of your body. Since your body is not immortal, it takes some time before it gets healed. You did tell me that you feel an immense pain when you arrive in the Hsien village, remember? Jinlong has always been the most skeptical among all the bearers so he will probably test you if you are worthy to become a Dragon Warrior or not - one of his test includes torturing my prospects before they meet him. I desperately want him to acknowledge you.' Ryuu explained to her. 'Meeting the Bearer of fire and heat can be a very painful ordeal. I want you to be strong because if you can't sustain his power, it may cost you your life.'

"So I have to go through the agony that may cost me my life before I become the Dragon Warrior?" Yan Mei Ling stopped on her tracks upon hearing his words. She said in disbelief, "I don't get it. As much as I want to be a Dragon Warrior, the thought of dying without saving the people that I love first is too much of a gamble that I cannot risk. My goal, as of the moment, is to save Li Lei Shuang and, for me to save her, I need to stay alive."

'Is that your way of telling me that you are a coward? And, when you say that you are willing to risk everything including your life to save Li Lei Shuang, it is nothing but a lie?'

"Don't you ever twist my words; you know that I am willing to do anything and risk everything for her! But if I die before I am able to save her just because of that Jinlong, then all that I've been fighting for will amount to nothing. He is not the reason why I come here, why should I die because of him?" Yan Mei Ling huffed angrily, her shoulders shaking from pent-up emotions. "And, you, baba - how insensitive is it of you to say that I am a coward and a liar, considering all the things that I have done!"

Ryuu momentarily fell silent but after a moment, he gently asked, 'Would you rather have it that you don't see Li Lei Shuang anymore?'

"No! Li Lei Shuang is everything to me. A life without Li Lei Shuang is worse than death itself... If I can't see her anymore; if I can't save the one that I love the most, then what is the point of being a warrior?" Yan Mei Ling cried in misery. "But you... you always talk to me in riddles and command me around without giving me a reason why. And, when I ask you questions, you simply dodge them with questions."

'Sometimes it is best to not ask too much.'

"But if I don't ask, then it is as if I am being treated like a brainless fool!" Yan Mei Ling raised her voice; her face turned red from being flustered. "I don't like it; it makes me feel uncomfortable!"

'Humans always find comfort in doing something whose outcome is already known but that's just too easy. Anyway, in due time, you will get the answer to your questions.' Ryuu sighed wearily, still not giving Yan Mei Ling a better explanation. 'Just put it in your mind that the only way for you to save Li Lei

Shuang is to become a Dragon Warrior and, you are simply and blindly following the Dragon god even if you think that it makes you look like a brainless fool.'

"Why not now?"

'You will know and understand everything in due time.' Ryuu repeated and emphasized patiently. 'Resume running lest everything will be too late, my child.'

"I still don't understand, baba." She sighed wearily in frustration, burying her face briefly with her other palm. "But I will do as you say for now..." She began to sprint through the hallway

'Good.' Ryuu commented apathetically. 'Now, prepare yourself, enemies are approaching.'

"How long will it take for my body to heal, baba?"

'Almost...' Ryuu replied evasively. 'Focus, my child, there are arrows targeting you! Lay down!'

Yan Mei Ling dived into the marble floor and saw several arrows propelling everywhere.

'The arrows are shot using a big mechanically-controlled equipment so the position where they could be shot was limited. Just stay still and you won't be harmed.' Ryuu informed her.

'How did you know about the arrows, baba?'

'Simply because I am the Dragon god.' Ryuu stated with a playful arrogance.

Yan Mei Ling scoffed ironically but she continued to lay down while the arrows were dashing above her.

'Do you see that humongous brass shield on the wall to your right side?'

Yan Mei Ling turned her head to the left and saw it. 'Yes'

'I want you to retrieve it when the shooting stops.'

'Why?'

'Don't ask, just do as I say.'

'Fine, baba.'

As soon as the shooting of arrows desisted, Yan Mei Ling went for a mad dash and leapt for the brass shield.

'Now what do I do with this?' Yan Mei Ling inquired.

'Toss it across as strong as you can and, then drop yourself immediately.'

She did as Ryuu said. The brass shield began to revolve around the room, destroying some parts of the walls. She could hear men screaming and running. When the shield finally stopped revolving, it fell on the floor, blood smeared its circular edges.

'Some of them die but a lot still survive,' Ryuu stated. 'Stand up and ready your sword, my child.'

Yan Mei Ling rose and held her sword; her alert eyes observed the room. No sooner, numerous Hsien soldiers appeared and stormed around her. She stood calmly, waiting for them to attack her.

'Why are they not attacking, baba?'

'All of them are afraid of you...' Ryuu told her. 'Initiate the attack.'

Yan Mei Ling vaulted over and rotated with her sword pointed to the soldiers.

Some soldiers were wounded but the others retaliated back by swinging their swords at her. She blocked their strikes and tumbled backwards.

Three Hsien foes attempted to trap her with their swords but she sprang above them. With her feet pointed above the ceiling, she sliced their faces into halves by dangling her sword vertically, its sharp end pointed down. She gravitated to the floor, diving into her enemies' puddle of blood.

'I never know that I can perform such a skill...' Yan Mei Ling uttered in bewilderment.

'That is just one of the many skills that you will learn once you become the Dragon Warrior.'

Yan Mei Ling smirked and wiped the fuller of her scarlet-coated sword with her index and middle fingers. She flicked the blood from her fingers to the side, bent her lower body down to a fighting stance, and beckoned her enemies invitingly with her palms.

"Agghh!!" The Hsien soldiers shouted in outrage as they hurtled to her direction - some jumped above her, while others strode towards her.

She swayed her jian to her attackers but they were hurled away from each other when the left side of the hallway exploded. She was violently slammed to the wall, spit escaped her mouth before she crashed down.

"Ehhggg..." She groaned while she grabbed her hair in an effort to reduce the pain in her head. "Baba?"

No response.

"Baba, where are you?" She anxiously called in the hallway.

Half the place was on fire but still there was no response.

Her entire body began to quiver violently as she felt an immense heat consumed her entire body. She panted heavily as her chest began to tighten, her vision covered in haze. She covered her mouth as she coughed; when she stared at her palms, she could see streaks of blood - her own - painting it.

"You left without even telling me..." Yan Mei Ling sobbed in disappointment. She struggled to stand up, searching for the sword that she lose somewhere in the hallway.

Despite the pain and her failing vision, she staggered and crouched, touching the marble floor, searching for her weapon. She encountered rubbles and dead bodies. She was reaching for the sword from one of the cadavers when she felt something eerily off behind her. She looked ahead of her and saw a distinctive shadow looming above. She swiftly rolled to the side, just in time that a jian hit the ground where she was crouching.

Still sprawled on the floor, the enemy pounced at her again but she parried his attack with her sword. He pushed his jian to her, overpowering her already depleting strength.

"You will die now!" Her opponent hollered, preparing to stab her with his sword but she managed to kick him in his groin. "Damn you, bastard!"

Yan Mei Ling hit him with her sword, mangling halfway through his torso. Blood spurted upon her before the dead body fell upon her. She pushed the corpse away. She allowed her exhausted body to recover before standing up; she retrieved her sword from the cadaver and plodded through the hallway.

Before she could move another step forward, another blast was heard; this time the foundation behind her came down, the beams missed her by a scant few inches. She inhaled and exhaled heavily, tears streamed down her eyes as her body fought to sustain the flame that was slowly eating her from the inside. Her ebbing eyesight was worsened by the fog of the burning establishment; from a distant she could hear the echoes of warring soldiers.

Yan Mei Ling stumbled when something dropped to her head. She peered around and realized that it was just a debris from the deteriorating ceiling that struck her. She warily touched her head and felt a sticky substance - no doubt her blood.

She scrambled to stand and paced slowly despite the smog that swallowed the entire place. The air that she was breathing was becoming too thin to the point that it was almost suffocating. She decided to use the sword as a cane to support her body. Behind the cloak of stinging vapor, she saw several shadows barricading the gigantic double doors at a distance away from her. She coughed again to expel the irritating gas that entered her lungs.

In the same way that half of the main wing was on fire, Yan Mei Ling's body felt the same. Is this because of Jinlong? She clamped her other fist tightly as the intensity of the pain that she was experiencing aggravated. She could feel her sweat escaping the pores of her flustered skin, pooling beneath her feet. Using her forearm, she wiped the perspiration from her forehead.

She wheezed through the haze, her eyes watery. The guards near the gigantic doors were struggling too. She closed her eyes and earnestly prayed to the gods and her ancestors, 'If my fate ends here, I beg you, please allow me to save Li Lei Shuang.'

Yan Mei Ling closed her eyes and allowed the tears to escape. Her throat was burning with sadness. She gripped her hand tightly onto her sword as the pain wracked her body again. She gnashed her teeth and bolted towards the doors; she leapt above the astounded guards and slashed their bodies with her sword. When the guards dropped into mangled pieces, she took several steps back and, with all the strength that she could muster, she thrashed the thick gigantic doors until they dismantled.

She gasped for air and stood for a moment, taking in the ostentatious place with her weary eyes. The harem's wing was extravagant with silk curtains flowing like a graceful waterfall on its ceilings and enormous windows; there were beautiful colorful paper lanterns flying like magical objects. The room was illuminated beautifully, the moonlight shimmered down on its floor like a milky ocean. She ambled down the marble floor which was equally as beautiful as the entire wing with its painted designs. In the middle, there was a marvelous fountain. 'Where are the women?'

While she examined the entire area, the sound of shattering ceramics resounded. Startled, Yan Mei Ling clutched her sword and gazed to the direction of the sound.

"Who are you? What are you doing here?" A girl who was about her age - probably an attendant to the harem considering her plain attire - freaked out.

Yan Mei Ling marched to the girl, raising her hands in a peaceful manner, but the latter cautiously moved back. "Don't be afraid of me; I swear I don't mean you any harm."

"You have a sword," the girl warily motioned to the jian in Yan Mei Ling's hand with frightened eyes. "And your clothes are ripped and dripping in blood... I don't think you are one of the guards."

"I am not one of the guards but I am here to save the princess and the women in this harem..."

The girl shook her head in alarm. "You... You can't! You don't know Lord Hsien Mao Dong; your efforts will only be in vain; you will only die!"

"What do you - " Before Yan Mei Ling could finish her words, an arrow shot through the girl's forehead, drilling through it before the shaft proceeded to aim for her. She managed to catch the arrow before it pierced her.

"Great catch..." A man chuckled in admiration. "I never thought you can kill all of my guards and manage to come here alive."

"You're evil - how could you kill the girl?" Yan Mei Ling demanded angrily. "Where are you, Hsien Mao Dong? Show your face, coward!"

Instead of getting an answer, several arrows were projected at her. She somersaulted and hid behind the fountain. She lightly thumped her chest when she felt a searing sensation inside; she coughed and blood escaped her mouth. Before she could wipe her mouth, a series of arrow jutted through the cascading lucid veil of the fountain. She reeled away from the fatal shafts and pushed herself to a handspring.

"Impressive for someone who is very young." She could hear Lord Hsien Mao Dong's fiendish voice resonating through the entire room. "I could use someone like you. What if I offer you something that will appeal to you? If you serve me, I will make you a jiangjun of my army."

Yan Mei Ling huffed in disgust. "I'd rather die than serve you!"

"You must be someone who is so arrogant to have the gall to refuse my offer." Lord Hsien Mao Dong commented. "But if you want to die, I will be more than happy to grant you your wish."

Another wave of arrows pursued Yan Mei Ling. She trotted away to a different direction when a gliding man assaulted her with a heavy sword, she evaded the attack by bouncing away - the huge jian hit the floor, smashing it into smithereens. The man promptly pulled the sword back and dangled it to her. She arched her body backwards but still the jian's point managed to sliver through her outer clothes.

Yan Mei Ling retaliated with a swing of her sword but the man managed to break the steel of her sword into pieces. She jolted back and somersaulted away from the man.

"I guess you know who I am." The man said with a smirk. He was wearing a long flowing golden silk brocade embroidered with brown and red beautiful dragon motifs - it was so exquisitely made that intricate patterns were printed from the side of his dress' opening to its hems. He was holding an elegant dragon-shaped long bow on his right hand and a hulking double-edged bronze sword to the left.

"Lord Hsien Mao Dong!" Yan Mei Ling spat his name with extreme revulsion.

"Who are you?"

"The last person that you will see."

"How ambitious," Lord Hsien Mao Dong remarked sardonically. "Pray tell, how will you kill me - with your bare hands and mediocre skills?"

Yan Mei Ling's pride was piqued by Lord Hsien Mao Dong's words but a terrible pain restrained her from reacting to it.

Lord Hsien Mao Dong smirked when he stared at the struggling boy, "I'm certain that my sword is not able to graze your skin but why are you in pain?"

She took a big gulp of air and snapped vehemently, "I'm not in pain! Where is Princess Li Lei Shuang?"

A brief moment of confusion crossed the warlord's wrinkled face but he immediately replaced it with a supercilious smile. "Hmmm... What business do you have with my fiancée?"

A burst of violent temper elevated Yan Mei Ling's already feverish body to the extreme. "She... She... She is not your fiancée!"

Lord Hsien Mao Dong crossed his arms in his chest and aloofly studied the young warrior in front of him. He calmly asked, "Who do you think you are to say that Princess Li Lei Shuang is not my fiancée?"

"I am the princess' savior. If you want to die a hasty death, give me the princess!"

"And if I don't want to give you the princess?" He asked in an amused tone.

Yan Mei Ling did a fighting stance and vehemently shouted, "Then what choice do I have but to kill you?" She sprang above Lord Hsien Mao Dong, did a back tuck and delivered a flying kick behind him.

Lord Hsien Mao Dong whispered, "I sure would appreciate a bit of entertainment." He levitated higher than the young warrior and threw a vicious butterfly kick at his opponent.

Yan Mei Ling was thrown to the ground, writhing in pain.

"What a weakling." The warlord sauntered in front of the young fighter and pushed his boot on her face. "But you look familiar..."

Yan Mei Ling sputtered blood and heaved violently.

Lord Hsien Mao Dong carried the young warrior with the bridge of his foot and flung her across to the left. "Did you not say that you will kill me a while ago? Why are you acting like a weakling right now? Stand up and fight me!"

Yan Mei Ling crawled and forced herself to bring her weight up with her wobbling knees. Her vision doubled as the heat in her body intensified.

"I can kill you right now but where is the thrill in that?"

She peered around and spotted several decorative spears on the walls. She rushed to the direction of the decorative weapons and lobbed them at Lord Hsien Mao Dong.

The warlord sundered the flying spears with his jian while pursuing his foe.

Yan Mei Ling saw a huge ceramic vase, carried it and, then hurled it to Lord Hsien Mao Dong. The latter kicked the vase to the floor when it was near him, destroying it. He managed to reduce the distance between him and the young warrior but the former immediately run on the wall and hurdled backwards. He targeted Yan Mei Ling by swaying his sword behind him but she managed to escape the blade.

Lord Hsien Mao Dong faced the warrior and remarked, "It had been too long since I fight someone whose skills are as impressive as yours. You amaze me more than anyone else, little one."

"I don't need your compliment!" Yan Mei Ling spat in rage. "Where is the princess?"

"Secret," Lord Hsien Mao Dong chuckled ironically and attacked the warrior with his sword again.

Yan Mei Ling pivoted away from the jian and threw a side kick to Lord Hsien Mao Dong who staggered to his knees.

"You actually manage to hit me - unbelievable."

"You are not that fast."

"You're ridiculous." Lord Hsien Mao Dong scorned at the youth's words. He gave his opponent a very thorough scrutiny. "Since you are here for the princess, what if we have a bargain?"

Yan Mei Ling's eyes narrowed skeptically. "Bargain?"

"Yes."

"Why would you strike a bargain with me?"

"Because I like your bravado and you impress me."

Yan Mei Ling scoffed, dismissing his words.

"Since you want the princess, I am sure this bargain is something that you can't refuse." Lord Hsien Mao Dong continued. He stared deeply into the young warrior and smiled in amusement as if he had known something that shouldn't be known to him. "You are not merely the princess' savior, aren't you?"

"Just what are you talking about?"

"I already remember... I think I know who you are." Lord Hsien Mao Dong smirked as he continued to look at the young fighter up and down. "How could I ever forget your face?"

Yan Mei Ling opened and closed her mouth in disbelief before saying, "Don't try to bait me with your deceitful tricks; they are not going to work on me."

"I know that you are aware of what I am talking about. Don't act as if you don't get what I am saying."

"You're bluffing!" Yan Mei Ling said in annoyance.

"I am not bluffing" Lord Hsien Mao Dong gave the young warrior a dark smile before stating, "little lady."

Yan Mei Ling blood run cold at what she heard.

"If I am not mistaken, you are the Ninja Boy."

"Yes, so what about it?" She said dismissively. "And you actually call me little lady - what a fool."

"Because that's what you are." Lord Hsien Mao Dong nodded his head in delight. "Aren't you going to ask me how I know you?"

"You don't know me at all." Yan Mei Ling muttered in agitation.

"Really?" The warlord smirked as he confidently crossed his arms. "What if I tell you that I know that you are Duke Yan Bao Rong's daughter; tell me, what's your reaction?"

Yan Mei Ling's mouth went agape with shock.

"How could I ever forget your beautiful face?" He strode in front of the stunned young lady. He closed the distance between them and softly caressed Yan Mei Ling's face. "Do you think that I can't see past your charade despite you wearing ugly rags?"

Yan Mei Ling remained petrified unable to move. It seemed that she was hypnotized into stillness.

Lord Hsien Mao Dong continued to caress her - her temple, side of her ears - before cupping her face. "Aren't you interested to know about the bargain?" He asked huskily; his eyes smoky with lust. He moved his mouth closer to her, with every intention of kissing her, when Yan Mei Ling stealthily moved to carve his face with her dragon-painted dagger.

"Fucking bitch!" The warlord exclaimed wrathfully. He was able to move away from Yan Mei Ling to avoid serious damage but she managed to inflict a superficial wound on his face.

"You are a disgusting perverted pig!" Yan Mei Ling hollered in indignation as she brandished her dagger at her adversary. "Do you think you can lull me, ugly old man? I don't need to know what bargain you are talking about because my answer will always be a 'no.' I am not that stupid to strike a deal with a conniving devil like you. What about if I change the rules of your bargain, instead - you kill me or I kill you and whoever remains alive will get the princess?"

"Feisty." Lord Hsien Mao Dong stepped back and wiped the blood off of his face. He gazed menacingly at the young warrior. "You are not in the best form right now - you obviously have a fever. Rejecting my offer for a truce that will benefit us both is a very, very stupid move."

"Don't dare insult my intelligence."

"For someone so young and a female, your arrogance is incredible." He stated cynically.

"Huh!" Yan Mei Ling scoffed. "I may be young and a female but for someone who is old and a male, your existence is a bane in the World under Heaven; you should be extinguished."

"Really?" Lord Hsien Mao Dong sniggered sarcastically. He treaded towards Yan Mei Ling, seemingly intimidating her. "Now, you pique my interest; tell me, how do you plan to extinguish me?"

"Go near me and you are good as dead." Yan Mei Ling threatened as she pointed the dagger to her approaching adversary.

"I'll take my chances..." Lord Hsien Mao Dong said under his breath as he moved to grab her.

Yan Mei Ling swept her dagger to cleave his hand off but her opponent eluded it. He attempted to clobber her with his huge sword but she slipped to the side and delivered a hook kick. Lord Hsien Mao Dong fell on his knees; using that opportunity, she jumped above to impale his rear side with her dagger. "Die, you demon!"

Lord Hsien Mao Dong reacted immediately by shifting his jian to his side before pushing it from behind him to stab the advancing warrior. The latter twisted her body away from the point of the sword and landed crouching on the ground.

Her jaw tightened as her body shuddered in pain. Her hand shook as she gripped her dagger and cried at the top of her lungs, "Baba, Jinlong, release me from this torment that you are putting me through! I don't want to be the Dragon Warrior; I only want to save my friend..."

Lord Hsien Mao Dong was seized into stupefaction at what he heard - how did she know about Jinlong? He gritted his teeth as his ire began to steam. "How presumptuous is it of you to claim that you are the Dragon Warrior - who do you think you are?"

"Presumptuous?" Yan Mei Ling huffed in an offended voice. "How dare you accuse me of that?"

"The Dragon Lord will never choose a weakling like you!" The warlord shook with tempestuous rage. His eyes dilated in realization, "You came here to steal the sword from me, didn't you?"

Yan Mei Ling's furrowed in confusion, "Sword? I came here to save the princess not for some piece of junk."

"Don't lie to me, you come here to steal the Huojian from me!" Lord Hsien Mao Dong barked furiously. "You will never take it away from me. I will kill you first, bitch!" He darted to her direction to finish her off with his sword but she was able to shield herself with her dagger.

"Your dagger did not break - how could it withstand my sword?" He exclaimed in shock.

"Is that what you call the Huojian?" Yan Mei Ling mocked as she pushed against her enemy's sword despite her juddering arms. "My dagger is more reliable." She swept her feet at her at him, throwing him off his balance and proceeded to run off to the vestibule which led to another room.

"Don't even try stepping into that room!" He yelled and began shooting arrows at her.

"Then try to stop me!" Yan Mei Ling dared him and evaded all the arrows being shot at her.

"You are as elusive as the wind," Lord Hsien Mao Dong simpered. "But I am certain that you won't escape your death this time!" He lunged to the far right side of the wall and pulled a string from a tiny wooden chamber.

Yan Mei Ling paused in wonder when the room began to quake violently. A moment later, she could hear something swishing from all corners of the room.

"Tang Lao Fang, run!" A familiar voice shouted a warning before she felt a strong kick that catapulted her to a sprawling position just outside the threshold of the adjoining room.

She groaned from the impact and opened her eyes. Her heart plummeted down to an unknown abyss where it was hard to escape from at what she saw. "Jinzhou Lu Wang Wei!" She cried at the top of her lungs when the blistering arrows incinerated his body from the top, bottom and, both left and right side.

"No!" She shouted again and again as she watched the blood exiting out of Lu Wang Wei's already dead body in a manic frenzy. "No..." She whispered in agony as she covered her face with her palms to weep.

"Bastard!" Lord Hsien Mao Dong hollered in rage when the arrows stopped.

"You killed him." Yan Mei Ling said in tearful contempt as she clenched and unclenched her fists.

The warlord strolled to Jinzhou Lu Wang Wei's corpse and booted it. "He is a nuisance."

"How dare you defile his body?"

Lord Hsien Mao Dong shrugged his shoulders casually and simpered. "If my message doesn't come across you, let me dumb down things for you, I don't really give a damn."

Yan Mei Ling stood, eyeing her opponent murderously. "I will kill you!"

"How many times have I heard you say that?" He mocked her as he waved his sword playfully. "I'm bored. When exactly do you plan to do that?"

She gnashed her teeth in annoyance and spat with a shaking voice. "I will kill you. If gambling my life is what it takes to kill you, I will gamble it."

"Oh, really?" Lord Hsien Mao Dong uttered in amusement as he strolled to the young warrior's direction. "Talk is cheap, little one," he bolted to her direction and, without warning, strangled her. "Action is what I am looking for."

"Aggghh!"

"Just one stab from my sword and your life is forfeited." Lord Hsien Mao Dong told her grimly. "You are hard to knock down and very stubborn to boot. But I think I am going to regret killing you." He eyed her seriously. "So I decided to give you a chance... If you swear to serve and commit your loyalty to me, I will spare your life."

She grimaced.

He loosened his hold and leaned near her cheek; he said in a low voice, "Don't worry, little one, I am not going to make you as one of the women in my harem. I will appoint you as a jiangjun in my army under the guise of a man. I may, however, require you to lend your body to my pleasure occasionally..."

"No! I've already told you that I will never strike a deal with a conniving devil like you!" Yan Mei Ling spat on his face. "You are revolting."

Lord Hsien Mao Dong turned his face to the other side, the pulse at the side of his temple ticking furiously. "Are you certain about that?"

"Which part of 'no' is hard for you to understand?"

"Very well," he muttered aloofly and moved to stab her with his sword. His eyes widened in shock when the end of the sword refused to penetrate through Yan Mei Ling's stomach despite exerting more force. "It is impossible!" He released her and said, "I only know one person who knows how to do it and that is Tang Jiao Quon."

Yan Mei Ling throw a punch on his face and retracted a few distance away from him. "Master Tang Jiao Quon is my teacher."

"How convenient," He exclaimed in disbelief and hilarity. "I have searched for him far and beyond but to no avail; and, now, I am facing his disciple. I never thought that this night has become exceedingly interesting."

"You failed direly in underestimating me if you think you can kill me so easily."

Lord Hsien Mao Dong nodded his head in agreement. "I have indeed underestimated you which is a huge mistake on my part. I don't really want to do this but since you are very hard to kill, I have no choice but to show you what I am capable of."

A creepy kind of darkness covered the entire place and the lanterns hanging in the room began to oscillate fiercely. Yan Mei Ling could hear the thunder cracking outside and the wind intensified as if a turbulent storm was coming. When everything calmed down, she stared at Lord Hsien Mao Dong. "What are you?" She gasped a question.

He looked different - he seemed to grow in both size and height. His eyes swirled with an eerie black color in it and a strong dangerous aura emanated from him. "I always wanted to rule the World under Heaven and be proclaimed as the strongest warrior in it. I did everything but it seems futile until I learn about the legend of the Dragon Warrior."

Yan Mei Ling's heart beat nervously as she looked at Lord Hsien Mao Dong's formidable form.

"I need to find the 6 weapons and tame the dragons in them to become one but I only manage to get one - Jinlong's Houjian." He narrated. "I am not successful in taming Jinlong but that doesn't mean that there is no possibility of taming him in the future. I learn that if I sell my soul to the Demon Lord, I will gain power to tame the dragons but I need to get my hand on the 6 jians first. So I razed and conquered villages in search of the remaining 5 swords - offering the blood of the casualties to the Demon Lord."

"I don't see the point why you are telling me that"

"Oh, there is," he stated. "You have mentioned Jinlong's name a while ago and that you don't want to become the Dragon Warrior. Where did you get the guts to proclaim that you are the chosen one?"

"You did fail to learn that the first step to become the Dragon Warrior is that you should be descended from the first Dragon Warrior."

"Really?" He asked with levity. "Are you implying that you are a descendant of the Dragon Warrior?"

"Yes, I am."

"Hahahah," Lord Hsien Mao Dong laughed with incredulity. "Fantastic! Absolutely fantastic!" His face hardened into a harsh scowl. "How presumptuous - you certainly are a delusional fool, aren't you?"

"You don't need to believe me"

"I find your tale hardly believable at all." He snarled. "Do actually you take me for a fool?"

"Yes, you are a fool!"

He swung his sword in the air and Yan Mei Ling was slammed hard against the wall. "How dare you mock me?"

She groaned in pain and muttered, "I will dare as I please!"

He beckoned at the young warrior with his fingers and she began to buoy up in the air.

"What do you think you are doing?" Yan Mei Ling struggled but it seemed that her hands and feet were tied - like that of what Ryuu did to her in the Sky Heaven's Landing.

He motioned his palm down and she was propelled to the ground, face down. "Do you understand why I don't believe you are the Dragon Warrior?"

Yan Mei Ling merely answered with a whimper.

"You don't have the strength; you are nothing but a weakling." He said in a taunting manner. "I have given you the chance to live and serve me but you merely laugh it off. Now, you give me no choice but to kill you. I swear that I won't give you an easy death; I will torture you until I break that stubborn spirit of yours and revel in the sound of your tortured voice." He upturned his palm and Yan Mei Ling was drifted in the air; he swung it to the side and she was flung inside the connecting room.

Her body was convulsing from the extreme pain. It did not help that she was already weak from the unusual fever that consumed her.

"See the consequence of going against me?" He lifted his hands up before clapping them together.

Yan Mei Ling bounced up and down before she was pushed down; her body outlined the ground. She struggled to stand up despite her worsening injuries.

"Oh, you are still alive?" Lord Hsien Mao Dong chuckled in feigned surprise and approached her. He grabbed her hair and scrutinized her bloodied face. "You're pretty hard to break. I am almost tempted to believe your tale."

"Monster, I will not die until I ensure that you're dead and Princess Li Lei Shuang is safe!" Yan Mei Ling said in a ragged voice.

Lord Hsien Mao Dong smirked. He slugged his fist repeatedly to her abdomen until she spewed with frothy blood. "Instead of begging me, you actually have the audacity to rile me!"

"Beg you?" Yan Mei Ling laughed hysterically. "You're dreaming."

He delivered a smashing blow which sent her flying to the floor.

Yan Mei Ling's eyes became blurry. She leaned against something but froze when she realized that it was a huge cage covered with red silk. She shivered from fear when she saw blood streaming from its side.

'It can't be...'

She could hear the irritating sound of the jian's end being dragged on the floor - exactly the same as that of her nightmare in the Chao village.

"Please don't let it be." Yan Mei Ling mumbled in grief.

Lord Hsien Mao Dong laughed diabolically and licked his jian's fuller. His eyes were dilated and frightening. He looked every ounce of the demon he sold himself to.

"Do you think you can save the Princess?" The evil man taunted. "You are weak and frail. You are nothing but a little girl." He laughed again.

Exactly the same words.

'Please let this be a nightmare.' Yan Mei Ling prayed with all her heart as tears refused to stop falling from her eyes. She wanted to pull the silk cover but she was afraid that her ultimate fear would manifest in front of her.

Lord Hsien Mao Dong was a step closer to her when she jumped to swipe at his face with her dagger.

"Die, monster!" She screamed angrily. She relentlessly attacked him but the latter merely eluded her.

"Is that the best that you can do?"

"Just die!" She foamed with white hot fury and stabbed him in the heart.

The warlord stood, chuckling at the girl who pushed her dagger against chest. "Do you think that I can't do tricks just like yours?"

Yan Mei Ling fell helplessly on her knees and sobbed in frustration. "Li Lei Shuang... Li Lei Shuang... I am sorry... I am nothing... I am weak; I am not even there to save you. It must have hurt you so much."

"You are right." Lord Hsien Mao Dong told her. "You are nothing; you are weak; and, if I may add, you are stupid."

Her shoulders heaved up and down in exhaustion. Her mind was blank and she did not want to fight anymore. Perhaps this was the real feeling of being hopeless - it wrapped around her like a depressing and constricting coil. Jinzhou Lu Wang Wei was dead; Li Lei Shuang was gone - whether she believed it or not - what sense was there to go on living? Nothing anymore.

"Why did you stop?" Lord Hsien Mao Dong asked snarkily. "Did you already give up?"

Yan Mei Ling continued to stare blankly into the space, ignoring everything around her.

"Pathetic," he sneered in derision. He took a handful of the unmoving girl's hair and touched his sword suggestively on her neck. "I am going to slice your pretty head off your body, aren't you going to do something about that?"

She remained unresponsive as if she drifted off to a deep sense of oblivion.

He shook Yan Mei Ling's roughly and whispered impatiently, "If you are playing tricks, I suggest you to not do it." The latter remained unmoved so he kicked her on the face. "Bitch, what exactly are you doing - trying to stir compassion from me? I have none of that!"

Still the same.

Lord Hsien Mao Dong gritted his teeth in annoyance when something came into his head. A sheen of lust shimmered in his eyes as his scowl transformed into a smirk. "You sure won't move, huh? I'll do anything I want to do to you." He grabbed the girl by her clothes and attempted to tear it off when a strong invisible force hurled them away from each other. His eyes widened in alarm when he saw that the young warrior landed beside the giant cylindrical fire pit where the Houjian was kept aflame.

'My child, don't just lay in there; stand up and fight Hsien Mao Dong. Get the Houjian from the pit!' Ryuu's voice came back, urging her.

"Baba?" She mumbled weakly.

'If you want to see Li Lei Shuang defeat Lord Hsien Mao Dong, get the Houjian now!'

"Li Lei Shuang is gone..." She sobbed as the tears escaped her shuttered eyes.

'Damn it, Yan Mei Ling!' Ryuu snapped angrily. 'I expect you to be tougher than this. Listen to me and listen very carefully; for you to see Li Lei Shuang again, get the Houjian from the pit and defeat Hsien Mao Dong.'

"She is not gone?"

'Time is of huge importance; save your questions later - do as I say now!'

Yan Mei Ling stood abruptly and took the Houjian from the flaming pit. She expected the flames to burn her flesh but something else happened. The moment that she pulled it off from the pit, the hilt melted into her palm and indescribable pain seared her entire body. "Agggghhh!!!"

A blinding light crumped from the girl's body, sending Lord Hsien Mao Dong farther away from her.

Blood began to escape Yan Mei Ling's ears, nose, mouth and eyes. Her body jerking horrendously. She tried to release the Houjian from her hand but it appeared to have been attached to her, like it was a part of her body. She levitated midair and a gargantuan fire dragon stared at her with angry red eyes.

'So you want to tame Jinlong?' Jinlong asked in disdain. 'How dare would a person of no consequence aspire to do that?'

"I may be of no consequence but I beg you please help me save the people that I love by lending me your power." Yan Mei Ling stuttered.

Jinlong scoffed at her. 'Typical words just like those fools who wish to tame Jinlong. What makes you different from them?'

"I only wish to save the people that I love and nothing else." Yan Mei Ling answered earnestly.

'Let's see.' Jinlong muttered skeptically and transformed into a huge man with a bald head. He looked utterly formidable with his blue flame eyes and puckered scar on the lower right side of his jaw. He wore a brick red steel cuirass embedded with a huge fire gem in the middle of the breastplate. There were carvings of dragons on his armor and luminous red tattoos covered his brawny arms. Cuisses made of intricately connected chains of steel plates covered his muscled thighs and red tassets were superimposed upon them; his boots were made of red-colored steel. He carried the girl by the collar and inserted his hand inside her chest as if it was invisible. Yan Mei Ling shook from the pang as more blood slobbered from her mouth.

Jinlong touched her heart while scrutinizing her. After a moment, he pulled his hand back - surprisingly his hand was nary of blood. He threw Yan Mei Ling carelessly to the ground and said, 'Jinlong sees through your heart - my power is yours.' He turned back into a dragon and his essence went inside her body.

Chapter 35

It hurt. It terribly hurt.

If she thought that the pain she felt when she took ahold of the Houjian was too much, the pain of Jinlong's spirit entering her body was horrible. Nothing could compare to it – the pain of being burned inside and out was a far dim comparison.

She was levitated in the air as she twisted and turn; trying to escape the tremendous pang that seared her from deep down of her body to the surface of her skin. Her flesh stung; her insides were being ripped apart; her eyes cried blood; her nose dripping convulsively; her mouth was uncontrollably disgorging blood; and her ears were deaf due to the crimson essence escaping from their holes. She had no idea how long her body endured the unspeakable pain but, eventually, her vision turned from hazy to utter darkness.

Lord Hsien Mao Dong's mouth went agape as he stared at the girl consumed by the infernal flame and agonizing pain. His jaw tightened in jealousy and his heart flaming with wrath. How dare she took Jinlong's power just like that when he had worked so hard and waited several years. He stood and with ire-filled shaking body, he brandished his double-edged sword and darted to Yan Mei Ling's direction. "Undeserving bitch!"

He jumped over the girl's levitating body, gesturing to hack her body in two when his sword's steel melted like an ice near a fire. He drifted down in shock. He clenched his fist, raised his arm and shouted at the top of his lungs, "Demon Lord, lend me your power."

A crack of vicious thunder was heard and a gloomy shadow pervaded the entire place. His body, who had grown in size a while ago, increased immensely to the width and height of a raging behemoth. His appearance changed from a giant version of himself turned to a monstrous giant with fiendish red eyes and protruding incisors extending below his lower lip. He had become excessively muscular with stone slab chests and thick veins snaking around his body; his thighs were enormous resembling that of the tree's trunks and; his hands were so huge that it seemed that they could grip the columns of the room without difficulty. His flesh transmogrified from tawny brown color to an eerie greyish brown. "Roar!!!"

The room shook violently as Lord Hsien Mao Dong's savage voice resonated. He jumped again and swung his elbows down to strike down his inert opponent. He and the girl landed on the ground but he pushed against her body to bury her deeper. He peered down the girl and cackled hysterically while he watched the flames slowly ebbing from her body. He raised and slammed his other foot repeatedly at her still unconscious body. "How dare you take what rightfully belongs to me?"

His voice was filled with acrimony as he continued, "You don't know what I've been through just to get my hands on Houjian and you get Jinlong's power just like that? Just like that?" His grotesque face was taut with indignation. "What is so special about a weak girl like you? I am stronger and I can easily kill you. In all aspects, I deserve to be the Dragon Warrior!" His arms began to tremble and, gradually, his hand extended into a narrow shape until it transformed into the head of a dagger-axe.

Yan Mei Ling finally gained consciousness and chuckled – there was still blood sputtering from her mouth. "There is nothing special about me but it doesn't mean that you are stronger than me." She gazed hard into his diabolical eyes and declared, "You are greedy and selfish. You sold your soul to the devil because deep inside your heart, if you still have one, you know that you will never be the Dragon Warrior." A light erupted from her, flinging the egregious lord away. She levitated and hit the ground in standing position. She clenched her palm tightly around the hilt of the Houjian, a white luminescent energy smoldering around her.

Lord Hsien Mao Dong ran to Yan Mei Ling's direction to attack her but she quickly met his weapon with the Houjian's blade. His arms trembled from the force. When he looked into the eyes of the girl, he could see flashes of thin red haze swirling inside her irises. He realized that he was not fighting the girl alone.

Yan Mei Ling expeditiously made a quick turn and strike her heel to his chin. He staggered back and threw spit in the air. She made succeeding attack by hovering above him and threw several aerial foot stamps on his face. She bashed him with her sword but he parried it with his weapon. They continued to assault each other with their weapons, none was willing to surrender.

"Die!" He hollered furiously and clobbered his foe with his weapon. She glided behind him and attempted to slice his back but he eluded her by sidestepping opposite from the direction of the Houjian's blade. He squeezed his hand and, when he opened it, a spherical gray matter was floating in his palms. He casted it on the girl and she was immediately flung to the far side of the wall.

The young warrior fell to the ground but she still managed to stand. She swiftly sprinted to her enemy and assailed him. They both exchanged attacks, sparks coming off from the friction of their weapons. Several claps of thunder shook the entire Hsien village as the two warriors continued to fight belligerently.

Lord Hsien Mao Dong extended his arm and, again, from his palm several gray balls came out of it, pursuing the elusive Dragon Warrior. Yan Mei Ling, on the other hand, deflected them using her sword.

"And you call yourself the Dragon Warrior?" The lord yelled bitterly. "You don't even have any power other than that sword!" He released a succession of gray orbs - two managed to hit the girl. "I will prove to Jinlong that he made a grave mistake by choosing a weakling like you."

Yan Mei Ling fell on her knees, her chests heaving up and down. She calmly rose and asked with a straight face, "Is that all you can do?"

The behemoth stood and snickered darkly. "Actually, no." The muscles in his arms jerked spasmodically and both changed into long beefy and spiky whips. He laughed maniacally and said, "Do you think you'll survive this time?"

The girl stood apathetically and answered, "You have forgotten that the Dragon Warrior managed to defeat hundreds of dark warriors alone. Look at you, you're just one dark warrior."

"You are not half what the previous Dragon Warrior has become!"

"Perhaps," Yan Mei Ling agreed aloofly. "But I will still defeat you." She moved towards the monster and contended against him. Lord Hsien Mao Dong reacted by lashing his lengthy whips at the approaching opponent. She stealthily avoided his dangerous scourge. She dived straight into him and delivered a number of butterfly kicks; she held her angled arm back and thrusted her fist onto his humongous nose. When he screamed from the pain, she immediately stabbed the Houjian into his bowels; she pulled back and distanced herself from him.

She watched as the dark lord shuddered vehemently while thick pasty black blood escaped from his wound. Her eyes wandered when something caught her attention; she turned to its direction and saw a group trembling and crying women observing them from afar. "Stay there and don't go near!" She warned them but one of Lord Hsien Mao Dong's arms extended to grab the nearest woman within his reach.

"Help!" The woman screamed in terror while the others wept, "Changchang!"

Yan Mei Ling tried to rescue the girl but the behemoth's other arm thrashed her away. "What do you think you are doing? Put her down, she has nothing to do with this!"

"Help me!" Changchang continued to struggle against Lord Hsien Mao Dong's grip despite the dripping blood from her punctured skin. "My lord, please release me. I beg you please..."

The monstrous lord seemed to lose his sanity as he loosely stared at his captive with clouded eyes, his mouth was trickling with a mixture of black blood and drool.

"I said put her down!" The young warrior demanded and dashed forward with her Houjian.

He responded to her with a whack of his other arm on the ground, catapulting her to the direction of the other women. Yan Mei Ling persisted but a few gray orbs where thrown at her, she warded them off to protect the women behind her. Seeing that his opponent was occupied, he bared his sharp teeth and plunged them deep into the neck of his captive, draining her precious blood.

"Changchang!" The women cried while Yan Mei Ling stood in shock.

He continued to chew ferociously on the flesh of Changchang until her head fell on the marble floor. His other arm shortened and he inserted it between her breasts, pulling her heart out. He threw the corpse aside and devoured the heart.

"Changchang..." The women grieved at the loss of their companions.

Yan Mei Ling noticed that Lord Hsien Mao Dong's wound slowly healed so she hastily turned to the other women. "You need to get out of here. This place is not safe!"

"We are trapped in the harem."

"There is nothing we can do..."

"He will kill all of us just like the princess!"

"What?" Yan Mei Ling paled at what she heard. "What do you mean the princess?"

"Lord Hsien Mao Dong's army has kidnapped a princess from another realm and, instead of making her one of his concubines, he is going to offer her as a blood sacrifice to the Demon Lord."

"Is she the one in the concealed cage?"

"Yes"

"Li Lei Shuang" Yan Mei Ling whispered in alarm and her knees buckled down. "Is she... is she..." She could not bring herself to utter the word.

"Do you know the princess?" One of the women asked; she was the youngest one among the group.

"Yes," Yan Mei Ling answered in anguish. Her tears held back, threatening to spill from her eyes.

"I don't think she's dead. The red moon will rise three days from now; only then will she be offered as a blood sacrifice to the Demon Lord."

"Do you mean that she is still alive?" A strong surge of hope was evident in Yan Mei Ling's voice.

"Yes," the woman replied. "I saw Lord Hsien Mao Dong tied her before imprisoning her inside the cage."

Yan Mei Ling's somber face cracked into a smile. "What's your name?"

The woman blushed as she looked at the beautiful warrior in front of her; she answered shyly, "My name is Sung Baozhai."

Yan Mei Ling stood upright. "Sung Baozhai, thank you for telling me." She took Sung Baozhai's hands with hers and said, "Lord Hsien Mao Dong's body is still recuperating. Our fight is still far from over. You need to get out of here, as fast as you can, lest you will get harmed. Don't worry, I will do my best to save you and all of your companions."

The women cried in happiness as they looked at Yan Mei Ling with love, respect and admiration.

"Step aside," she commanded all of them. The women complied and watched her clutched the sword hard until a bright flaming energy swirled around it. She slashed her Houjian to the wall's direction and destroyed it with the flaming energy. The demolished wall created an exit for the women but the outside was as dangerous as Lord Hsien Mao Dong's monster form with the rumpus of the soldiers at war and toppling debris from the devastated buildings. She created a shield around the women and her when a nearby building shattered.

"I need to go back inside and kill Lord Hsien Mao Dong, do you know where to go from here?" Yan Mei Ling asked the women behind her.

"Yes," the oldest one among the group answered.

"Good. My shield will last for a few minutes or as long as I am not dead." Yan Mei Ling informed with a wary haze in her eyes. "Make sure to exit the village and, if you see anyone from the Imperial Army, go to them and tell them that the Ninja Boy seeks their help."

"Thank you," the women responded in unison and gathered around her.

"Is Ninja Boy really your name?" Sung Baozhai inquired for the last time.

Yan Mei Ling smiled gently. "That is how I want to be called."

"Ninja Boy..." Sung Baozhai murmured reverently. "I will never forget you. Please take care of yourself."

"I will." Yan Mei Ling said and exited from the shield. "Go now and don't fear the falling objects or anything for as long as you are inside the shield, no one can harm you."

As soon as the women travelled a few distance away from her, two spiky long objects grabbed her by the arms. She tried to escape but the spikes only penetrated deeper into her flesh.

"Struggle and you will tear your flesh," the young warrior heard her nemesis' evil voice. She clenched her jaw when she was dragged near the grotesque dark lord.

"Do you think you can escape and survive this time?" He spat furiously, his big mouth foaming with spit and blood. He was huge, his size alone could equal four grown men put together. "You've overestimated yourself and even committed a graver mistake by helping my wives escape!"

Yan Mei Ling did not move too much to avoid serious damage to her flesh. Instead, she tried to put on an apathetic face despite the outrageous biting pain. "Obviously, none of the women regarded you as her husband. Let me guess, you force your despicable self upon those helpless women because no one from them would be willing to tie herself to an abomination such as yourself. Am I correct?"

Lord Hsien Mao Dong gritted his teeth in anger and tightened his grip at the annoying girl.

Yan Mei Ling grimaced but she quickly displaced it with a smirk. "With all the wealth you have amassed; all the land that you have conquered; and all the people that you ruled over, you still do not get what you truly want which is real power. Do you want to know why?"

When the lord did not answer, she continued, "It is because you are evil and selfish! People only bow down to you not because they love nor respect you but because they only fear you."

Lord Hsien Mao Dong laughed at what he heard. His laughter melted into a scowl and low growl. "You're utterly naive, aren't you, little girl? I don't care about how they feel about me as long as they fear and tremble down to me."

"You get your power from those people you have full disregard of!"

"I don't give a damn." He muttered coldly and tightened his hold on the girl, drawing more blood from her perforated flesh.

Yan Mei Ling held the whimper in her throat, refusing to show vulnerability.

"Do you really have the power of Jinlong – why can't I feel it?"

She smirked at his words and taunted him, "Simple, because you are weak. Weak creatures can't feel Jinlong."

"Bitch!" He railed and lengthened the spikes on his lashes.

"Why are you not killing me yet?" The young warrior asked in a bored tone. "Do you actually expect me to whimper and beg you?"

"Arrogant are we?" Lord Hsien Mao Dong smirked sarcastically.

"Watch me." Yan Mei Ling stated. The color of her irises in her eyes began to glow once again. The temperature of her body increased and, soon, her body was literally aflame.

"Ahhhh!!!" The dark lord screamed from the intense heat; the spikes dissolved into ashes and he was left without any choice but to drop the girl on the ground.

She landed in her feet. The holes on her flesh healed quickly before the fire surrounding her body went out. Her eyes still held the flame in them; she spoke, "Do you actually think that you can fight Jinlong, lesser demon?"

Lord Hsien Mao Dong grumbled angrily. "I am not a lesser demon! I will show you my unlimited strength!" Several dark shadows began to swirl inside the room and a succession of thunder bellowed in the sky like a blitzkrieg.

Yan Mei Ling watched both in awe and amusement as her enemy's body convulsed like an epileptic. In a few moments, his body expanded both horizontally and vertically until his head elevated above the ceiling and destroyed the entire roof of the harem. She levitated away before a huge debris crushed her to death. Her nemesis continued to grow, his snout elongated and the color of his skin changed. His back bent irregularly and spikes came out of it. His eyes turned scarlet red and his face had gone from ugly to appalling. When his transformation ended, his appearance resembled that of a gargantuan wolf crossed with a porcupine.

The fighting soldiers began to stop fighting as they stared at the massive beast in horror. The beast began to take a swipe at them, not caring if they were Hsien or imperial soldiers, and viciously gobbled those he caught.

Yan Mei Ling held the Houjian and glided towards the enemy. She raised her sword to destroy him but the latter shoved her with his giant claws. She stuck the point of her sword to the ground, leaving her in a head first vertical position to avoid injury. She removed her sword and flipped into the air. A huge shadow block the light of the moon from her and, then she realized that the giant monster almost scooped her. She floated to the side and took a swipe of her sword on his left elbow, wounding him deeply. Lord Hsien Mao Dong howled in pain and the black blood from his wound rained down the village.

Some soldiers sent their cannons flying at the immense creature but they barely created a damage on him. The beast retaliated by sprinting towards them, the ground shook heavily with each of his step, and grabbed a handful of soldiers while the others desperately ran for their lives. He ate his captives and triturated them until their flesh had the consistency of mashed vegetables. The spilled blood and body parts of the eaten soldiers laid like clutter in the ground.

The young warrior headed to the monster who was chasing after the attacking soldiers. She used the Houjian's fuller as a shield, stopping the beast from advancing further. He pushed against her but she pushed back despite the vibrating pain in her arms. He used his free hand to grapple her but she flew behind him and delivered a straight kick to his nape, reducing him to a kneeling position.

Multitude of cannons projected to the Lord Hsien Mao Dong's direction until he was all wrapped in fire and smoke.

Yan Mei Ling distanced herself from the smog and shouted, "Stop firing your cannons – it won't kill the monster!"

"You are not our superior, why should we follow your orders?" One of the imperial soldiers mocked.

"Ping, do as the boy say." A ranked soldier reprimanded Ping and all of the cannoneers ceased from firing.

Yan Mei Ling looked at the man and her eyes widened in recognition – he was Jiangjun Chonglin Da, her father's subordinate and trusted right hand. But where was her father? Her jaws hardened in ire and she moved to the beast when he emerged from the waning smog unharmed. She brandished her sword and he met her attack headlong. She severed his forearm with an adroit sweep of the Houjian. The monster screamed in pain; he jumped above her and pummeled her towards the ground. The Houjian escaped her grasp but she managed to survive when she inserted herself between a huge rock and the soil. The rock began to grow heavier as the monster continued to push his weight down.

"Jiangjun, the boy is not emerging!"

Jiangjun Chonglin Da's eyes narrowed and a thought came to him. "We will divert the monster's attention from the boy to us by shooting cannons"

"It is suicide, Jiangjun Chonglin Da!"

Jiangjun Chonglin Da aloofly gazed at his subordinate and said, "If we don't help the boy who is the only one who could contend with the monster, we will die just the same. If we will just die, we might as well die courageously and honorably." He directed his stare to the cannoneers and ordered, "Men, prepare the cannons! Shoot the cannons!"

The imperial soldiers directed their cannons to the raging beast and blasted at him. The monster was riled with the action that he shifted his attention to the soldiers and vaulted in front of them.

"Whether we run or not, the monster will still catch us. Do not stop!" Jiangjun Chonglin Da hollered at the soldiers.

The beast was about to hit them when Yan Mei Ling materialized in front of him and intercepted his attack with the Houjian.

The event became a show of strength as the beast pushed his tremendous weight against the fragile-looking warrior.

"Get away from here, all of you!" Yan Mei Ling shouted to the soldiers and they immediately complied. She looked at the raving monster straight into his eyes and snarled, "I am tired of playing games with you, lesser demon."

Lord Hsien Mao Dong raged and gave her several wallops. The young warrior responded by thrusting the tip of her sword to his fist and shot him with a white energy ball, the impact threw him at a distance. He writhed deliriously but he stood and raised his arm, gathering a gray-colored force in his palms. The girl did not waste any time and immediately soared to his direction to deliver a strong punch in his jaw. The beast landed on the village houses, utterly wrecking several of them. She pursued him further and stabbed his chest. A geyser of black blood drenched, it felt like acid in her skin. Her enemy groaned in pain and swayed his unsliced arm aimlessly until he managed to knock the girl away.

Yan Mei Ling was shoved against a village house. Her entire body shaking from the painful impact. She barely recovered when a gray ball was hurled at her. She coughed and sputtered blood as she stood erect. She wiped the blood from her mouth and smirked when the beast's gravitating body almost smack her down. She bounced away and drifted to Lord Hsien Mao Dong's face. "I told you, I am tired of playing games." She gripped hard at the handle of her sword and her body was wrapped in flames. She swung her sword far behind and lashed out at his head, sending a ball of bright vertical light.

"Roar!!!" Lord Hsien Mao Dong screamed in agony as his body jolted violently. Dark shadows danced frenziedly around him as his size gradually decreased until what was left of the gargantuan monster was his bloody and naked dead body.

Yan Mei Ling glided down to Lord Hsien Mao Dong's corpse and she stumbled exhaustedly beside it. She heaved up and down, using the sword as a cane to support her. She whispered coldly, "That is the limit of your power, lesser demon."

'So what do you want to do next?' Ryuu inquired as he casually squat beside his daughter.

Yan Mei Ling gasped in surprise upon seeing her ancestor, she had gotten used to him communicating to her telepathically. "I need to go back to harem and free Li Lei Shuang from the cage, baba."

Ryuu momentarily fell silent before nodding his head. 'Yes, you need to go back to the harem.'

Yan Mei Ling eyes hardened to a glare as she stared at her nemesis' body. She gnashed her teeth in wrath as she grabbed a handful of his hair and cleanly sliced his head off his body.

'That is not necessary!' Ryuu admonished her.

"I could have mutilated his body!" Yan Mei Ling clenched her palm on the Houjian's grip in exasperation.

Ryuu shook his head in disapproval. 'You have already done it. There is nothing I can do. However, in the future, I don't want you to do that; you need to control your anger.'

"I have no plans of being a Dragon Warrior after I save Li Lei Shuang."

'Oh, but it is your destiny.' Ryuu said with finality. 'You can't escape your destiny.'

She stood when she recovered, Lord Hsien Mao Dong's head was still in her hand. "I don't care. My destiny will solely be based on my choices, not what others write for me."

'You will say that for now; you will eventually change your mind later on.' Ryuu said before he disappeared.

Yan Mei Ling ran to the direction of the harem while reflecting on her divine ancestor's words. She shrugged it off her mind and headed to the ruined building. She tried to fly but, to her disappointment, she seemed to lose the ability. "So Jinlong's power only last for a short moment." She uttered and decided to leap through the wreckage until she located the concealed cage.

She was still holding Lord Hsien Mao Dong's head when the beat of her heart became erratically fast. She swallowed the hard, the tears in her eyes were streaming down in excitement. "Li Lei Shuang, we will finally be reunited." She unwrapped the cage and her entire body had gone cold at what she saw. "Li Lei Shuang?" She croaked and buckled down, a great wave of pain wash over her. She threw Lord Hsien Mao Dong decapitated head and bawled in anguish, "Li Lei Shuang! Li Lei Shuang! No!" She cried over and over again, extreme sorrow racked her entire body. "I tried..." She shook her head to verify if everything was just a nightmare. "I did my best but... No..."

'Why are you crying, my daughter? Aren't you going to save the girl inside the cage? She needs your help.'

Yan Mei Ling stared at the owner of the voice and muttered tearfully. "Ryuu!" Her grieving face turned into a scowl as she inveighed, "I have saved a lot of people but I am not able to save the one that I love the most. My efforts are all in vain and please do not call me Dragon Warrior – I detest being it!"

'So you are telling me that you're just forced to help other people?'

"You are wrong." Yan Mei Ling shouted in aggravation. She harshly opened the cage and released the wounded girl from the shackles that bound her wrists and ankles. When she stepped out of the enclosure, she told Ryuu, "Understand the part that I am grieving too – I am only human!"

'I do understand you, my child.' Ryuu earnestly told her.

Yan Mei Ling gently cradled the unconscious girl in arms. "You do not."

Ryuu ignored her hostility and interjected, 'What if I tell you that Li Lei Shuang is alive and safe?'

Yan Mei Ling froze as a new spark of hope conquered her body. Tears began to fell from her eyes. "Do not give me false hopes because it will only make things worse. I'd very much prefer the harsh truth than sweet lies."

Ryuu opened his palm and a bright ball, the same as that in the Sky Heaven's Landing, appeared in it. Yan Mei Ling's eyes widened when she saw Li Lei Shuang sitting in her wing's garden. Her best friend looked sickly pale and thin as she stared impassively into the space.

"Li Lei Shuang..." Yan Mei Ling tried to reach out for the ball but it vanished the moment that her hand made contact with it. "Please let me see her, baba. I beg you please."

'Do you really want to see Li Lei Shuang?'

"Yes, baba." –

'Go home and you'll see her.'

Yan Mei Ling inclined her head and, once again, he disappeared when the sounds of footsteps behind her became prominent.

"Young man," someone called her.

She turned her head and saw Jiangjun Chonglin Da smiling as he went near her.

Jiangjun Chonglin Da turned his head at the trail of blood and saw Lord Hsien Mao Dong's head; he strode and picked it up. He bowed on his knees and said, "I, in behalf of the Son of Heaven, would like to thank you for helping us."

Yan Mei Ling kept her head down to avoid recognition and responded, "You are welcome."

"If it is not much to ask, may I please know the name of our hero?"

She carefully thought for a moment before answering, "Please call me Ninja Boy."

Jiangjun Chonglin Da's eyes widened in surprise at what he heard. "I heard of your greatness although I was not there during the Imperial Tournament. I did not imagine that you will exceed my expectation. You can equal the Dragon Warrior himself!"

She did not bother commenting on the Jiangjun's remark.

"I know that we can't pay you enough but is there anything that you would like to ask? I can negotiate with the Unit Commander to reward you appropriately for your astounding heroism."

Yan Mei Ling contemplated until she slowly nodded her head. "I need a horse."

"A horse?" He exclaimed in astonishment. He actually expected more.

"Yes, a horse. I want to go home."

"Are you not going to ask for anything else? I can surely arrange..."

"No, I just need a horse, nothing else." Yan Mei Ling interrupted him.

Jiangjun Chonglin Da beamed brightly. "Very well. I will give you a horse."

"And where are the women?"

"Women?" Jiangjun Chonglin Da blurted out in confusion.

"I think she is referring to the rescued harem women." One of the soldiers answered from behind.

"Oh," Jiangjun Chonglin Da remarked. "Do you happen to know where they are?"

"They are outside of the village under Bohai's care."

Jiangjun Chonglin Da bobbed his head before facing the Ninja Boy. "They are all safe."

"I'll go to them. If you can please guide me as to where they are." Yan Mei Ling told him. "I have one of their companions."

"Certainly. We will also prepare your horse."

"Thank you."

"My pleasure," Jiangjun Chonglin Da said and tended his gaze at the girl in the young warrior's arms. "Do you want me to help in carrying the girl?"

"No, I will manage." Yan Mei Ling shook her head in refusal. "I'll bring her to her companions and, then take my leave when the horse is ready."

"As you wish, Ninja Boy."

Epilogue

When I arrive at our village after a long arduous incessant journey, I get off my horse and cry at the wreck that my village has become. I feel a singe inside my heart but what shatters it into terrible pieces is seeing my father kneeling like a hermit beside a hut made from the remnants of the village rubble.

He is facing the Mountain of Dark Skull; his shoulders slump in defeat; his eyes watery although there are no tears falling from them. I, however, can see the toil of sorrow and exhaustion in him; the despair and helplessness that literally emanates from his mighty posture. It does not suit him but I'm certain that I am the one who reduce him to this pathetic state. Why have I ever done this to him — my very own father?

I hold back the lump in my throat and try not to stutter as I call him. "Baba..."

I watch him close his eyes slowly and the tears that he has been holding back stream down. "Ai Nyu, it has been a long time since I have heard your voice but I want to tell you, I miss you very much. I really miss you. This might have been too late but I want you to know that I love you and I am extremely proud of you. I might have not told you but the happiest day of my life is the moment that I first hold you in my arms; I am thinking during that time that you are the gods' greatest gift to me. You may be stubborn but you are strong and intelligent. You are everything that I wish that my daughter should be even if I have never told you." He presses his face against the ash-filled ground and weeps agonizingly. "Please talk to me for the last time, I don't mind if I will be insane until the rest of my life as long as I hear your voice today. I beg you."

"Baba..."

"I am sorry for not being the best father to you; I am sorry for neglecting you; I am sorry for not taking care of you in a way that a parent should; I am sorry for not living up to the promise that I made to your mother to always protect you. I am the worst person — the worst father. But even if everything is too late, I will always love you and no one can ever replace you inside my heart. You will always be my beloved daughter. Wherever you may be, I hope that you will be happy at and peace."

"Baba, don't!" I cry and rush to my father unable to take his torment. I try to assist him to an upright position but just like a vegetable, he staggers back.

"Ahhh!!!" He wails to the ground like an infant as his shoulders shakes convulsively. The guilt and anguish that I feel magnified; I wish the ground will just swallow me.

"Hhhhh... I am the worst person. I am worthless — totally worthless."

What have I done?

"Baba, listen," I shake my father, trying to put some semblance of sanity within him but he just continues to cry. "Please, baba, I beg you listen to me. I am not dead! I am alive. Please don't do this! I can't stand you crying for a worthless daughter like this — I don't deserve your pain and sorrow..."

My father looks at me; the cloud in his eyes still hovering over them. "Did you know that your mother tells me that you look just like me?" He laughs tremulously before breaking down. "I told her with pride in my heart, certainly, after all you are my daughter. My very own and flesh blood. Your mother loves you and before she breathes her last breath, she beseeches me to give you love and affection that you may not feel the need for any maternal love." His face twists into self-loathing. "I promised her but I haven't fulfilled it! I have treated you coldly because I am being a coward and I let my grief pull me down. I should have done better as a father but no, you're gone. You're viciously taken away from me!"

My chest tightens from the heaviness inside.

"Remember your cousin, Princess Li Lei Shuang? You are very fond of her. I saved her and killed her abductor. I know this will make you happy because you love her very much."

I smile in relief upon hearing his words but I need to bring back my strong father who never cries and is always looking brave. The father that I very much admire and look up to; the person who inspires me to be a warrior — my father; my hero. "Baba, I am alive. Please stop crying. I never died; I was somewhere safe and... the villagers are safe too. They are currently in the Mountain of Dark Skull." I lift his face and wipe his tears. "I am strong just like you, remember? It will take more than the entire Hsien army to kill me. I am, after all, your daughter; your very own flesh and blood!" I lift my arms to flex them.

My father chuckles but this time out of humor. "Am I not talking to my daughter's ghost?"

"No, baba."

He exhales deeply and smiles. There are still tears in his eyes but those are happy ones. "I am happy that you are alive." He pulls me to him and engulfs me in a warm embrace. Surprisingly, a memory of me surges through. A memory of him cradling and comforting me, an infant me, lovingly in his arms as I cry.

"You say that the villagers are alive?"

"Yes, baba..."

We both stand up and he tells me, "Good. We better hurry and fetch them so we can start rebuilding our village."

"Yes, baba." I reply. "Oh, I have something to ask of you."

"What is it, my daughter?"

I bow my head respectfully and request, "Please allow me to become a warrior, baba."

There is a moment of silence so I start to blabber, "I mean, I don't need to join the military since females are not allowed but I really want to become a warrior..."

My father smiles and I know that I get his approval when he taps my shoulder. "You are my daughter. Being a warrior is in your blood so there is no sense saying no to you." He looks behind me and say, "I see that you have something with you."

I touch the linen-wrapped sword hanging at my back. "It is a jian given to me."

"I see." He comments while nodding his head. " Anyway, I haven't told you this but we are actually descended from the first dragon warrior."

"What is his name, baba?"

My father beams brightly and looks ahead. "Well, I will tell you everything I know about him while we walk to the Mountain of Dark Skull, how is that?"

I bob happily and we start to walk to do the direction of the mountain.

The moon looks glorious as it stakes its claim on the milk-streak dark sky. It's light shone like a glimmer of diamonds descending down the World Under Heaven. Beneath the light-splashed cape of darkness, a gentle fall of thin snow cascades down to the sparsely covered wet ground.

The trees and plants in the garden are in hibernation but nonetheless they still look beautiful in the winter-conquered land. But their beauty lack a certain luster, maybe because of the somber palette or the absence of colorful butterflies and playful birds that are conspicuous during the spring and summer; or maybe something else.

Li Lei Shuang stares listlessly around, noticing the dreary stillness of her garden. Everything may have looked beautiful but it feels so unnatural.

'If winter comes and you feel sad, just call me, and together, we will reminisce the wonderful memories that happens during the last spring season.'

The princess breaks down in tears at the recollection.

'I promise that I will become the strongest warrior in Chixian Shenzhou because I want to protect you. I will never leave you, Li Lei Shuang.'

Words so sweet to hear; promises laden with passion and spoken with utter honesty but they only end up like a distant reminiscence in the past. Unfortunately, they are naught but unfounded promises and painful relics of the past.

A nightingale sings from a distance. It surprises her considering that it is something rare especially during the winter. The bird's song is so beautiful although a bit melancholic or maybe her perception is mirroring what is inside her heart? But it's wonderful melody resonates throughout the garden, singing to her heart, appealing to the longing that is within.

It is hopeless — utterly hopeless. What is the sense of longing for someone that you know will never come back? What comfort will she get in longing when her heart breaks every time she remembers the sad and even the happy memories? However, she has no choice for those memories will always be a part of her. Maybe she'll keep them as souvenir for her to dream on whenever she is asleep. At least in dreaming, she finds a real refuge that makes her forget the bitter reality that is constantly smothering her. Perhaps it is better if she dies, then she won't feel this heart-wrenching pain.

The moonlight continues to bathe her with its majestic radiance but it does not give her any comfort. In fact, it's beauty seems superfluous, seemingly mocking her. Why doesn't it when her life has become too ironic amidst the wonders that surrounds her?

A gentle sound of footstep is heard but the princess pays it no heed. Whoever that person and whether he kills her or not, she doesn't care. Her heart, that once beats with emotion, is now filled with void.

"Li Lei Shuang..."

Li Lei Shuang's heart thudded violently upon hearing that beloved and familiar voice. Is she the one who invoke it? Does her sorrows drown her into its abysmal depths which makes her delusional? She turns her head to its direction and her heart comes to a halt. She must have been tethering precariously in the ropes of insanity if the vision projected in front of her is Yan Mei Ling.

"Li Lei Shuang," the precious voice calls again.

"Yan Mei Ling?" The princess' voice comes out like a hoarse gasp.

Her beloved best friend stands a few distance away from her, staring at her as if she is the most precious person in the World under Heaven; her beautiful dark eyes shine like gems, reflecting a love so great, it is astounding.

Unable to contain the excitement and emotion that are simmering inside my heart, I run to my best friend and warily settle down in front of her. I swallow the heaviness in my throat as my tears start to mimic the snow that descends from the sky. "I am here, Li Lei Shuang. I am here..."

"Is that really you, Yan Mei Ling?" Li Lei Shuang asks, her pretty pale face is still full of doubt.

I'm reduced to silence as I gaze into her and without restrain, I tenderly touch her face which is something I have dreamt of doing during the lonely times I spend at the campaign; I lovingly trace her features in a way that a sculptor will do to its priceless craft; and softly I wipe the tears the smear her beauty. "Yes, it is me. Please don't think that I am just a figment of your imagination. I am real and I am alive. I made a promise to you, remember?"

Li Lei Shuang whimpers dejectedly upon hearing her best friend's words. In a angst-filled voice, she admonishes Yan Mei Ling, "You told me that you will never leave me but where were you when I needed you the most? You didn't have any idea of what I felt when I learned that you were dead! It literally killed my soul! I felt so lonely that even the mere act of breathing was so hard to do."

"I'm sorry." My voice quivers in guilt and anguish. If Li Lei Shuang will lash out on me, I will gladly take it if that will ease even a bit of the enormous pain that I have caused her. "I know that asking for your forgiveness will not undo the pain that I've done to you so if you will hate and get angry at me, I will not stop you." I take her hands and press it to my face. "If you want to hurt me for hurting you, do so. I will not mind because I deserve it not the tears that fall from your eyes."

The princess stares at her best friend blankly before her teary face softens with affection. She gingerly strokes Yan Mei Ling's face with her hands, feeling the warmness that emanates from her best friend's skin to her fingertips. She carefully withdraws her hands and patiently waits if the vision before her will fade but then, Yan Mei Ling remains and never leaves. "You will never leave me again, won't you, Yan Mei Ling?"

I gaze into Li Lei Shuang's eyes through the tears that obscure my vision and earnestly vow to her, "Yes, I promise you that I will never leave you again, and this time I will do well with my promise."

Li Lei Shuang closes her eyes and sheds more tears as a poignant emotion overwhelms her entire being. She shortens the distance between her and Yan Mei Ling, and places an affectionate kiss on the latter's forehead. "I love you, Yan Mei Ling."

"I love you too, Li Lei Shuang." I answer back and find myself snuggled into a tranquil sanctuary that is her arms.

The moon illuminates above and I am certain that the goddess Chang'e is smiling down at us. I can hear a distant nightingale's serenading the garden but I am not exactly sure as to where it is. But I really cannot care anything less as long as I feel the warmness of Li Lei Shuang's embrace and the wonderful scent of her silky black hair wrapping around me like a protective curtain.

My painful and weary odyssey is over. I am finally safe now.

www.ingramcontent.com/pod-product-compliance
Lightning Source LLC
Chambersburg PA
CBHW070434170726
48291CB00002B/503

* 9 7 8 1 9 3 3 1 2 1 5 7 4 *